Behind the Face of Winter

Behind the Face
of Winter

H NIGEL THOMAS

We acknowledge the support of the Canada Council for the Arts for our publishing program. We also acknowledge support from the Ontario Arts Council.

National Library of Canada Cataloguing in Publication Data

Thomas, H. Nigel, 1947-
  Behind the face of winter

ISBN 0-920661-95-5

  I. Title.

PS8589.H4578B4 2001   C813'.54   C2001-902421-5
PR9199.3.T455B4 2001

Printed in Canada by Coach House Printing.

TSAR Publications
P. O. Box 6996, Station A
Toronto, Ontario M5W 1X7
Canada

www.candesign.com/tsarbooks

To the memory of my maternal grandparents,
Hester Roban-Dickson and John Dickson,
for the nurture they gave me and the values
they instilled in me

Prologue

JANUARY 6, 1986. 4.10 AM, my watch face glows angrily at me. My luck to be awakened by a nightmare on my twenty-sixth birthday. I sit up in bed, get out to turn on the floor lamp beside my desk a few feet away, and look around to orient myself—even if this has been my bedroom for some nine years.

Outside, the wind hisses—at the buildings, the naked trees, at everything in its path. The usual clamour from squeaking brakes, screeching tires, humming motors on Victoria Avenue—even at this time of morning—or Côte des Neiges, depending on the direction of the wind, is absent; absorbed into the wind and falling snow. The curtains are open, but everything's blotted out, even the light from the street lamps. Snow. Feathery white dots linking heaven and earth. Weaving about earth a burial shroud, pristine white, which will turn into grey slush in less than a day. Like life. *Wash me in the blood of the lamb/ And I shall be whiter than snow.* My first snowstorm a windless mid-December day eleven years ago, when the clouds crumbled, leaving their pallor in the air, and covered the earth, even the dog turds scattered about the sidewalks, a gleaming white! With something of the breathless, excited eagerness of a virgin bride, I'd hurriedly dressed and bounced rather than walked up the stairs to join the sudden carnival of youngsters and grannies converging like metal objects pulled by a magnet on the single large now snow-coated lawn a little way down the street. Explosions of uncoiled mirth erupting everywhere. Snowballs flying from mittened little hands. Stout, bundled-up, breathless, sallow-faced grandmothers steaming at the nostrils like locomotives, pulling sleds of pink-faced babies up and down the lawn and on the sidewalk. A week later, when liquid ice poured from the sky and moulded a fiery-cold armour on every outdoor thing, the virgin bride had already turned drudge.

I stare at the white gyprock walls—my head pivoting—so different from the green wood walls of my grandmother's house I left almost twelve years ago. Unsure now what's home. *"A long ways from home."* Choked by sorrow, Sister Agnes could not finish it at my mother's funeral six weeks ago; Sister Andrews did.

Grama's place. Eternal summer. Flowering trees always, even in the dry season; for flame trees and poui, especially the dry season; hibiscus—pink, white, salmon, magenta—their petals nectar for glossy, topknot, blue-throat humming birds; oleander, queen of flowers, bougainvillea; jasmine perfuming the night air year round, drifting in through the window. Mrs Duncan, our neighbour, grew them all.

Summer. What a lying seducer! Heat defines cold—as day defines night, as wet defines dry. There's lots to life stripped to twigs, and stalks, and bark; to an anemic sun shortening its journey, delivering cold light to an ice-wrapped earth. With wonder I watch the trees denude themselves in fall. When, elsewhere, the rains refuse to come, year after year, as in Ethiopia, where these days the land's a crematorium, one's got to be real smug to never wonder: what if winter never ends, never gives over the reins to summer.

We no longer feed the sun, won't even acknowledge we're its fruits, its labour.

Still I long for the onset of the tropical evenings of my first fourteen years when the Caribbean Sea and the tops of the mountains hugging Hanovertown turned from pale yellow to bright gold, then purple, until everything got swallowed up in charcoal grey twinkling with emeralds; for clear windless evenings when the Caribbean Sea mirrored the stars, the moon and Hanovertown with just enough shimmer to create the feathery edges that distinguish photographs from paintings, and slobbered the shore with kisses just loud enough to remind us of its presence. My grandmother was sure such scenes would be a pot of honey to sweeten all future bitterness.

I put on a green, corduroy dressing gown my mother gave me for Christmas a few years back and go to sit at the kitchen table, a chrome-and-white formica affair with four matching vinyl chairs that Sister Andrews gave Ma when we moved here. I turn the light on and watch roaches scamper like tiny brown bullets across the white vinyl floor. *Cockroach don't get justice in fowl cock courts.* These escape to fortresses where poisons never reach. Above me and under the counter, the white melamine cupboards are crammed to bursting with dry and canned food my mother always bought whenever it was on special. Crowded behind the table is a freezer a woman she cleaned for gave her; it too is full of frozen specials. There's a few years' supply of toilet paper in the bathroom cupboard. Two months ago, she would have been stirring now. I would have heard, except on those rare mornings when I was asleep, the bathroom water running, later the opening of the kitchen cupboards, the fridge, the bread popping up in the toaster, and eventually the coat closet opening, the inward rush of air from the corridor, and the click of her key locking the apartment door. I tried never to think of her cleaning houses day after day for a living.

I'll sit here and watch the day come to life, listen to the snow ploughs. There's nothing special to be done. I have been waiting since last May—it begins to feel like the early Christians tarrying—for a teaching job. Today I must do something else, try perhaps to make sense of this life of mine, to unwrap some things, look behind, mindful of Lot's wife—annoying that she wasn't given a name—for I'm shut, it seems, in a dark cavern and must find or make an egress to the light. *Caution.* The unexamined life is not worth living, but the over-examined life is beyond enduring; romping over memory can be like ice you're standing on one moment and drowning under in the next; and journeys mostly end where they begin; and naive fools with butterfly nets, which is how we all start, end often as senile fools recounting nursery rhymes. Stuff of and stuffing for nightmares.

Face crouched on the living room floor when I awoke; heart thumping. On my back in an open field. A dozen soldiers—African, Asian, European—their rifles pointed at me, surround me in a horseshoe. "Fire!" the command sounds. But spit comes.

Later it's World War II. I'm being hunted. For a while I carry Bobby

3

then lose him. I crouch. Behind tree trunks. Boulders. In ditches. Over-
head thundering planes circle. Next I'm in treeless space. Later in a
yard fronting a farmhouse, in the presence of a couple and two adoles-
cent boys. The woman's face is Ms Mackenzie's, my ex-high school Eng-
lish teacher. I speak, relieved—in English, in French, in Spanish. She
doesn't recognize me. They shake their heads, are frightened, and push
me into the house and through a trap door into a dark cellar.

I had nightmares like this during my first months in Montreal, and they've returned and have been chewing up my sleep for the last five years. But the sleepwalking's new. As far as I know. The spitting too; its origin I know; thought I'd nixed it. *A mock execution.*

My mother died six weeks ago, my "father" eleven years ago. One must find out what's truly dead and burn it. *Burdens.* My mother talked often about putting hers down—but never got beyond talk. My grandmother's cousin Mavis had tried doing so with religion but got trapped in an insane cul de sac. Where's the map, blueprint, formula, for these things? Metaphors. No metaphor how I'll pay the bills Ma had been paying when the fifteen hundred dollars she gave me on her deathbed run out.

1

A SATURDAY IN 1965, when I was five years old, Grama, Ma, and I were driven to the airport, a long stretch of asphalt on the other side of the hill on which we lived, where a bamboo placed across the highway stopped the traffic whenever planes were alighting or taking off. Ma cried before boarding the plane, and Grama, wiping her eyes with a white kerchief, her head wrapped in a blue-and-red plaid one, cried too and said she would probably never see Ma again in this life. Two foolish people, I thought: if they wanted to see each other, then why was Ma leaving? I didn't say it because whenever I stated my thoughts, they said I was rude. I'd already concluded that children weren't supposed to think and so I didn't want them to know that I was thinking.

A few weeks later, Grama received a letter from Ma. Grama sent me a short way up the hill to call Brother Shiloh, who read it aloud to us. Ma said she'd arrived safely; she hadn't yet found a job, but several people she knew were helping her to find one, including Louisa, whose rich mother, Mrs Manley, lived in a big pink house on the bank above us. She said that for reasons Grama would understand her name was now Millicent Brady, not Isis Moore.

"Ma get married?" I asked Grama, because when big-bottom Shirley Brown got married and everybody threw rice at her, which the fowls from all around came to eat, Grama and everyone else started calling her Mistress Yearwood, and I figured it was because she was married to Yearwood. Wagging his finger and brandishing a machete, Yearwood had told Saul, "She is me woman now, so keep yo' dirty looks to yo'self, else, so help me God, I will break every single fowl bone in yo' ass."

"No, yo' mother don' get married. Stop asking me stupid questions."

So I didn't know why my mother's name had changed. I began to wonder too if I would be able to recognize Ma if I saw her. I'd heard Grama and Mrs Duncan talking about a man who turned into a woman after leaving Mount Olivet. I hoped my mother wouldn't turn into a man, and wondered why strange things happened to people when they went to live across the sea.

Before Ma left for Canada I'd already known that the food Grama went down the hill in Hanovertown to buy was with money my mother brought when she came home every Saturday evening before leaving again on Sunday evening.

"Why Ma always leaving and only coming back on Saturday?"

" 'Cause she have for work."

"Why?"

"You will feed us?"

For three Saturdays after Ma left for Canada, Grama bought no chicken. All of the first week there was no fish or flesh of any kind. The Friday morning before I left for school, Grama sent me up to Brother Shiloh's wife to beg for a cup of sugar and to borrow twenty-five cents. On the way home I was to buy bread from Mrs Bibby with the money. Sister Shiloh gave me a bag with a pound of sugar, a pound of flour, a pound of rice and a dollar to take back to Grama. Her face, round black, and smiling, dough on her fingers, which she wiped on a red apron she was wearing, she said, "Tell Ma Moore I say she don't owe me nothing. We all got to help one another stay above water."

"God make mouth and He provide bread," Grama said when she heard Sister Shiloh's message.

Wednesday of the next week, I had finished looking over my reader, as Miss Bonnie had told us to do when we got home. I knew all the lessons by heart. I even made up my own stories about Miss Tibs and Mr Grumps—Mr Grumps wanting to marry Miss Tibs and Miss Tibs thinking Mr Grumps too ugly. What would their children look like? After all Miss Tibs was a goat and Mr Grumps a pig. I noticed that Grama hadn't lit the primus stove. Usually, just as the sun was disappearing behind the Hanovertown hills we would be eating. The sun was already doing that and Grama was still sitting on the settee. At noon that day I'd had a bun and a cup of lemonade. It was a mile to and from school. I was usually hungry by the time I got back to school. I'd learned since I was about three to keep my hunger to myself, because whenever I said I was hungry, Grama would ask me if I wanted her to steal to feed me. One time she said that people who weren't satisfied with what they had ended up in prison, such people wanted to fly in the face of God. And since God sent people He was angry with to hell, I didn't want God to get angry with me. Another time—it was the last time I ever complained— Grama had slapped me. Then, holding me by the hand, she had taken me up to the corner shop and asked Mrs Bibby to credit her some crackers until the following Saturday. Mrs Bibby said Grama's bill was too high already and that Grama had to pay it off before she could get any more credit. Grama pointed to me and told Mrs Bibby that I was hungry. Mrs Bibby said if she gave credit to all the hungry people in the world she would go out of business.

"You is worser than a dog," Grama told her.

"But I is top dog. Is you that want credit and I what have credit to give. Get out o' me shop!"

From that time I never told Grama I was hungry, and if she asked me if I was, I'd bow my head. So that late afternoon terror gripped me. When it got dark, Grama lit the kerosene lamp, gave me a glass of water, and told me to go to bed. I now slept on the cot, which used to be my mother's bed whenever she'd had her day off, up from the floor where before I slept on rags. I knew what was happening. I'd heard Grama say many times that people give you when you ask once, but if you keep going back they get tired of you.

Later, when Grama thought I was asleep, she stood over me and prayed aloud, "Lord what going happen to this child? I is old and on my way out of this world. Please, God, don' make this child suffer."

Next morning Grama killed one of three laying hens she kept in a coop behind the house and exchanged half of it with Mrs Duncan for rice and other things. She made rice soup, which I ate for breakfast, lunch, and supper that day.

That afternoon when I came home, Grama wasn't there, and Mrs Duncan, whose house was on the lot beside ours, going towards

7

Hanovertown, told me that Grama said I was to remain at her place until she returned.

"Where you went to?" I asked her when she returned at dusk.

"None o' yo' business."

I was silent. Later she said, probably realizing that she needed to solicit my cooperation, "I been to look for work."

I knew that at her age—she was in her mid-sixties—she shouldn't be working. I was silent and guilty because I knew that I hadn't succeeded in hiding my hunger, and that had made Grama go out to find work. I wanted to ask her if she'd found work, and who would take care of me. For me, work for women was leaving on Sunday evening and returning the following Saturday evening.

"You don' want to know if I find a job?"

As it turned out she'd found a job, for both of us. That question too broke down the question barrier, for although sometimes she'd say, "Children should be seen and not heard," or, "You is too inquisitive," more often than not she was glad I asked her questions.

It must have been around this time that she told me I was ugly; that my hard hair, which had broken several of her combs, and my wide nostrils, round face, and dark skin were ugly (she never mentioned my chin). She said my buttocks were two crocus bags of coal and that she'd cook with them if she were ever out of fuel. I knew that people asked God to change things they didn't like, so every night I begged God please to make my buttocks like other people's, and, "Please, don't make Grama cook with them." It must have been around this time too that she heard me singing lines I'd picked up from my schoolmates—*Hark, the herald angels sing: Ginger beer and pound cake bring*— and laughed and told me I was making fun of God and He would strike me dead with lightning.

She and Mrs Duncan once said that I'd been born with a caul. It should have given me extra sight, to see ghosts; but they had burned it and dissolved the ashes in water, which they'd made me drink to see normally.

In her youth and even after my mother's birth, Grama had been the laundress and housekeeper at the Linton "greathouse." One of the Linton boys, she said, had always been partial to her. He was now a lawyer and married with two children. She had gone that day to find out whether he needed someone to do the laundry. She later found out that he had taken the job away from someone else so she could have it. "Poor people always have for fight one another for the bones white people don't want," was all she had said when she found out the truth.

The highway Mr Linton drove on into town passed in front of our house. He dropped the soiled laundry off on Mondays and picked up the laundered clothes on Thursdays. Grama got two large drums, which I had to fill with water on Saturdays. It took several trips to the standpipe, which was about 150 feet away. She used a tailor's goose to iron the clothes, and whenever charcoal was scarce it became my job to go up into the villages in the hills above Hanovertown in search of it.

She continued to do laundry right up to the time I left for Canada, at which point there was electricity in the house, and tap water in the yard and in the shed at the back that served as a shower. My mother had sent money to do all this and to add two more rooms to the original two rooms of the house. One room became a kitchen and the other was my bedroom.

By the time I was seven Grama had begun discussing almost everything with me. She said that my mother had gone to Canada illegally, which meant that the police were looking to pick her up and send her home. She had borrowed fifteen hundred dollars on the land to pay Ma's travel expenses. The bank had to be repaid before we could even eat, otherwise the bank would seize the land and the house, and we would have to live in the street. I didn't need an explanation, because, earlier that year, accompanying Grama to the annual missionary meeting, I had on the way back noticed the beggars under the gallery of the hardware store. I asked Grama why they were there, and she said they had no place to go.

"What they do when rain falls?"

"They get wet."

Grama told me that when I said my prayers before sleeping and upon waking, I was to beg God to keep the police from finding my mother. Each night and morning I did just that.

For about three years after those crucial first weeks there was food, very little meat and fish, but food in the house. Mrs Duncan sometimes pretended to need me for some errand but it was usually to give me something nourishing: a hard-boiled egg, a slice of cheese, or a glass of milk. "Yo' grandmother is a proud woman; don' tell she I giving you anything fo' eat."

My mother even sent a package with a burgundy dress and a pink housecoat for Grama; some stockings for Mrs Duncan; and two pairs of long pants, two shirts, a pair of dress shoes and a pair of running shoes for me. (I became one of the fifty or so students who didn't go to school barefooted.) What a relief not to have to walk barefooted on the asphalt at lunchtime! I often hear stories of people walking barefoot on fire; they should try Hanovertown's asphalt at midday.

About three years after my mother's departure, the bank had been repaid and Grama was able to spend the money Ma sent instead of turning it all over to the bank.

Six months later I outgrew all my clothes and began to be top in my class, which prompted Grama to say, "Good, you got brains. It will get you far if you have the will for use and control it."

2

UP TO AGE ELEVEN I spent a week or two each August in the country with Cousin Lucy, one of two first cousins of my grandmother (the other one was Mavis, who's still alive). I loved to be with her older boy Bruisee—a name he got because as a child he was constantly wandering away and returning with bruises. They were "hands" on a large plantation, which had remained, it was boasted, in the same English family since the beginning of colonization. Bruisee's two older sisters worked as chambermaids on Baleine Island (one of the islets that together with Isabella Island comprised the state of Isabella Island and the Dependencies). Whenever they overnighted on Isabella Island, they stayed with us in Mount Olivet.

The last time I spent a week with Bruisee, Cousin Lucy was ill, having had some kind of surgery, after which she became an invalid. Grama said it was because the wards for poor people weren't clean and Cousin Lucy had got gangrene and blood poisoning and had been "out of her head" for two days, and afterwards it was like she was afraid of people and would sometimes talk nonsense, and her legs got rubbery so she could no longer stand or move about.

Bruisee was nineteen when I made my final August visit. I arrived on Saturday. The following Wednesday night he went hunting with Boley, a short half-Carib fellow who spent his spare time playing a harmonica and lived with his mother and brothers and sisters further down the dirt lane in a room like Cousin Lucy's. They caught two opossums (manicou) weighing less than a pound each. When Bruisee came in from work that Thursday, he took over most of the cooking from Emmeline. She was fourteen and in her last year of school. She kneaded the flour for the dumplings while Bruisee peeled the ground provisions and kept the fire blazing under a smoke-blackened, tripod iron pot in which the opossum was cooking.

Their cooking was done in a small shed built of palm fronds and bamboo poles. It was a neat little affair. One side was left open. During nights and in the rainy season they blocked it with an old oilcloth. The fire hearth was raised to stomach level. The three stones on it were arranged so that either of their cast-iron pots sat on them evenly. Their fuel was coconut fronds and shells. They had lots of it, for coconuts were the mainstay of the plantation.

They made a manicou stew, putting in it all the odds and ends they could find and a plentiful supply of the broad-leaf thyme and pepper that grew right beside the bleaching stones out front in the few square feet of a yard they shared with the family in the adjoining room. And the aroma made us salivate.

When the cooking was almost done, about fifteen children of all ages stood around. Periodically their mothers came to get them, but they dodged them or pretended to go along only to return. Dora, a bright-eyed one—flames seemed to shoot out from her eyes—kept circling her mother—a palmlike figure, curved like a comma, face hard like coconut shell, a suckling baby at her breast.

"You carrying on like if I don' feed you. Wait 'til yo' pappy come home. I will make him cut yo' ass." But Dora's mother went back to her room alone.

Bruisee shared the stew, serving what remained of the manicou to his mother and me in porcelain bowls and to his three sisters, Bobby and himself in calabashes. Into three more calabashes he poured stew for three other children. While they ate, others waited anxiously for the calabashes that the eater would generally give to a younger brother or sister. I never did note whether Dora got any because the food ran out before everyone had eaten. I hoped she didn't get beaten. It is astonishing how many children are beaten because they're hungry, but I'm getting ahead of my story.

Bruisee's sisters washed up afterwards, making several trips to the standpipe where Mr Amasser drew water for his horses. Bruisee and I sat on the step, his lean, sinewy, blue-black torso bare. Even his gums were black. His eyes were amber where other people's were white. Meanwhile Emmeline prepared her mother for bed. The other sisters and Bobby sat silently on the bleaching stones.

Bruisee snapped at them easily and hit them if he found he had to tell them something they should have figured out themselves. They were never angry with him, just ashamed that they added to his burdens.

When Grama and I had visited the year before, Uncle Ambrose, their father, was still alive. Their mother wasn't yet completely bedridden. But a month after Grama and I returned to town, we'd had to make a return trip to attend Uncle Ambrose's funeral. His job on the estate had been the care of a hundred and fifty beef cattle. One of the bulls had charged him while he was bent over some work. By the time help arrived, he had lost too much blood to survive.

The Isabella-for-Isabellans Association advised Bruisee to sue Mr Amasser. The lawyer Bruisee consulted must have informed Mr Amasser, because Mr Amasser told Bruisee he knew he'd contacted a lawyer, and he would evict them if they attempted to sue him. The lawyer charged Bruisee $50 for the advice he gave: not to sue Mr Amasser, since every judge would "say Mr Amasser right. You follow me? Mr Amasser is always right."

On the day of the funeral, Major Dobby, Amasser's chief overseer, brought a wreath and sat through the funeral service in the nearby Methodist chapel. Later in the afternoon, Amasser's oldest son brought four bottles of rum for the wake. The Christmas following, their cook brought two tins of sardines and a tin of rolled oats.

That summer when Bruisee was nineteen he was no longer the Bruisee I looked forward to being with every August. I had gone ready to upbraid him for the bamboo flute he had promised to make for me a year earlier. On evenings after we'd eaten he used to play one he'd made. His father had had one too, and sometimes they played together. He and Uncle Ambrose had taught me to play "Baa Baa Black Sheep." I'd played on it on both of their flutes.

But Bruisee was too tired to take me anywhere or to play the flute, or do anything. He worked half day on Saturday and spent the other half day in their garden plot on the slope of the mountain, where Mr Amasser did not see it worth his while to farm and allowed his "hands" to keep vegetable gardens, provided they paid him a yearly rent for the privilege and did not grow more than they could consume. The year before, Bruisee had taken me up into the mountains and shown me a wild parrot's nest with turquoise eggs in it. He kept several manicou traps up there that he baited with bananas, and he had taken me with him on his daily trips to check them.

Those trips up into the mountains. The spongy feel of the forest floor, texture of life's cradle, like a placenta—nurturing-cushioning-cleansing prebirth. The forest vapours and perfumes: life's smells—a commingling of live breath, of trunks, leaves and branches dissolving into food for the living. This is my body broken for you. All meaningful religions derive their inspiration from nature. The wind moving through the forest, spreading a euphoria that sets the trees dancing, their leaves upcurled in gratitude. The antiphonal chorus of birds, enriched by the bass Who-who-who're ye? of the mountain parrots and the euphony of the trees, each species a different octave (I wish I had asked Bruisee for their names), interweaving with the constant rush and fall of water as it circumvents or cascades over rocks. Nature's symphony. The forest a stretch of endless green, pliant, undulating beneath the wind's caressingsweep—emerald where the sunlight bathes it, jade where it doesn't. Soothing to a boy from town whose soul's been scorched by midday asphalt, bruised by concrete, soiled with civilization's dung. My love for mountains and trees started then. Perhaps too my ambivalence for society.

At the other end was the sea. And it was merely a question of where I had chosen to look, even when we were up in the mountains. In later years, the Atlantic bordering the Amasser plantation made me think of lungs—the earth's—as the water heaved in and out, as if the earth were in the race of its life, albeit unending; occasionally it ran a flat stretch, even less occasionally down an incline. When I'd first observed the Atlantic there, I'd imagined a billion frothing hungry bulldogs bent on breaking their chains: snarling, roaring, rushing towards the land that must surely be food. I cannot remember a time when the Atlantic did not frighten and fascinate me. But Bruisee and Bobby and their sisters loved its hurling waves, would let it strike their bodies, and would come out of it bruised by the pebbles and grit it had scrubbed them with.

When Uncle Ambrose was alive and Cousin Lucy was well, we all went to the garden plot on Saturdays. Cousin Lucy spent the first few hours cooking. We the younger ones imitated the older ones at pulling up weeds until, bored, we wandered off to the nearby stream, scaring away the fish in our clumsy attempts to catch them. Around four, we'd begin again the two-mile trudge back to the village, everybody except Grama and I carrying something. They said Grama and I were from town and would collapse on the way if we carried anything heavier than the clothes we were wearing. The following week when we headed back to town, Cousin Lucy and Uncle Ambrose loaded us down with yams and other root tubers that would have lasted months, if Grama hadn't shared them with Mrs Duncan and Sister Shiloh and others.

That Sunday Bruisee put on one of his two Sunday shirts, a clean pair of trousers, and shoes and went to the Methodist chapel a little way from the village, where it was his duty to pick up and count the collection. Along with him were his sisters and Bobby, wearing clothes my mother sent from Canada once or twice yearly.

Around two, we had pigeon-pea soup, served in the porcelain bowls reserved for Sunday and special occasions. After dinner all of us were in the room. Bruisee lay on the other settee that was his bed; Cousin Lucy lay on her bed; some of us sat on the settee that was my bed while I was there; Emmeline sat on the floor. The air felt heavy so I went outside, although I knew that on Sunday, the Lord's day, after church and dinner I should stay indoors and rest. Bobby followed me outside.

"Where you get yo' pretty clothes-them?" he asked.

"My mother sends them."

"Why my mother not in Canada too?"

"Because she's sick."

There was fear in his eyes. Bobby was around seven, so he would have remembered a time when his mother was healthy and his father provided for them. I saw in his eyes the same confusion I'd felt when my own mother left for Canada and food almost completely disappeared from the house. Bobby had visited us a month before. He'd come with Emmeline when she brought Cousin Lucy to town for her annual checkup. Grama had just enlarged the house. Bobby had looked on bright eyed.

Around sunset Bruisee came out and sat on the steps. He was thoughtful and taciturn. All his laughter, you might even say his youth, had vanished. There was a harshness in his face that hadn't been there a year before; a vacant dullness too, in his eyes.

"When you going join yo' mother in Canada?"

"I don't know."

He looked at my clothes, then out over the coconuts at the raging Atlantic, and fell silent. About an hour later, Emmeline brought us tea and bread. Mine was buttered. Nobody else's was.

When I returned to Mount Olivet, I told Grama to send Cousin Lucy a pound of fish and a pound or two of flour and rice on Thursdays. Right after the manicou stew they'd had trouble scraping together every meal until the Saturday afternoon when Bruisee got paid. Grama started asking me why but never finished. She continued to send them the groceries up to the time Cousin Lucy died, the April before I left for Canada. Bobby was dead too, from a wound which had turned septic. *I am still dreaming of him, losing him in my escape.* Her remaining children were by then scattered. They no longer lived on the plantation: Mr Amasser had died and his children had sold it. I never went back to spend a week with them. Grama and I overnighted a few times when we visited Cousin Lucy, but we always took the next-morning bus back to Mount Olivet . . .

Grama's other cousin, Mavis, was a half-sister to cousin Lucy; they had the same father, who was also Grama's uncle. She showed up irregularly at Grama's up to the time I was about seven. She'd always bring me coconut buns. She smelt like a blend of nutmeg, coconut oil, lemon oil, and raw tripe. Grama said it was all the "stupidness" that Bozo, the man she *they-with*, made her rub with. Grama herself left urine to ferment all day, and on evenings, an hour before bedtime, when she was sure no one would visit, soaked rags in it and bandaged them to her knee. Before going to bed she removed them and rubbed her knee with salt. She said it was a remedy her dead mother had given her in a dream for her rheumatic pains. Once I had twisted my right ankle in a rut which a rainstorm had created in our yard, and it was swollen and painful and I couldn't stand on it, and Grama had stewed rotting banana root and vinegar and mixed it with a rotten avocado and bandaged it to my ankle for four days. It stank, but when she removed it, the skin was all wrinkled and bleached but the swelling and pain were gone. Once when Mavis was visiting, a donkey several houses away kept braying, and Grama said that Cousin Mavis's smell had disturbed it. Mrs Duncan, who was present, told Grama that it wasn't a nice thing to say. But Cousin Mavis only grinned.

After that we used to visit her the first Sunday of every month at the insane asylum. Every couple of months my mother sent ten, occasionally twenty, extra dollars, which she said were for Mavis.

I was able to reconstruct Mavis's story from Grama and Mrs Duncan's conversations about her. Mrs Duncan would sit on the step with Grama and bring two oranges—sometimes golden apples or plumrose—and peel them and put the skins in a hollow she made in the skirt of her dress, then divide the fruit, keeping half for herself and giving Grama the other half. They'd sit there and talk about Mavis, about the dreams they'd had and what they were foretelling, about who'd got saved, who'd backslid, who'd had an abortion, which young girl had just fallen, which women were "butting" their husbands . . . About Mavis. She had begun speaking of visions, and went on "her knee" despite being warned by her pointress (her guide) not to do so. The night when thousands of people came from all around to hear her tell her wonderful visions, she was "dumb silent, as a rock." The pointress had had to beat her in the presence of all the people to get her to say what had blocked her. But Mavis did not confess, and the pointress had beaten her until she'd become too exhausted to continue. Shortly after that Mavis went mad. Mrs Duncan said it was because Mavis had poisoned her husband because he used to beat her. Grama said she didn't know anything about that. Mrs Duncan said it was because Grama didn't want to know. "I would o' kill him too, Ma Moore, and live with a bad conscience after. Mavis stupid to think she could o' have it all. That ain't how life is. Imagine she going on mourning ground after she done kill him! She should o' know she would o' get blocked. Besides Pointress Billy did done warn her. She bring that on sheself, Ma Moore."

3

FOR NINE AND A HALF years I did not see my mother. Like the golden apple tree at the back of the house that got noticed only when the ripe, juicy fruit began to fall, she was interesting when money orders and packages of clothing arrived but ignored otherwise—except during those three years when the bank had to be repaid. Grama cashed the money orders at the post office after Brother Shiloh had signed them. As for my father, they told me that he lived in Trinidad but was sort of dead. I remember my mother laughing and telling me that she hoped I wouldn't be an outhouse like my father.

"Where my father?" I asked her then. She and Grama disagreed over whom I "favoured."

"In Trinidad chasing down every frock tail his eyes 'light 'pon."

"Don' tell the child stupidness!" Grama reprimanded her.

I broached the subject of my father with Grama at various times. "He not worth knowing," she'd always reply. Once I even asked Mrs Duncan what my father looked like. She chuckled and her eyes twinkled and she said, "I don' want for get in you-all commess. When you reach big man, yo' mother or else yo' grandmother will tell you."

Around the age of ten I became very conscious of my name, to the point of checking it out in a dictionary of names in the library. I was flattered by what it meant. When I was able to ask my mother why she'd named me Pedro, she said that in Trinidad she'd worked for a Spanish couple who had a very "obedient, sweetheart of a boy named Pedro," and she'd promised herself that if she ever had a son she'd name him Pedro. "You nothing like him though, neither in looks nor behaviour."

"*Looks!* Was he white?"

She nodded.

She'd have preferred a white child!

"You didn't know what the name meant?"

"No."

"Do you know what your own name means?"

"No. I like how it sound though."

I'm sure that neither Apis nor his parents knew what Apis meant. Apis MacHutchinson. He was from Mount Olivet. We called him Apish sometimes. Sometimes Dog. Never when the teacher was distant, for Apis was around fourteen and a lot wider than we. Grama would have punished me if she'd found out I was doing this. Apis got beaten after every dictation. A story went around that he once wrote Apis Dog at the top of his dictation page, and he explained to the teacher—Beulah Billy—that by the time he got through writing *MacHutchinson* the dictation was usually over.

He cooperated fully in his humiliation. One end of term he wanted to be on stage reciting, so we created a passage for him and taught it to him.

London is the capital of Paris
And France is the capital of Spain.
Prince Charles is the son of Queen Elizabeth.
We get wet when we go out in the rain.

"Pedro, why yo' chin backwards?" he'd ask. "That is the first chin I see what look like a hoe." And so I got the name Hoechin.

I always hated my chin. My mother's deathbed confession makes me think it's a deformation, something like what happened to the thalidomide babies, but less serious.

Often Apis, looking at me and laughing, would imitate my pigeon-toe walk. One recess he asked me, "Boy why you let truck run over yo' nose? Tell yo' Grama to put a clothespin on it at night when you go to bed and 'noint it with soft candle for give it a bridge." Afterwards, whenever my classmates wanted to irk me they'd say, "At least truck didn' run over me nose, and you can't weed garden with me chin." I did try the clothespin. Once. It was painful and, I suspected, useless.

I must have liked elementary school, although I was flogged on a few occasions for not paying attention. On hot, sticky, rain-free Isabellan days our teachers took us out into the schoolyard so others could do arithmetic and dictation, subjects we couldn't do standing. It seemed we got beaten less outside, where we sometimes read aloud or recited, and got the occasional strap for reading too slowly or pronouncing badly. Strapping was plentiful on recitation days. "The Mothers of the City" . . . "They have dug for the yam and the yampie/ They have grovelled potato hills/ They have dug the red clay where the spider/ His fangs with his venom fills." I certainly learned that one, but most of my forty-four classmates got flogged for not learning it. Yampie, we all knew, was the yellow or green mucus we wiped from our eyes when we woke up. When we were older we found out it was the Queen's English we should talk —not our mothers' and grandmothers'. Yampie was some blue-eyed, pink-skinned man's mispronunciation of food we called by its African name, some white man sent out to the colonies to make the curriculum relevant and compose poetry for recitation in Her Majesty's schools.

That teacher—Beulah Billy—a woman with a round brown face and deep dimples and no more than an elementary school education herself, did not understand "The Mothers of the City," or much more than the strap (which kept us quiet) and her monthly pay packet (that got her pretty dresses).

Miss Bonnie knew those as well as the meanings of the words and their political purpose. She made us repeat aloud and sing over and over again until we got it:

Once I made a snowman—
So big and tall and fat.
I dressed him like a gentleman
In daddy's cane and hat.

One sunny morning
I sadly woke to find
My snowman gone,
But he had left
His cane and hat behind.

Miss Bonnie was outraged that we didn't know where the snowman went and flogged us soundly for our ignorance.

On my first trip back, in 1976, when Grama died—I returned once after that, in 1981—I visited Miss Bonnie, by then principal of John Wesley Elementary School. The school looked small and dingy. I'd never thought it was. Even the steeple of the church in whose shadow it stood—a blessing on hot days—had begun to rot. A piece had already broken off. In its place a fern grew like a venereal wart. The school's outer walls were covered with a greenish black mould with a rank smell. Miss Bonnie herself looked shrunk. While I was in her office, she strapped six slack-skinned, hollow-eyed children for crimes ranging from incomplete homework to nodding in class—probably because they were hungry—for Miss Bonnie was paid to maintain order and no doubt had an order to maintain. Her office was dusty and made me sneeze. Piles of damp-smelling paper were on the floor with football size chunks of basalt to keep them from blowing away. In one corner was a floor fan but it was turned off. On the wall directly above her desk was the mandatory portrait of Queen Elizabeth and HRH the Duke of Edinburgh.

"Is Canada as nice as they say it is?" she asked me in one of her intervals between strapping, fingering a string of white costume beads. Her hair, cut short, was grey nearest the scalp and ranged from auburn to ebony elsewhere. I'd never known her to grin but now she was a lavender-reeking Cheshire cat.

"It's alright."

"Alright? I don' know anybody that wouldn't give everything they have to go to Canada. I always regret I didn't move out when I was young. Last year I went to England on a conference. The Methodists sent me. To represent the Guides. When I saw all those big buildings and all that progress, everything—I realized what a fool I was not to go to England when I was young. I hear Canada even nicer than England."

She stared at me intensely still fingering her costume beads, expecting a response.

"Did it snow while you were in England?"

"No. It was summer. I hear the winter so cold, I didn't want it to catch me there." She was silent for a while, as if she perceived some contradiction in what she was saying. "I hope some place opens up, because all Isabella Island producing is children, and if they can't leave, they will have to eat one another."

"At least there'll be something to eat."

"What sort of stupidness you saying?"

"Never mind."

"So what you studying to come? Doctor or lawyer?"

"I don't know yet."

"You better don't come back home when you finish your studies, to take 'way a job that somebody who didn't have your chance to go abroad can get. I know the Prime Minister always saying how Isabellan nationals overseas should come home. The other day I ask his secretary what they going do when they come back. She said the Prime Minister knows that Isabellans overseas got sense enough to hold on to the bone and leave the shadow alone." She paused and smiled, at some joke she alone was aware of. "All the big houses you see building round the place is America, England, and Canada money that building them."

I'd heard they were being built with marijuana money.

She looked around her office then with her forehead all screwed up, as if some unauthorized person had entered it. "It's reality," she added a trifle uncertain.

On my way back to Canada, I laughed at Miss Bonnie, even at her light complexion—still an asset in today's, postcolonial Isabella Island. Maybe she knew she could do nothing with it in England, Canada or the US, where "niggers" come variously pigmented. She attended the Methodist church every Sunday, was one of the top ten beggars for missionary funds, and a member of every church organization, including Methodist Mothers. She had no children and people said she'd joined to atone for those she hadn't brought to term. But all that had got her her "principality." She didn't even have to sleep with the minister, though many swore and were probably right that she did—in her imagination at the very least.

She'd asked me to talk to the students so they'd see they could get somewhere if they worked hard, but I'd told her no.

She'd replied, " You is—are—a selfish young man."

No. Miss Bonnie did not get her exhibit of former-pupil-who'd-made-good. I was not going to give her another excuse to flog bored, hungry Caribbean children who were expected to know where snow-men go.

Last year I heard she was senile. A snowwoman at sixty, probably reciting to herself the nonsensical ditties she'd been ordered to mystify us with, as if life isn't mystery enough. To survive in a colony, you begin forgetting a lot before you are six and there's a lot you dare not learn in case you live to a lucid hundred and six.

Even if my mother knew her father, she was only slightly luckier than I. She was nine at the outbreak of World War II, when the British conscripted Grampa. They told Grama that he went "a wall." When she recounted the story she included a "to" or "behind" to that description, in an attempt to make sense of what she thought they'd told her. Several times she had asked the colonial authorities if she wasn't supposed to be getting a pension. They told her they paid pensions to the spouses of those who'd died serving the British military. Grampa, they said, probably "liked it in North Africa and went a wall. Lots of men did. It's only natural." She'd repeat the story in sad, slow tones and add resignedly, "Cockroach don't get justice in fowlcock court."

It wasn't until I was thirteen that I understood what the clerks who'd spoken to Grama had meant to tell her. They were probably too arrogant to provide her with the explanation she needed. Every time she had asked to see the "head man," she was told that he was either busy or wasn't in his office. Once she'd asked a clerk, "What you mean, he went to a wall?" And the blasted nigger boy, not too long outta diapers, looked at me, old enough fo' be his grandmother, and buss out a laugh: Laugh at me 'cause I ask him for explain what he tell me. Pedro, I walk out o' there quick 'cause I been so angry no telling what I might o' do to he. Fresh! Pissing tail country bouqie!"

At thirteen I'd wondered what had caused my grandfather to go AWOL, and whether my grandmother had been told the truth. I'd wanted to explain to her the implications of going AWOL, to convince her that it wasn't a story to repeat. But I could not bring myself to soil the image Grama had of Grampa. She'd invested a lot of time weaving that tapestry. Unravelling it would have unravelled her. Many of her listeners found her story about Grampa's disappearance bizarre. I saw it in their eyes, in their half smiles, but they were too polite to ask an old woman to explain herself. Only once did someone venture, "Ma Moore, you sure you heard the story right?" She'd flown into a rage, and the woman had apologized.

Grampa was her favourite topic of conversation. "He loved for read books. You couldn' put nothing over him. And a man that listen when people talk. And always sift things: take out the nourishing part and throw 'way the husk. Wherever you find fighting and confusion, you didn' find him. He used to say, 'Muriel, I married you 'cause you walk with yo' head high, an' you know how for move in an' out o' trash and leave it all behind you.' Yo' grandfather was a model of a man.

"He been poor just like me. When the Soufrière erupt, he been in hospital, and it kill all his family. That is what they tell him becausen he wasn' a year-old yet. People in town raise him. But when he reach big man, he move 'way from them becausen—Lord—them use for blows him! And work him! From the crack o' dawn 'til midnight! But he get a little schooling. Not like me. My mother did think that I did only have for learn for sign my name. I didn' spend more than two years in school, and I clean forget everything I learn there."

Around age eight I would interrupt her at this point in the story. "Grama, I can read. I can teach you to read. What I learn in school I will teach you when I come home."

"Good. But you must do that after you done rest up," she'd answer with a smile that warmed up her face and puckered the corners of her eyes and put tears of joy in her eyes.

She would resume her story, "And even them two years, sometimes I didn' go, becausen some Monday mornings my mother didn' have the penny that we all had for carry, so I would stay home for that whole week. Every year my mother give birth to a child. Them never used for live, but she keep me home for look after them till them pass on.

"This piece o' land here and this little house, yo' grandfather and me put away penny after penny in tin pans and hide them under the bed 'til we could buy the land, becausen the bank never used for lend black people money. Sometimes the estate—them use for sell hill land to black people. And you was suppose for pay off for it while you working it, but when the time come for you get the title, the estate never give it. So when the people that done pay for the land die, them children couldn' get it.

"You can be proud o' yo' grandfather. No white body could o' push they fingers in his eyes. No black ones either. If you take after him you going get far. What the white people-them say 'bout him is for humour me. Them know he dead; themself done kill him—push that wall down 'pon him. Come telling me he gone a wall, like if they think I dotish! He been always one for put white people in they place. Is paying me the money that bothering them. I know when he dead too. Was a night that didn' have no wind at all and a tree break in the front yard and make a big groan. Next morning when I wake up and for three days the house been full o' his scent. Even your mother did notice it. His sweat did smell like grind-up plum bush. He does visit every couple o' weeks. When that plum-bush smell in here I know Bertie by my side and I feel glad." Occasionally she'd ask, "You smell that smell, Pedro? Hmm!" I always said yes.

"Never mind them. I looking forward to the time when I going join yo' grandfather in heaven. What a sweet tenor voice that man did have! He uses to sing in the church choir. Bye and bye, I will hear him sing in God's choir.

"Black people don' have no business in white people war. He used for always say that." They'd taken him illegally, for he was over thirty-five. Occasionally Grama said black people had to protect their most precious possessions from white people. At other times, she said that black people were worse than white people, and that she was better off with white people any day. It depended on the race of the person who'd got on her wrong side that day. She kept a

26

faded photograph of Grampa in his army uniform in a tin frame. At ends-of-term, when I brought home my school report and read it to her, she'd look at this picture and say, "Where yo' grandfather is in heaven he looking down right now, and he is smiling and proud o' you."

"You know," she said to me one day, "I not suppose for believe in spirits but I know that yo' grandfather spirit watching over you, 'cause children that got young mother and father home for control them not half as well behaved as you is. Pedro, you is a sweet boy."

I hung my head and could not look her in the eye because the week before, Benjy had seen her with her market basket waiting at the in-town bus stop, and had come to the gate and told me to follow him. Mrs Duncan wasn't home and there was a fair chance that Grama would not know that I'd left the house. In any event I had every intention of returning before she got back. We climbed the steps to Miss Haynes's yard and walked towards the back of Mrs Manley's property. Several of her fruit trees towered above her corrugated galvanized fence. One was a julee mango, the juiciest and most delicious of all mangoes, and it was laden. Sometimes I smelled them from the road and my mouth would water. A branch of the mango tree reached over the fence. Benjy stood on my shoulders, caught it, hoisted himself up and was soon where the best mangoes were. He threw me three halfripe mangoes and put a few in his pockets. But before he could come down Mrs Manley showed up, a walking stick in hand, and ordered him to come down. "I will fix your business," she said, brandishing the stick. I crouched behind the fence, so she did not see me. Benjy began to pelt Mrs Manley with green mangoes, deliberately avoiding hitting her. "Murder! Help!" Mrs Manley bawled. This time Benjy hit her with a mango and said, "Shut up! You *sookoona* bitch!" Shocked, Mrs Manley did. *Her business fixed*. Benjy jumped outside the fence. We ran, leaving the mangoes behind. At home I hoped Mrs Manley's servants hadn't seen us, felt guilty about what Benjy had done, but brushed that away with thoughts that Mrs Manley was preparing to beat Benjy, gave away nothing, except funeral wreaths, rarely spoke to the neighbours, and was, Grama and Mrs Duncan said, a "sookoona"—a *soucouyan*.

27

Grama never found out about this. I loved it when she praised me, and did little things for her just so that she would praise me.

Sometimes she and Mrs Duncan talked about Miss Haynes's grandson, who "cause that poor woman eyewater to run all the time. That boy start running that woman blood to water since he knee-high. Imagine when he start smelling heself." Mrs Duncan said that half of it was Miss Haynes's fault.

I wondered what Grama meant about boys smelling themselves. She was sure that Grampa's spirit looking over me wherever I went steered me away from evil temptation. "I don' care what Reverend Abrahams want me for believe, I know Bertie guiding you."

But that wasn't how Mr Sam explained it. He said a person's shadow was his guardian spirit. It appeared to people in dreams to warn them about things that could happen to them. If someone wanted to kill somebody, all he had to do was catch the person's shadow and seal it in a bottle. After that the person would shrink to almost nothing because then he'd be without his protector, and all the evil forces in the world would suck the strength out of him until he was too weak to live. Reverend Abrahams saw such beliefs as hindrances that Blacks brought from Africa.

Mr Sam was one of those who'd hidden from the conscripting parties. The earth rises up in vengeance, he said, against those who stupidly spill the blood it gives them. According to him, what's red in nature, especially blood, is sacred.

Every year on Remembrance Day, we were marched by our teachers to the War Memorial in Trafalgar Square right in the middle of Hanovertown. When we learned in school about Trafalgar Square in London, I wondered why this one was also called Trafalgar Square and whether the nondescript male statue there was also Lord Horatio Nelson. And it wouldn't have surprised me if one day I found thousands of pigeons there. The British Administrator, to a fanfare struck up by the police band, would mount a scaffold erected for the occasion and tell us how brave the Isabellans who had fought in two World Wars had been. A dozen or so survivors were always on display at the foot of the scaffolding. There were always three or four who had lost a leg or an arm—the lower half of the empty trouser leg folded neatly up against the upper half and held in place with a clothespin or large safety pin, a crutch standing in for the missing leg; or the empty collapsed shirt sleeve tucked into a trouser pocket. The first time I was taken there, I was so engrossed with their missing limbs, I heard not a word the Administrator said and was ashamed of myself when I got home and couldn't tell Grama what he had told us or why I couldn't remember his speech. In subsequent years the Administrator told us that the veterans were brave men whom we should cherish, respect, and emulate if the need were to arise. They had saved Isabellans from slavery and certain death. Those who had died—their names were on the War Memorial (Grampa's wasn't on it)—had done no less than sacrifice their lives for the freedom all Isabellans enjoyed.

Following this the Administrator descended and took a wreath the Chief Minister handed to him and placed it at the foot of the War Memorial. A short distance away, in a street that was cordoned off with red, white, and blue rope, the police, in white bowlers, grey shirts, red belts, and black tunics, would stiffen as if falling to attention and bring their shining brass instruments to their lips and play, the crowd singing along with them, "Onward Christian Soldiers Marching as to War." When the band stopped playing, the Anglican bishop, his silk surplice rustling, would mount the scaffold and ask the Lord to bless the veterans, to grant peace to the dead and the living . . . world-without-end-amen. Finally, with the bugle wailing, the police band played "Day is Done, Gone the Sun." *All is well. Safely rest.*

 The exercise was again repeated the Sunday after Remembrance Day by the four main Hanovertown denominations: Anglicans, Methodists, Presbyterians, and Roman Catholics, but without the Administrator and the police band.

It was all right except when it was raining, which, November being Isabella Island's rainiest month, was almost always. And we couldn't complain because there was the strap, and more than that, although wet, we were alive, and free, and mobile compared to others who had been maimed or killed so that we could be free. Mr Sam said it was all British bullshit.

He wanted to marry Grama. "I don' know if my husband still living. What if he come back from that wall? I can' married you," Grama repeatedly told him.

Once I told Grama that Mr Sam was a nice man who wouldn't beat her, and she should marry him. I'd had visions of my grandmother in a white dress with a train and lots of flowers and hundreds of people eating "sweet food," and musicians playing, and people dancing and giving speeches.

"What you know 'bout such things? If I marriage him I will have fo' give up my church. And I don' want for do that. 'Sides what if I ups and marriage him and my husband what went to a wall show up?" She said it with a deep sadness, her eyes looking far off into the distance.

She allowed me to visit Mr Sam regularly. He lived a short way downhill from us on the bank above the highway in a two-room, unpainted house whose boards had been bleached silver on the outside. He was very proud of his two-room house. It was *clean*. I never went into his bedroom. He'd made it clear that I was not to go in there. There were no curtains in his windows. I asked him why. He said he had nothing to hide. Only evil people had things to hide, which made me wonder why he didn't want me to go into his bedroom. In the room in which he did everything except sleep, wash, and void (he called it his hall), he had a small dining table and two chairs directly under one window. On the opposite wall he had three shelves that ran the length of the room. The topmost shelf stood about three feet from the floor. On it he kept his Primus stove and his kitchen utensils—two enamel cups, two enamel plates, a few spoons, cutting and peeling knives, a pot, a saucepan, a frying pan and a dishpan. He kept his groceries on the lower shelf. He had a butterscotch cat that was almost always in his lap when he was sitting, or lying beside him when he was outside working. It behaved more like a dog than a cat. He kept three thatched sheds outside. One was his outhouse, one his work shed, which he used only when it rained, and the third he refused to talk to me about—except to say it was off bounds and if I were to enter it a bolt of lightning would strike me dead. I defied him once but found the door locked. He made bamboo baskets for a living. He had a huge testicular hernia (bamanko) that killed him two weeks after I left Isabella Island. It used to swing from side to side when he came down the hill with as much as three feet of bamboo lace piled on his head.

Not knowing that I was hearing them, Mrs Duncan and Grama had one day talked about his *bamanko.*

"Ma Moore, if you married him he won' able for comfort you. That *bamanko* will keep everything down."

"He not studying 'bout that, Patience. All he want at this stage o' his life is somebody for wash his clothes, cook a piece of food for him, and keep his house clean."

"And what 'bout you, Ma Moore? You have needs."

"What needs, girl? At my age all I studying is my Bible and how to keep my soul clean."

Mrs Duncan laughed. It began deep within her, mounted on a crescendo, where it lingered a while before falling, like a stretched-out hen's cackle. "Look at Anderson. Eighty and got a two-year son. And mistress, wife, and heself living in the same house, sleeping in the same bed!"

Grama laughed: three staccato notes repeated once with a short pause in between, her laugh that said she was tickled all the way to her entrails.

"Anderson wife older than you, Ma Moore; and you know what she been saying in the market the other day? 'You all should come and listen to what my moves does do to he. And Andy tell me that I is better than that other Jezebel.' And then she start knocking her chest and bragging, 'Young as she is, I is better than she. Put that in all yo' pipe and smoke it!'"

Grama laughed again. "Hope none o' the two o' them don' have a heart attack."

"What I is telling you, Ma Moore, is, compare to Mistress Anderson, you is a pullet."

"That woman was talking 'bout she *husband*, Patience! I don' have a husband. Now if Bertie was alive—" she stopped, probably shocked by what she almost said.

Mrs Duncan fell into a long laughing fit.

"And what 'bout you?" Grama turned the spotlight on her. "I don' see no man visiting you since Duncan dead."

"These wutliss men round here, Ma Moore! You must be joking!"

But their relationship wasn't always this cordial; it came closest to breaking point in their attitudes to carnival.

Some of the bands passed in front of Grama's gate on their way into town. Mrs Duncan jumped up in the Mount Olivet Band. A day after one of Ishtar's goats had ravaged her flower garden and she and Ishtar had quarreled, she sweet-talked Ishtar into helping her make a carnival outfit. They'd sat on her porch all afternoon cutting yellow felt into banana shapes and sewing them on to a black belt. She said it was her Josephine Baker outfit. Grama told her, "Take care no man molest you, 'cause the magistrate will say is you what cause it. I don' know why Duncan don' put his foot down."

"Ma Moore, ain't you know the body got needs the soul don' know 'bout? Why you always vex when people having fun?" Mrs Duncan told her, smiling.

That carnival Tuesday she wore her Josephine Baker skirt over black knickers and covered her breasts with a red halter-top. Her thighs parted the banana shapes as if they were strands of beaded curtains. Grama looked at her, raised her eyes to heaven, and looked at her again.

I too stared at her. She came onto Grama's porch where I was, ruffled my hair and said, "See that look in yo' eye? You is definitely cream from the old goat."

Grama slanted her head towards me, sucked in her cheeks and spiked her lips, severity in her eyes—a wordless command not to respond to Mrs Duncan's statement. I wanted to go down the hill with her, to see the costumes, to dance and listen to the music.

At the carnival two years later, three months before her husband's death, she had ripped off her blouse and brassiere in a music daze.

Mrs Duncan! She knew where and when every dance was going to be held, and would have gone if Duncan had permitted her. As soon as Duncan died she bought the biggest stereo she could find—with Duncan's insurance money, the neighbours said—and every dance record released. Petite, pale skinned, with semi-straight hair, she blushed at every male who looked at her, but she didn't sleep with them. Whereas most people in her age group sang hymns, she sang calypsos. Grama called her home the den of sin. But the little tensions between them never penetrated to the bedrock of their friendship. Grama admired her for her generosity. She remained celibate after her husband's death, confounding everyone who'd said, "Duncan got his hands full satisfying that slut." Saul "Tomcat" said Duncan had to do it with his hands—and "Duncan ain' will be in the ground nine days before men start lining up in front o' that house." She must have known those opinions: discretion was not a trait cultivated or encouraged by Isabellans. And she was no stranger to scandal. Duncan was not her first husband. There was a rumour that she was responsible for her first husband's death. The story went that he'd had another woman, to whom he gave his wages. One night when he opened his supper bowl a live frog jumped out. He got it in his head that it was sorcery and began to waste away. One evening, six months later, he jumped to his death from the precipice at Fort George. But Duncan was not your average husband, and people said it was because he was afraid of her special powers or because he was under her influence. He told Grama, in one of his rare conversations, that he'd married her because he'd wanted a wife capable of fighting her own battles. I doubt there are any actual adulterous acts in her "dark closet." Fantasies aplenty though—of the men she'd not slept with, including my father.

Someone had come running to call Duncan, "Come quick! Yo' wife up at Crossroad, naked as she born." He slapped her back into reality—he was no wife-beater—took off his shirt, wrapped it around her, and led her home. Come to think of it, he was already on sick leave.

Grama, who felt that any festivity without hymns and prayers was against the Lord's will, did not allow me to go into town on either carnival day. The closest thing resembling carnival that she took part in was the Methodist parade, which was held two or three times yearly. To the drumbeat of the police band they marched through the streets of Hanovertown, belting out "Onward Christian Soldiers." *Forward into battle see His banners go*. I can see now why she hated carnival, especially the songs that went with it: "Me bucket got a hole in the centre / And if you think I telling lie, shove yo' finger"; "The big bamboo"; "One plantain could full up your pot /Especially when hot!"

Too hot for Grama's handling.

Mr Sam said that his grandmother had told him that when black people were still slaves, carnival used to be at the end of the sugar cane harvest. Then, Blacks used to put on black and white masks and act out the injustices of slavery on the lawns outside the plantation houses.

"Weren't they afraid of being beaten?"

"Some masters never used for allow them. Sure they was afraid. But they was used to getting beat. Once in a while they get good results though, like a time when a slave master free all his slaves after he see the performance."

The February before I left, thousands of people had lined the highway from Mount Olivet into Hanovertown to watch a man do the downhill journey on his hands and head, to the beat of a drummer gyrating behind him. That year Mrs Duncan's costume was a loose, army-green canvas frock with a hood that covered her face. Circles of mirrors were glued onto the frock where it covered her face, breasts, crotch and behind. Her eyes, nose and mouth showed through slits in the facial mirror, mingling with reflections and drawing fascinated stares.

"When people look at you is theyself they see," Grama called out to her as she stepped from the porch into the yard. "I don' get the point at all."

"That is the point, Ma Moore," she replied, focusing her mirrored face onto Grama's before turning around and wiggling her behind with blinding glares from the mirrors.

"Pedro," Mrs Duncan said, beckoning to me, "come with me; le' we go play 'mas. Leave yo' Grandmother to pray. You ain't have no life in that house. You ain't do nothing fo' be in prison."

"You not going nowhere," Grama said.

"I want to go," I told her.

"Ma Moore! Stop cooping up that boy under yo' frock tail!

Caramba! What yo' think he is?"

"You is not going!" Grama said with a vehement stamp of the foot. "Patience, the devil send you for my soul today? He not content with yours, he have for have mines too?"

"Ma Moore," Mr Sam's voice sounded from the gate. He came into the yard; he had on a toga made from a crocus bag, his face blackened with ground charcoal, a spear of bamboo in his hand. "Patience," he said with nodding approval, his eyes roving over Mrs Duncan's body, "You is a artist for true, gal." To me, he said, "Where yo' costume, Pedro?" Then he turned to Grama and winked, "You not feting, Ma Moore? Where yo' costume? Come le's go in town and do a lil' win'ing."

"What you is? Since when you know I involve in devil dealings?" Grama replied, already conceding.

"Loosen up, Ma Moore. You too tie up in yo' soul," Mr Sam said.

It was my cue to defy her. I went inside and got dressed and went into town with Mr Sam and Mrs Duncan. That year *The Isabellan* awarded Mrs Duncan the prize for the most imaginative, inexpensive costume. Her picture was on its front page.

I made sure they accompanied me home, just in case. But Grama only said, "You getting fo' be more than I can handle. Soon you will ha' for go and meet yo' mother. I can' take care o' no own-way pickney."

Up to the time I was nine (the practice died out after that) *mardi gras* revellers gathered at the Mount Olivet Crossroad around five am Ash Wednesday and threw their masks and costumes into a bonfire. Those without masks or costumes sacrificed a piece of valuable clothing. If they were Catholic, like Mrs Duncan or Anglican (like Ishtar), they later headed off to church and returned with a patch of ashes on their forehead. As usual Grama did not allow me to see the bonfire. But even if she spurned the pre-Lenten pleasures, she spared herself and me none of Lent's privations. Every Lent I had to spend an hour each week with one of the shut-in Methodists, and read aloud to Grama for thirty minutes from the Bible on Saturday and Wednesday.

Mrs Duncan stopped wearing shorts and eating meat during Lent and tried her best not to sing calypsos. On Holy Thursday she had to stay pure to do the Stations of the Cross on Good Friday. When she got back from church, Ishtar and she would each crack an egg and pour the white into a glass of water, which they put on a chair out in the sun. Depending on whether it formed a ship, a church or a coffin, it foretold travel, marriage, or death. Grama often joked that Ishtar's would show a coffin. The year Mr Duncan died Mrs Duncan insisted that her glass had shown a coffin. In any event Duncan had already been sick.

4

ON THE JANUARY 24 following my thirteenth birthday, I was in the living room listening to the radio. It was the holiday that celebrated Columbus's discovery of Isabella Island. A Carib leader on the radio was saying that his people were tired of being shat, pissed and spat upon year after year, first by the British, and now by the leaders of independent Isabella Island. The news followed. The newscaster spoke of various happenings before saying—he had a deep, melodious voice, and seemed more interested in showing it off than in reading the news—"Just in from Trinidad and Tobago: an ex-Isabellan, Patrick Percy, has been charged with the murder of his live-in mate. Neighbours began noticing that they hadn't seen either of them for four days. When a foul smell began issuing from their shack, the neighbours searched it and discovered the woman's already bloated body. This morning the police apprehended Percy, who confessed to having committed the deed."

Grama was in the kitchen and hadn't heard the news. Almost instantly, I heard Mrs Duncan's running footsteps outside. "Ma Moore," she shouted, out of breath, "the news just say that Patrick Percy kill a woman in Trinidad."

"Sh-sh," Grama said. The remainder of their conversation was carried on in whispers.

What was it that they did not want me to hear?

Grama had cooked pigeon-pea soup with lots of salt beef and corn dumplings. It was one of my favourite dishes. She had taken to asking me what I would like to eat; once she did so in Brother Shiloh's presence. Brother Shiloh had shaken his head and told her, "Ma Moore, you not training this boy right. It's like he is the man o' the house."

"Shiloh, what other man you see 'round here? Pedro is the man o' the house, yes. And Pedro know that he have for protect me." She winked at Brother Shiloh, and Brother Shiloh and I laughed.

At the table she would sometimes stop eating and stare at me while I ate, pleased that I enjoyed her cooking. Sometimes she'd say, "I have for stop feeding you like this; you is outgrowing yo' clothes too fast." But today she was tense, staring off into the distance and striking the table with the palm of her hand. When she turned to me she realized that I was looking at her. "What is the matter with you, boy? Why you only picking at yo' food?"

"Nothing."

"What you mean, nothing? Up to 'bout a hour ago, you was out here reading and listening to the radio—what come over you all of a sudden?"

What had come over her?

I asked her why she and Mrs Duncan did not want me to hear their conversation about Patrick Percy.

"Look, boy don' turn my soul wrong-side out today! You hear me?"

"Grama!"

She gripped her side of the table with both hands and took several deep breaths. Even so, when she spoke there was a tremor in her voice, and when she stopped holding the table her hands shook and she perspired profusely.

"Yes, lots o' people, lots o' people—Oh God!—done fall in Patrick Percy trap-them. Is 'bout time he fall in it heself. Is 'bout time! I pray God that poor woman don' leave no motherless children behind. His neck will wring *this time*. It should o' wring before he scatter his misery 'pon this earth."

I had never seen my grandmother so emotionally wrought.

She paused. "Eat yo' food." But her lips continued to move in a silent conversation with herself, and she stared blankly into space. Eventually she left her place at the table, came to stand behind me, and patted my hair. "Poor boy! One o' these days, you will find out all 'bout Patrick Percy, but now not the right time. Don' make Patrick Percy deeds upset you."

"Grama, you're the one upset. Is Patrick Percy our family?"

"Your family. Not mine. Oh God! What foolish questions you asking me! Look boy, eat yo' food. You hear me? Don' turn my soul wrong-side out. You making me say stupidness." I knew that if I'd been looking at her, her eyelids would be winking fast. She was trying to hide something.

"What is Patrick Percy to me, Grama?"

"Stop questioning me! You is not no lawyer and I not in no court. You better don' mention that man name again—in this house or anywhere else."

Who was Patrick Percy? How closely were we related? Why was Grama afraid to tell me? The rest of the day I wondered who my father was, how closely he was related to Patrick Percy, and decided I would follow the Patrick Percy story in the newspaper and save the clippings.

That afternoon, still thinking of all this, I walked down to the wharf, using the very steep side road instead of the footpath beside the highway. The area had changed. In the odd place there still remained the gable roof, two-room shacks that had covered the slope when I first started school. Two-storey cement houses, many still incomplete, their corrugated steel roofs painted red or green, now covered the slope all the way down to the Hanovertown plain. I walked to the centre of Hanovertown, traversed the Quadrangle there where on regular days the women haggled their produce in the open-air market (it was quiet today), and headed over to the Hanovertown Gardens, before returning again into town. It was suppertime when I got back home. All the while I thought about the men I knew who mistreated their women and children.

Of Mathilda—she lived five houses in from the road, uphill from us—telling Percival just in front of Grama's house, "The pickney you breed me with hungry. What sort of man you is for see yo' child hungry and don' feed it?"

Percival was a dung-gut fellow on bandy legs that touched at the knees and then angled outwards, thighs, knees and legs forming an X (women he made lewd remarks at told him to run along with his "twis'-up self" unless he wanted their husbands to straighten him out); his nail-keg chest was pushed out in front of him and his bottom trailed a ways behind. He barely opened his eyes that always seemed half shut and told Mathilda that she didn't have proof he was the child's father: "Nobody didn' see me fucking you. Shell corn," he grinned broadly, his lips pulled back like a braying ass's, "don' know what cob it come from."

Mathilda displayed the child she'd been clasping with one arm against her chest, raised her eyes to heaven in a silent plea to God to bear witness, and shook her head slowly. She pointed her free arm toward Percival, waving her finger at him furiously.

"Percival," Grama said, without removing from her mouth a sprig of mint she was chewing, "That child is yo' spitting image. You is the corn cob." While she spoke she moved into the road to where Percival and Mathilda were battling it out.

Mrs Duncan, who was sitting on her porch fanning herself, laughed.

I tensed. Percival was notorious for the four-letter epithets he hurled at everyone, including the Hanovertown magistrate. Once he'd told Mrs Duncan, who usually called him Goatman, that her "cunt" wasn't big enough for his "dick"; and she shot back, in a voice of fake pity, "Poor thing! Such a little head and all it got in is dick!" And one time Puckett had kicked him over the bank further down the highway, vowing to "untwist" him, because of obscene gestures he'd made to his wife. Now, instead of answering Grama, Percival pushed his hand into his pocket, pulled out a wad of dollar bills, peeled off a dollar, and pushed it towards Mathilda, who looked at it and spat.

"You see? I just gi'ing she this dollar 'cause I feel sorry for the starving child." Turning to look at Grama, he continued, "Ma Moore, you is a respectable, church-going lady. Don' get mix up in all this man-'oman nastiness, else you will reach heaven still smelling o' it." Again he brought out the wad and peeled off a two-dollar bill, which he added to the first and handed to Mathilda.

Mathilda looked at Grama, who shook her head.

Eventually he increased it to ten before Mathilda took it. Then he tried to encircle her with his free arm. "After all this, you mean you

40

not even giving me a kiss?"

"I don' kiss dog," Mathilda replied, snaking herself out of his attempted embrace.

Was my father like that?

Was he like Saul (Tomcat), Percival's cousin? Tomcat owned the countryside lot beside Grama's house as well as the back lot adjoining; his four-room, gable-roofed, boardhouse, painted green, the galvanized roof red, stood on cement stilts on the back lot. Ishtar, his wife, reared the goats which were tied to the stilts; she fed them vegetable scraps and weeds gathered from empty lots and the roadside. On days when the sea was almost silent, and no wind came sweeping down the hill, and no vehicles were going up and down on the highway, I could actually hear the cru-cru-ing of their chewing; sometimes too they got untied and headed straight for Mrs Duncan's flower garden, causing Mrs Duncan and Ishtar to accuse one another of being without bloomers, throwing away children, working obeah on their husbands, roasting in hell already; and to play games a day or two later to make up. A footpath ran through the front lot to the house on the back; behind the house the land dropped in uneven steep terraces down to the sea. On either side of the footpath the earth was heaped into mounds in which arbours were staked to support the vines of yams Tomcat cultivated. Scattered across the lot were pigeon-pea shrubs. A couple of papaya trees grew on it; Ishtar cooked the green ones—for her mother's diabetes, she said. A hedge of hibiscus and cattail supporting a mass of morning glory vines that Grama had planted separated his land from ours.

People rarely spoke to Tomcat. This was probably what he wanted, since he made his statements sound like snarls. Mrs Duncan was the exception, her taunts made him laugh sometimes and sometimes curse. It was she who'd named him Tomcat; he'd grin and take it as a compliment when she called him that. When speaking about him she and Grama called him Ishtar's Tomcat.

He was in his mid-forties, was molasses-brown, and had red bulging eyes—from the hellfire inside him, Grama said, but it was because he drank heavily. He had spiky, hedgehoglike hair, and looked hardly more substantial than a five-foot string; he was

"Ishtar piece o' twine." He went around mostly with his torso bare, and you could sometimes discern his ribs, his sternum, and his vertebrae outlined under his skin. He was incapable of remaining still. He and Mrs Duncan's husband were drivers of Public Works Department trucks.

Tomcat used to beat Ishtar almost daily—"at tea, breakfast, and dinner," Grama said; "for entertainment," Mrs Duncan said. He called Ishtar a mule; he said he'd made her respectable, had rescued her from having to sleep with every man who wanted her, only to have her abort his children with help from her mother. He had several women, rarely slept at home, and was rarely there longer than it took to eat his meals, work in his garden, and beat Ishtar. Once one of his mistresses was hospitalized for months, and he brought her three children and ordered Ishtar to care for them. Ishtar's mother, Mother Branch, a Shango priestess, lived with them, but she was bedridden. And when Saul hadn't fully spent his cruelty on Ishtar, he'd turn to cursing her, calling her a sorceress and abortionist whose sins had crippled her. Grama would shake her head and say, despite her hostility to Shangos and Spiritual Baptists, "Everybody say that woman lead a clean life. In due time God will call Saul to reckoning."

"How you managing, Ishtar," the women around asked her in their daily greetings; and she would say, "Poorly, yes. Poorly." If she was still smarting from the bruises Tomcat had left on her body, she would say, "Water more than flour." Miss Haynes would always say, "But all the same, you is a forbearing woman, Ishtar. I would o' done kill Saul long time and heng for it, or else tame him with a lil' som'n from Kimbo" (the Obeah man). Apparently that was what Cousin Mavis had tried to do, but she'd miscalculated the dosage of the potion Kimbo had given her.

Short, wide, yellow-skin Ishtar waddled to and from her yard and downhill into Hanovertown, putting most of her plentiful weight on her right foot, dragging the left (hurt from a beating by Tomcat), her red calico shift sticking in the crease of her bottom, her breasts bouncing under her shifts.

Once she had run into Grama's house to escape a beating, Tomcat on her heels, naked except for a bath towel. Grama stood blocking the doorway and told me to bring the bread knife quick. Ishtar slept in Grama's bed that night. "Strange man," Mrs Duncan said next day, "beating his wife while he naked."

The morning after Ishtar returned home, I asked Grama if Grampa used to beat her. Grampa didn't indulge, she said with a long, drawn-out sigh, "in low-class wutlisness."

Tomcat, Percival (Ram Goat) and Percival's brother Joseph were first cousins. Joseph had been caught doing it with a donkey. (Thereafter he became Back-Back.) A night when there was a full moon, they'd "hanged" him at Crossroad, after a trial by " judge and jury"—Mr Sam and twelve villagers. Two persons, one playing Joseph and one disguised as a donkey, acted out what Joseph had done. The village calypsonian was "the attorney for the defence." His brief was a sung calypso that accused the donkey of bewitching Joseph, and featured Joseph begging in a spasmodic voice, *"Please, Miss Donkey, don' back-back on me. You go make the people-them catch me. I can' leave this tree. I can' resist you, honeeeey! Don' back-back on me."* Next they'd stoned and afterwards burned him in effigy. For a long time people sang "the defence attorney's song"; and "back-back" and its variations expanded the Isabellan lexicon: *to back-back, back-backed, back-backing, back-backer, backmenter, backmenting, backmentment,* and *backmentation.*

Grama said often that they were a blighted breed, that a curse was on them (all except one brother who'd done well, who was a solicitor in England and never came home because, Mount Olivetans said, he was ashamed of his relatives). Afterwards she'd look at me guiltily, as if she'd mouthed an obscenity. Once after she'd said it, she'd held me ferociously against her, to the point of suffocation almost, and sobbed, her tears falling on my head.

The night of January 24 I dreamed my mother had returned from Canada, and was with a tall, lithe, handsome, pale-skinned, straight-haired man from Trinidad. The man said his name was Patrick Percy and that he was my father. Mathilda was in the dream too, though I couldn't remember her role. The police came to arrest him. I saw them coming but did not warn him, was angry with him for saying he was my father. The nightmare woke me, and in the sleepless hours that followed, I wondered how closely Patrick Percy and I were related. All I knew was that he was on my father's side of the family, since he was no family to Grama.

While heading home for lunch next day, I bought a copy of *The Trinidad Guardian*. A photograph of Patrick Percy, handcuffed and flanked by police officers with drawn pistols, was on the front page. He had a bony, oval face, wild eyes, narrow shoulders, and he looked half the size of the cops on either side of him. There was no resemblance between him and the man in my dream, and I felt relieved. I felt a deep loathing for him, and wished Grama hadn't told me he and I were related. A full account of the murder was on page two. He said he hadn't intended to kill the woman, hadn't known that the blow he gave her would be fatal. The neighbours said they'd heard the beating; it wasn't unusual; he accused her constantly of sleeping with other men; he never worked; spent his time "catting and playing pan"; she paid the bills.

5

IT WAS NOT UNTIL the night before I left for Canada that Grama raised the subject of my father again. With her arms spread out on the dining table, she told me as much as she felt comfortable saying. My father was an outstanding steel band player and a skirt chaser. In her twenties Ma had lived in Trinidad. About two years before my birth, Grama suffered a slight stroke, and Isis returned from Trinidad to take care of her. Shortly after she came back she took up with my father. She knew of the many children he had in villages all over Isabella Island wherever he went with his steel band, but she fell for his talk, "cause he didn' have looks for speak 'bout; just like a congo snake, if you ask me; a gut string stuff with filth. And Pedro, like the old heads-them say, 'Wha' sweet nanny goat does give her belly-runnings.'"

I didn't like Grama's likening me to diarrhea.

"Yo' father turn his back on yo' mother before you born and go way to Trinidad when you been 'bout three-months old. Isis stay right here 'cause life a Trinidad just as rock-stone hard like 'pon Isabella Island."

"I feel we should o' tell you everything soon as you old enough for understand. Yo' mother did want you for think yo' father die before you born." She looked away, weighed her words, before saying, "People here that you will shame for associate with is yo' close family. Them say blood thicker than water, but water better than that kind o' blood, and you is better off not knowing you have it." Lowering her head, she said, "Saul is yo' second cousin."

She left me to figure out that Percival and Joseph were too. Yes, I would have preferred not to know. So that was why she looked so guilty each time she'd said they were cursed. Grama believed firmly that depravity was inherited; that what was in the goat was also in the kid; that Guinea hen couldn't "bring" ram goat. But she also believed in the power of prayer. She must have prayed that day when she'd held me against her, almost cutting off my breath, that I would be spared the curse of the "Percy Breed." That night I understood that she'd kept me away from other children to prevent the seeds of "disgraceful behaviour" that she was sure I carried from sprouting. I could not help, given the tower of morality Grama was, seeing my mother as a cheap, ordinary, bottom-of-the-heap woman, and I felt less desirous of going to live with her.

"You still didn't tell me my father's name," I reminded Grama after I realized that she was staring at me with a worried look.

"Name? For now jus' call him Bogus."

"*Bogus?*"

"That is what I just done say: *Bogus*. That is what he is: a bogus what-you-ma'-call-it" (her substitute for sonofabitch). "Child, yo' mother will have fo' tell you that she own self. Why you so taken up with knowing who yo' father is? I didn' treat you right? Look at all the children 'bout here that know they father? All the lot o' them get from they father is constant beating. I ever beat you yet?" Her face was relaxed, her eyes beamed with pride. I felt guilty pressing the issue. My intuition told me that my grandmother had done the best parenting job she was capable of, and I truly loved her in a way I would never be able to love anyone else.

I'd by then celebrated my fourteenth birthday and it was rare that I hadn't felt lonely, especially in later years. There was never any question of my being close friends with anyone my age. She invented excuse upon excuse to make me come home immediately after school. She'd heard Reverend Abrahams preach against marijuana-smoking, and periodically she asked me if I'd started smoking marijuana yet. One time she said, her hands rapidly whipping up the soapsuds in an aluminum washtub full of clothes and her eyes blinking wildly, that someone had seen me puffing a marijuana cigarette. "Grama," I told her, "you've been dreaming again."

She forced me to join the Methodist Boys Brigade. I hated it. Some of the boys in it were bullies. They called me "Sissy" and

"Mamselle Moore." "Hoechin" didn't follow me to Grammar School. On my own I joined the Methodist Youth Fellowship. I liked Reverend Abrahams. In Boys Brigade, whenever we played cricket, the ball was never where I saw it, and the team had an agreement among themselves to aim the ball at my head (they couldn't match me in the quizzes and extemporaneous public speaking, which we did in Youth Fellowship), and I was ducking the ball more often than hitting it, defending my head instead of the wicket. During brigade drills, I often turned right when the captain said, "Left!" mostly because I have always had difficulty telling left from right. Even when the turn was correct it was badly timed and out of step. I begged my form master to write a letter to persuade Grama to let me join the Debating Society and used this to bargain my way out of Boys Brigade.

In Grammar School I'd tried to befriend a group of boys. But they always said nasty things about the size of my bottom. With finger gestures and grunts, they speculated about which of the buller men would be delighted to poke around in it. Sometimes they'd say, "Imagine, big man like you still sleeping with yo' head under yo' Grama nightdress!" Benjy was part of their group and he sometimes joined in the teasing.

Chauncey *was* a storyteller. Chauncey—the wide space between his bowlegs, his rocking walk, boulder-broad shoulders, bull voice. I would have worshipped him if he'd been kind to me. Lots of students would come to listen to him tell "clean" stories in which a legendary village fool called Doum-Doum was the protagonist. I stayed on the periphery of the listeners. After a while Doum-Doum was one of the names they called me.

Chauncey was also captain of the junior cricket team. A couple of times they invited me to play with them, saying they would teach me how to play. The first time I was bowled out by the second ball. The second time I'd let drop a ball that was easy to catch, and Chauncey clouted me, shouting, "Me sister play better cricket than you!" A third time he pulled up a wicket and threatened to beat me with it. The final humiliation came one day when he asked me when was my birthday, because he intended to buy me a frock.

In form one, Andrew Samuels, our English teacher for half a term—he was nineteen and had just passed his A levels—gave Chauncey a hard time. One day Chauncey asked to go to the toilet and Samuels said no. Chauncey said, "But sir, I have to shit."

"Indeed you have to. I'm not preventing you. But *respectable* people say *defecate*; and so that you won't forget it, you will write it out three hundred times. Def-e-cate," he pronounced slowly. "You think you'll be able to get it right?"

A few days later he told Chauncey that the English language came out of his mouth "bruised and battered and tortured, bitten where it should have been caressed, scratched where it should have been stroked." We all laughed, and poor Chauncey did his best not to cry. Under his breath he vowed he'd make Samuels pay.

Two weeks later Samuels asked Chauncey what work the women of his village did. All hell broke loose. Not instantly, because no one in class understood, but overnight we'd had time to check. Chauncey was from a village called Petit Bordel. Samuels, who was mulatto, was no doubt biding his time until the opposition party, of which his father was a henchman, came to power so he could get a scholarship to an American, Canadian or British university. It didn't help that Chauncey's riding was one the opposition could never win. Neither did it help that Chauncey was gruff, rough mannered (probably couldn't eat with a knife and fork), tar-black, had big feet, legs that widened into an arch, a thick flat nose, and hair that curled into tight tiny balls resembling black pepper grains: "country bouquie" traits that put him at the bottom of Isabellan colour caste and made him a prime target for mulatto "humour."

Next morning Chauncey told Samuels to say his prayers, and got up to kill him. Samuels ran to the principal's office (another, but "enlightened," mulatto as Samuels belatedly discovered) with Chauncey in close pursuit. We later joked that had we known we'd have clocked their speed, which had to have been faster than any Olympic record holder's. Samuels' teaching career ended that day and the principal apologized to Chauncey.

(On my 1981 trip to Isabella Island I asked him what had become of Samuels.

In khaki shorts and sandals, legs curved like horseshoes, belly now a dome under his yellow tank top—no longer the athlete I'd once admired and unconsciously lusted after—face darkening, brows wrinkling in what had been his glass-smooth face, ridges in his jaw muscles—he seemed to be choking, unable to answer. "Sorry. Forget it," I said, fearing I'd dug up a painful memory he'd buried.

"He's in the madhouse. He went to Cave Hill to study—law, I think—but came back crazy." He stopped briefly, stared at the ground, his face slowly relaxing. "What he did to me was foolishness. You know, at that age . . . showing off . . . I don't hold it against him."

I nodded, touched by his forgiving spirit, and looked intently into his eyes, registering their deep-brown gentleness, remembering my seemingly innocent dream of eight years before.)

Whenever my classmates teased me I found myself resenting Grama. If she'd allowed me to hang around with Mount Olivet youngsters I'd have learnt to play cricket and known stories that I could tell. All the village boys wandered about with their friends on Saturdays and during school holidays. Every night, too, for the three days before a full moon and on the night of the full moon, Mount Olivet children gathered at Crossroad and sang and danced or listened to stories adults told. One of their songs ran,

The man in the moonlight [a lead voice]
Aye ya yaye! [chorus of dancers]
Planting potato.
Aye ya yaye!
A man come and steal it.
Aye ya yaye!
My oko! My oko!
Aye ya yaye!

I asked Benjy what the strange words meant. He grinned with contempt, creasing his moonlike cinnamon-coloured face, and tossed his head and shoulders from left to right, before saying, "That is we secret." Mr Sam was no help: part of some African language, he believed, that Isabellans had long forgotten.

Grama said such full moon fun was "primitive" and I could not go. Such children, she was certain, had no future. I loved their present and wanted to be in on it.

One evening when the moonlight tinged the earth silver and the sea below us was one vast glow, I had a stronger than usual urge to be with the singers and dancers. I listened for Grama's snoring, quietly opened the door, sneaked to Crossroad, and joined the dancing circle there, but just as I was wondering why no one was asking me to "waltz out of the beautiful garden"—

How would you like me
To waltz with you, Darling,
Waltz with you,
Out of the beautiful garden?"—

a heavy hand came down on my arm, and I turned to see my grandmother's silhouette behind me. She promised to tan my behind good and proper for disobeying her. I was contrite for several weeks, and she forgot. Thereafter, other than lengthening my face when the singing and dancing and storytelling began, I did nothing about it.

One day Chauncey challenged me to tell a story. "If you tell we a joke or else a story, we going stop calling you Miss Moore."

I said nothing but was tempted. I knew several but not how to tell them.

The wake for Mrs Duncan's husband had been the week before. Hundreds of people came. During the evening and night on the day of the funeral, they sang and told stories. Grama didn't go. She said that she "wouldn't be caught dead at them kind o' common-class carryings-on." I wasn't allowed to go because it went on past midnight and it wasn't a fit place for decent people. But from my bed I heard the entire performance. It lasted until the wee hours of the morning. A male voice I didn't recognize told a Doum-Doum story:

"Doum-Doum did married a pretty woman call Mattie. If you see the hips and the behind 'pon she! So after the reception they go home. Mattie take off she clothes. And what Doum-Doum see frighten he.

"Doum-Doum take a good look. 'This look like a sore,' he tell heself. 'How me will enter that and no' hurt Mattie, and it will start for bleed too.'"

(Laughter.)

"Poor Doum-Doum, ain't know the score.

"Mattie start for worry if Doum-Doum funny 'cause she ain't see nothing stirring. 'Wha' hol'ing you back?' she ask him. She sit up in bed and reach over and try for pull him on she. He stiffen and pull 'way. 'Wha' wrong with you?' she ask him. "You lose yo' nature?"

"'I 'fraid I will hurt you,' he tell she.

"She take a good look at it and suck she teeth."

(Loud laughter.)

"But Doum-Doum ain't hear a word she saying. Doum-Doum decide he better go call on 'Nansi for advice. You see 'Nansi was his close pardner and the best man at the wedding.

"So Doum-Doum and 'Nansi come back to the house. 'Nansi go in the bedroom where Mattie is, and 'Nansi say to Doum-Doum, 'Watch me, pardner, watch me.' 'Nansi start for go away at it, and Mattie start for groan.

"Poor Doum-Doum! Think that is bawl Mattie bawling. And he go outside and get a big stick. When he come back, 'Nansi and Mattie groaning harder, thick in they sweetness. Doum-Doum let go the stick 'pon 'Nansi, and 'Nansi jump up. Mattie jump up too and she grab that stick from Doum-Doum and she start for beat him with it. Doum-Doum run out the house and Mattie behind him without a stitch on, beating him with that stick. People say it was something for behold.

"When Doum-Doum come back Mattie did done put his things out on the street. And 'Nansi did done move in with she."

"Lawd, Doum-Doum stupid," several voices exclaimed.

"Wire bend and story end."

But I didn't tell the story.

"See? You is a Doum-Doum for true! Sister Petra Doum-Doum Moore! I going get you a wimple and a pair o' false boobs. Don' know a single story! Only know for lick Miss Cameron batty for come first in English an' get book."

Mrs Cameron had given me two books as prizes: *Oliver Twist* and *Robinson Crusoe*, and lent me several others and would let me have her sons' magazines when they were finished with them.

6

AND MR SAM TOLD me smutty stories.

When I was around eight or nine, I told him the story I'd heard in Sunday school about Dives, who went to hell while the beggar he'd refused food to went to heaven. Mr Sam pulled on his pipe and listened attentively. When I finished, Mr Sam gave a big grin but continued pulling on his pipe until the tobacco was finished, knocked the ashes out of the bowl, unscrewed the stem and methodically cleaned it with a thin wire spike—before he responded.

"I know the story a different way. The great God make a lot of lesser Gods—like how the estate owners have managers that do the things the owners don't want to do."

I nodded to let him know I understood, all the while thinking that there could be only one God.

"These Gods was jealous o' one another and they use for try to outdo each other. Only one o' them was smart and wasn' greedy. Later on the Great God put money on earth for tempt the greedy, and only one did know for give the Great God thanks and not for have greed in his heart. He was the only one that the money didn' eat up."

"The money didn' eat up!"

"Son, money always hungry and on the lookout for greedy people to eat. Smart people make it their servant. Only the one that wasn't greedy that it didn' destroy."

I asked him if he'd like to be rich like Mrs Manley. Mrs Manley got her riches from witchcraft, he said; that when she was leaving heaven to come to earth she'd asked for riches but not the wisdom to use it. He wouldn't be rich, he explained, because when he was leaving heaven riches wasn't one of the things he'd asked for. "What a person live out on earth is the destiny they ask for before they come to this world."

"What did you ask for?"

"Peace of mind."

I wondered if this were true and what I'd asked for.

In Mr Sam's story of the Flood, a God and his followers had climbed up on a coconut tree into heaven and everything that stayed on earth got drowned. "That why every Shango temple got a tree trunk in the middle the spirits descend from."

The stories Mr Sam used to tell me! Sometimes I would giggle and Mr Sam would say, "We two is men, and between men we can talk openly 'bout every thing." One about a man with an erection who chased a woman but couldn't catch her, and when he came upon a pumpkin, had no choice but to penetrate it. And the pumpkin exploded, scattering seeds all over the world! "That why pumpkins grow everywhere."

Another about a man who badly wanted to fuck (the word he used) a woman, and a beautiful woman appeared in front of him. He started to feel weak and could even see the woman's nipples throbbing under her blouse. Then he found himself and the woman standing on the edge of a cliff. "'If you ha' the courage to jump over this cliff,' the woman tell him, 'I will give you what you want.' Instantly the fool jumped. When he open his eyes, the woman was standing over him naked and beautifuller. 'You is a brave man,' she tell him. 'Now you can have me.' But he been already numb from the waist down: he did done break his back."

Another about a white man's daughter who was sick and about to die and who said that only a man with a foot-long thing could cure her. And her father went all over the world trying to find a black man with one that long. When he got back home empty-handed, his son saw him all dejected and asked him what was wrong, and the father explained the cure his sister needed. "The son say to his father, 'Papa, I think I have the answer. Mine is fourteen inches.'"

His father turned white like starch as he remembered the rumours he'd heard but never believed—couldn't believe, the man was white—about the farmer next door. "If the sonofabitch was still living, so help me God, I would kill him."

He asked me never to repeat this story, "leastways to white people. It got a moral to it that white people won't want to understand. Not them that live on Isabella Island, at any rate. They certain for punish you if you tell it. That story hand down all the way from slavery and I passing it on to you now."

I couldn't identify the moral then and was afraid that if I'd asked him what it was, he would have thought me stupid (now I know that the first place I ought to look for monstrosity is in myself).

One Saturday afternoon I found him cooking. Two huge egg-shaped things that looked like yellow fat sat marinating in a bowl. I asked him what they were and he said bull's balls. "They good. Good for yo' back. Make you into a real he-man. I have a butcher that save them fo' me every Saturday." He winked at me as he said this.

I giggled.

"Don't laugh," he reprimanded with mock severity. "This is serious business. You will hear people say sex bad. Don' believe them. Sex bad if you don' do it right." He was silent.

I looked at him, expecting him to continue. But he didn't. After about fifteen minutes he said to me, "You sure you don' want to find out what I mean when I say, 'Sex bad if you don' do it right?'"

I nodded.

"Well, you must ask questions. That is the way to learn."

He was the only adult I knew who ever said this to a child.

"All I mean is that you must respect the woman you have sex with, and you mustn' have sex with a woman you don' love and respect, that can' be yo' wife."

He had no woman that I knew of, probably because of his *bamanko*. He said he'd been married a long time ago. He and his wife didn't have any children for about ten years. Then she conceived but died in childbirth. The child, he said, had changed its mind about leaving heaven, but it wanted its mother to return with it to heaven.

His religion, not his *bamanko*, was probably what caused Grama to reject his marriage proposal. He was a Shango servitor. I realized later that the thatched hut he warned me never to enter was his shrine. There were days when I went to his house and saw on his closed door two palm branches taped there in the form of an X; and his thunder staff, carved from mahogany with the figure of Shango holding an axe in a striking pose above his head, would be suspended from a hook above his door. And I would know it was one of his holy days, and I was not to disturb him.

He gave some of whatever he ate or drank to the earth: the ancestors' portion. This too was one of the things I wasn't supposed to mention to Grama.

One day while visiting him—I must have been around twelve—there was a rainbow in the sky, and he motioned to me to be silent; he bowed his head and kept it bowed until the rainbow disappeared. His answer to my "Why?" was: "Is a holy act." Once, during a thunderstorm, Grama said that she hoped he wasn't outside trying to see his God "'cause if lightning miss him cold will definitely get him."

He was the only person I knew who did not hate snakes. In his religion snakes were sacred to God (probably Mawu-Lisa, the Benin male/female twin God, or connected in some way to Damballah and the Abomey Serpent; women after menopause and men held equally powerful positions in the religion).

The Shango doctrines were African. Reverend Abrahams opposed them. When Grama was a young woman a British Methodist missionary told her that Shango's followers worship the devil, and she had continued to believe it. Mr Sam said that a Shango woman whose daughter had won the Methodist scholarship to Expatriates Academy had stopped following Shango and joined the Methodists, because the church board opposed giving the girl the scholarship unless her mother renounced Shango. The woman told the Methodist congregation that Shango's followers sacrificed human flesh in the forest at night whenever there was a full moon—exactly what the white missionaries wanted to hear. They took the woman to the hamlets of Isabella Island to testify against Shango. Within a month she began to waste away. When it became clear that she was dying, she sent for the Shango leader, who told her she had to recant her lie. Four persons carrying her on a stretcher bore her down the hill to the Hanovertown Methodist church one Sunday morning, where in a feeble voice she said that she had lied. Gradually she got better and resumed following Shango.

Once Grama asked me if Mr Sam was teaching me his religion. I shook my head. "Well, he better don't else I will stop you from going to his house." I told Mr Sam of Grama's fear. He held my hand and squeezed it and said, in a theatrical whisper as if he was afraid someone nearby might hear us, "If you can keep a secret"—he winked—"I can too. We two is men, right? And what men talk 'bout between them not for the ears o' women. Right?"

"Right," I agreed, feeling proud.

"Then it's a deal."

He released my hand, and we slapped palms.

He told me then that Shango had called Grampa just before he'd been conscripted. Grampa was thinking it over when the conscriptors caught him, but it was Shango who'd turned Grampa over to Ogun, the war divinity, because Grampa had taken too long to make up his mind, had snubbed Shango. "He probably been afraid Ma Moore leave him if he follow Shango."

He lowered his voice to a whisper. "Remember? What you must remember?"

"Not to repeat what you tell me. But why?"

"You is too young to understand," he taunted.

I held his plaiting hand so he could not continue his work. "Please, tell me!"

"If you ask the wrong questions you get in trouble. Ask Brother Shiloh what trouble is. He know a lot 'bout trouble."

"But you told me to ask questions."

"You must know which questions to ask and which questions not to ask. All right. White people hate Shango followers. A lot o' black people depend on white people to eat. And white people fire them from their jobs if they don't show and say that they is enemies o' Shango. One time—not long ago neither—they used to arrest all Shango followers and throw them in jail."

Even at fourteen I kept an open mind about Mr Sam's Shango beliefs, but I did not believe that Mrs Manley was a *soucouyan*. She was a bony, tall, half-white woman in her early sixties. She carried herself stiff and straight—because of the whalebone corsets she wore, according to Mrs Duncan. She never came outdoors without sunglasses. I was told I should not look into her eyes, and if by accident I did, I should say, "Jesus, protect me." There were several steps from the main road to her house. Once you mounted them you came to a gate, which had a bell. She herself didn't use these stairs. Her garage was built into the roadside bank and had stairs to the inside of her house. Her large, wooden, pink house, in which she lived alone—her maid and gardener came and left every day—and her spacious yard of at least two acres were fenced in, initially with barbed wire; but around the time I was nine, she replaced the barbed wire with corrugated steel. It was the only fenced property in that part of Mount Olivet. "And with bell 'pon top o' that. Ma Moore, we is not supposed to go to places where we is not wanted"—was Mrs Duncan's reaction.

"If she stay inside that galvanize fence of a night we all going sleep peaceful," Grama replied.

Laughing, Mrs Duncan said that when Mrs Manley was thirsty for blood, nothing, not jail, not even God himself, could hold her. "One night somebody will find her skin and lace it good and proper with salt and pepper. All that communion she take of a Sunday, in yo' church Ma Moore, won't cool that pepper."

The rest I learned from Mr Sam. He said that Mrs Manley bore all the signs of a *soucouyan*, that one night at a dance, a friend of his had met a woman who he was sure was Mrs Manley; this was before she got married, but she had given him another name, "seeing that she in a class that she think better than him"; he and she had danced close, and as the dance was coming to an end they'd both felt sweet, and he was about to take her to his house when he looked down at the floor and saw a cow's hoof protruding from under her floor-length gown; "she would o' certainly ride him that night."

"How you mean?"

"They turn you into bull and ride you all night. Then they bring you back before sunrise and turn you back to a human being. They puncture yo' skin and put something in yo' blood that prevent you from waking up. You only find yo'self tired next day and yo' body bruise up, especially your back."

"I have seen her in slippers. She has feet like everybody else."

"Yes, she normal like everybody else when she normal. But when she want blood and she turn *soucouyan* her feet-them change. Is the only way you can tell them from real women."

I shook my head. "If she was a *soucouyan* her husband would have known."

"Her husband *dead!*" He paused for a minute before adding, "When she dead, they should take her body up into the mountain and flog it."

"Why?" I was frightened.

" 'Cause is the only way she wouldn' born again. And even that not a guarantee."

I didn't understand but fear kept me quiet.

Long afterwards I reflected that she would never have gone to the dances Mr Sam's friends went to. She was too meticulous about class rules. She grew up on a plantation thirty miles away. Her father was the manager. She'd only moved to Mount Olivet in her late twenties after she'd married Mr Manley who, Grama said, did not act like he was better than other people even though he had "couple dollars well" and used to own one of the biggest stores in Hanovertown and at one time almost half the land in Mount Olivet.

Sometimes the neighbours "threw words" at her, indirectly telling her that she sucked people's blood and that they had guards posted to see where she put her skin when she took it off. It didn't seem to affect her. She ignored them and moved about as if her taunters spoke a language she did not know, or as if they were roadside weeds unworthy of her notice. Most of her visitors were white or part white and drove expensive cars. Brother Shiloh was the only person she spoke to; she invited him to her dos but he always declined. She always made wreaths from the flowers in her large garden for the village dead. But she did not attend the funerals. We used to wonder how she knew. But it was probably because of the obituary announcements at noon and at 6 pm on Radio Isabella. Besides her housekeeper and gardener were from Mount Olivet.

The villagers pumped them for lurid tales but got nothing except that she paid them well, was always polite to them, and wasn't stingy. Once Mrs Duncan wondered out loud whether they were in league with her, but concluded that since Mrs Manley did her dirty work at night, her servants were none the wiser. That was one reason too why she had to sleep alone.

Her foot ended up in her mouth most times she tried to make contact with us. One afternoon she stood at Grama's gate with a bulging shopping bag and called to me to come and get it. I took the bag from her and was surprised by how light it was. In it were four one-pound, saffroncoloured, empty Ovaltine tins. Mrs Duncan, who was sitting with Grama on the porch, raised her eyes to heaven, bit her lower lip, and shook her head.

"Lord, give me patience," Grama said, also raising her eyes to heaven. "Ovaltine tins!"

"She want you for help she get rid o' she garbage. You can never say she don't drink Ovaltine. Why she didn' send you a full tin for fatten yo' blood, Ma Moore? It would o' been a good investment. You better climb she stairs and tell she you can afford Ovaltine too. Pedro, go put them in my garbage drum."

I did but saved the shopping bag, since shopping bags were not free.

According to Grama and Mrs Duncan people were always on the lookout for *soucouyan* skins, which they'd salt and pepper, and the *soucouyans* drowned themselves because they could no longer reenter their skins.

Eventually I asked Reverend Abrahams if *soucouyans* existed. He said, no—in a real sense—but yes, in people's imaginations. "Do you know anyone who's accused of being one?"

"Mrs Manley."

"She isn't. She is disliked. That's it."

"Because she has fenced her property in?"

"Yes. And she has more wealth than most people and she doesn't share it. People who are different are sometimes hated. It's called scapegoating."

A week after my conversation with Reverend Abrahams, Grama

woke up one morning complaining of having been ridden all over Isabella Island that night. "I know it!" she exclaimed. "I know it! As sure as the sun rise this morning I know it! Look at that, Pedro! Look at that!" She pointed to a large discoloured area on her left calf. "That *soucouyan* woman ride me all night and suck my blood. Why somebody don' find her skin?"

"Reverend Abrahams says *soucouyans* don't exist."

"How he will know? His nose always in the Bible. It can't smell anything else."

I laughed.

"The day a *soucouyan* suck his blood and ride him the length and breadth o' Isabella Island, he will sing another tune. When you come home from school I want you to go up to Royal Hill and pick a wad o' corile for me. I going be drinking a cup every night from now on. If my blood been bitter that woman wouldn't o' come near me. Take two dollars from under the teacup at the front o' the china closet and buy a bag o' camphor balls at the drugstore on yo' way home from school. The only thing *soucouyan* 'fraid more than God is camphor."

At that point she left off kneading the dough for the johnny cakes we were going to have for breakfast and went into her bedroom. "Pedro! Come here!" she called angrily from her bedroom.

When I entered, she asked, "Where my Bible is?"

"In my bedroom."

She swung her arm to hit me. I moved out of the way. "Don' ever move my Bible from the night table! And where the scissors I keep on it?"

I pointed to the drawer where I'd put it.

"Ask Reverend Abrahams for give you yo' own Bible. I keep my Bible here with a scissors on top of it, in the shape o' the cross, for protect me from evil. If you didn' disturb it that woman wouldn'o' been able for ride me God knows where and suck out all my blood."

"She didn't."

"You keep on saying so and see if she won' ride you every night when she not able to find anybody else. You better start drinking corile tea too. Mark my words, you and Reverend Abrahams!

Giddy-up!" She made the motion of whipping a horse.

I laughed.

Poor Mrs Manley. I wonder if she was as impervious to our cruelty as she'd let on. She became a protagonist in stories that should have been about mythic figures in mythic places.

Ansel on the other hand was a historical figure who seemed to have come out of a fairy tale. He was the only Carib I knew, though Ansel never said he was one. Mount Olivetans suspected that he was from Carib Country—a village at the foothills of the volcano, where the British had forced them to live. In the 1901 volcanic eruption hundreds were killed. But he'd probably lived abroad, possibly England.

To get Ansel to reveal his identity, the villagers asked him all sorts of questions:

"Who is yo' father?"

"The sun."

"So if we ask you, 'Who yo' mother is?' you will tell us 'the earth'?"

"Absolutely correct."

"And the sea, and the rain, and wind?"

"They're my uncles and aunts."

The questioners were amused and exasperated.

He stayed in the village for roughly eighteen months. He was obviously a well-educated man whose poverty and barefoot wanderings were an enigma. He seemed to be in his sixties but the villagers had no way of telling. I was intrigued by his almond-shaped eyes, high cheekbones, mass of long, unkempt salt-and-pepper hair, his rusty-iron complexion, his stories and, above all, the way he lived, exactly like the lilies of the field. He had a fruity odour, like a freshly broken cocoa pod; sometimes we smelled him before seeing him. He'd just shown up in the village one day in 1972 with nothing more than the clothes he wore, and people lodged and fed him in no particular order. He slept in the house where night met him, on a blanket on the floor—never anywhere else—and he never used a pillow. He ate with whichever family he happened to be with at mealtime. If there were weeds in your yard he came and cleared them, or trimmed your hedge if it needed trimming—always borrowing the machete he did it with; if there were rotten boards in your house, he'd ask would you like to have them replaced. He'd tell you how many square feet of lumber to buy and, borrowing the tools of some carpenter, he'd do the work. He'd replaced some rotten wood in Grama's house, using Mr Duncan's tools (Duncan was already dead, and Mrs Duncan had offered him the tools to go earn a living with, and he'd asked her what was a living). Grama offered him money for the job; he laughed at her offer and told her to give it to her church.

He told stories incessantly, in impeccable English, about a time when the earth was peaceful, about the coming of corn and the war promise made in return for the gift of corn, of broken promises to God, and of punishments that included the coming of the white man. But the story that indelibly etched itself in my memory was the one he told—it wasn't his most frequent—about a mountain of gold.

"Shortly before the French and English overwhelmed Isabella, our priest was visited by an oracle. He told us that before long most of us would perish, and the few of us who would survive would not look like our ancestors. And then he showed our priest a vision.

"It was a mountain of gold that glowed like the sun. Thousands of people from all the world's races stood on a plain some distance from the mountain. A voice spoke to them. It said, 'Go to the mountain and take only a few pieces of gold, as much as one hand can hold; you do not need more. Anyone taking more will be cursed. He will wake up one day and find that in order to live he will have to amass gold that would be of no use to him. He'd even find himself forced to turn people into gold.'

"People on the plain gasped that there could ever be people so absurd and bestial.

"'Go now and help yourselves. Don't forget the warning.' The voice disappeared after pronouncing these words.

"The people began to move towards the mountain to collect their handful of gold. But before they could even start out, some pale-skinned people surrounded them with contraptions that belched lethal fire. The pale-skinned people commanded all others not to touch the gold and those who'd taken up some to drop it—because, the pale-skinned people said, they were the people chosen by God to have gold; it was for that reason that God had armed them; and their destiny was to control the unarmed.

"At that point the vision ceased and the oracle disappeared, and the priest called all the people together and informed them of the dire times ahead. We have seen half of the prophecy fulfilled. We are still waiting for the curse."

He disappeared as suddenly as he had come. Some villagers found him dead on a ledge of rocks below Saul and Ishtar's house. The official cause of death was said to be a heart attack, but everyone believed he had simply gone there, on the ledge just above the shore where the water was turquoise in colour, beautiful and calm, to become one again with the earth, his mother. Everyone who could attended his funeral.

Six years later, as a result of studying Thoreau's *Walden*, I would see him as one of the most valuable persons I'd ever met.

7

TOWARDS THE END OF 1973, my mother wrote that the Canadian government had declared an amnesty for illegal immigrants, and so she was going to try her luck. She had hesitated asking the people she worked for—she continued to work for them until I got to Montreal—to sponsor her. People who'd done so had had bad experiences. Their employers cut their wages and reported them to immigration if they fussed. One woman was forced to have sex with her boss when he found out. It was too risky. *But before Christmas that same year she informed Grama that she'd got her "stay."*

Ma would be able to come home now like all the other people who came home often from Canada, I thought. I could even go to visit her. Benjy had visited his mother. The way he spoke about Niagara Falls and Toronto City Hall and the Saint Lawrence River, anyone would have thought that he was the only one privileged to see them, or that anyone who hadn't seen them was undeserving of a school certificate, or couldn't go to heaven. Chauncey had asked him if there were standpipes at the street corners dispensing free milk and honey. Benjy said he hadn't seen any but he'd been able to eat all the meat and ice cream he wanted. I looked forward, too, to Grama's visiting Canada, like Benjy's Grama, and bringing back all sorts of things people at home couldn't afford, and feeling important because of the things she would be able to give to the neighbours.

Mr Fraser, my geography teacher, felt that I should join my mother in Canada. Fraser had studied at McGill. In an earlier conversation I had told him that I wanted to become a medical doctor. I was taken with Reverend Abrahams's advice to serve others and had visions of making poor, sick people well, people like Cousin Lucy who couldn't afford the fees of most Isabellan doctors and developed gangrene in the wards for the indigent and died or became invalids. Around the time that my mother got her visa, Fraser asked me whether my mother was in a position to send for me. He told Grama that the high schools in Canada would prepare me better for the sort of studies I wanted to pursue. Grama worshipped teachers only a shade less than she did Methodist ministers. She made Fraser wait while I went to get Brother Shiloh, whose wife had died suddenly. Grama now did his laundry and prepared his evening meal. Brother Shiloh had a large garden plot from which Grama got most of the vegetables she needed.

Fraser repeated to Brother Shiloh what he had told Grama, and Brother Shiloh said that if the teacher said so, he must know what he was talking about. "The man who's already walked the road knows it." That same evening Grama dictated a letter for Isis, my mother.

Isis replied that she didn't have the money. She worked as a live-in maid. "You-all don't know that. If Pedro come to Canada right away, it will put me in expenses I can't afford. Right now, because I live-in, I don't have expenses for light and so on. I don't even have a telephone. You-all see the barrels and the money coming but you-all don't know the price people over here have to pay to send them."

Grama wrote back, "Pedro is your responsibility, whether you can afford it or not. Now that you have your papers, make a move. Your son's future is the important thing. If I have to I will take out another mortgage and send Pedro up to Canada to meet you." It was I who wrote this letter and Brother Shiloh looked it over to make sure that it was all right.

My mother replied that it was such a long time since Grama was young that she'd forgotten you have to crawl before you walk.

"If she was in front of me face she wouldn't o' dare to say that," Grama shouted, her face taut with rage, as I read aloud the letter to her. "I would o' slap her down so hard she wouldn' o' able for crawl, creep nor walk, let alone talk. Fresh! She should o' think 'bout that before she go down on she back light and get up heavy."

By June 1974 everything was processed for me to join her.

It was only the week before my departure that I began to wonder what was to become of Grama. From the time I turned thirteen she would occasionally say, "This house does feel so empty when you not here. Thank God Patience does come sit on the step and talk with me days else I will turn jumbie in here." I'd hear in it her fear, stated aloud, that I might begin to defy her and stay out late, "now," as she'd put it, that I'd started "to smell" myself. But I had come to love solitude and the company of books. Besides, even if I couldn't admit it then, I knew that I would have failed the womanizing tests Isabellan society had waiting for me, so I sidestepped society and hid behind the abstinence Methodists preached profusely but practised sparsely. But Mrs Duncan was too worldly wise to have been fooled. (On my 1981 trip, she asked if there was love in my life and without batting an eyelid added, "Don' make what people will say stop you from looking for the kind o' love you want.") Grama and I went to church together on Sunday mornings. We no longer walked but took one of the many minibuses that plied the route. She had stopped going on Sunday evenings, and she didn't insist that I go, preferring that I spend the time on my schoolwork. Outside of school and church and my occasional visits to Mr Sam, she was my entire world. And I was hers.

Two days before I left, when I went to carry Brother Shiloh's supper, I spoke to him about Grama's being alone.

Brother Shiloh told me not to worry, that my grandmother was a survivor, was tougher than I thought, and was determined to live until I came back to Isabella Island to give her medicine in her old age. "Yesterday she told Ishtar, 'Me grandson leaving fo' Canada for learn doctoring.' You better don' disappoint her. If loneliness is the price she has to pay for you to *learn doctoring*"—he had a conspiratorial grin—"she's prepared to pay it. But she won't be lonely. We will look out for her—Mrs Duncan, Mathilda, Ishtar, Reverend Abrahams, myself. Your grandmother is a mother to everybody, so we will treat her like she's our own mother. Put your mind at ease."

He always spoke like that, Brother Shiloh. He loved to bring people together, to get them to end their quarrels and to make up. He read and wrote many of the villagers' letters, helped them prepare their wills and looked over their legal documents to make sure the lawyers weren't swindling them. He was the only person in whose presence Percival watched his tongue. Before we had running water, he would insist that I shower at his place. He was a Methodist lay preacher. Grama said that he had been a primary school principal but lost his job in 1948 because a black person looking for promotion had reported that he'd said that if black people can spill their blood to protect white people from Hitler, they could have voting rights too. The administrator had ordered his arrest for sedition and later ordered that he be fired. "And the Methodist missionaries-them what he been counting on to put in a good word for him didn' as much as cough." It was the only time I ever heard her criticize Methodists. His son and only child—an average-height, silent man, chubby like his mother, prematurely grey—was a chemist with one of the Trinidad oil companies and a Cambridge graduate. Every Christmas he came home. They lived in a house he'd built them and on money he sent them. Grama said God's blessing followed children like him.

The year I left, Isabella Island was having its worst drought in fifty years. Some preachers said it was God's punishment because Isabellans had embraced diabolic television.

My last full day home I looked at the ground in front of Grama's house, brown and cracked, powdering into dust. I reflected on how as a child I must have rolled in this soil and eaten it, as all children do. I stood back from the boundary between Grama's house and Mrs Duncan's to take one final stare at the splendour of a royal poinciana aflame between two blooming poui trees, one pink, one yellow. They tinted the light a pinkish yellow the length of the boundary between Grama and Mrs Duncan, where they grew in a line, and perfumed the air with what smelled like a blend of rose petals and lemon rind. I remembered their first blooms, somewhere around the time my mother left Isabella Island. Then, they were just a few feet high. Now they were at least twenty.

The poui and poinciana were blooming—celebrating the drought. Everything else was dying. The guava trees behind Mrs Duncan's house were curled up, their shrivelled branches ash-grey, their leaves clay-dry, looking like corpses in rigor mortis—dead despite the mixture of tap water and urine Mrs Duncan had been giving them. At the front, where she grew gerbras and roses, she had pruned the roses to within six inches of their roots and kept them from burning up with her bathwater.

I walked to the back of Grama's house, beyond our golden apple tree and the croton and hibiscus Bruisee had planted there two years before—now dead from the drought—beyond Ishtar and Saul's house to the uppermost ledge of the plateau and stared at the sheer ledges, each a few feet narrower than the one above it, all the way down to the sea. It was if I had to stamp their shape in my memory for when I could no longer see them. There was a cruise ship in the harbour and several smaller craft. At the Dependencies Wharf, a short distance to the right, about five hundred feet in a steep drop below me, passengers were embarking. Further right in the distance, across from the Hanovertown Harbour, at the outer northern end of the horseshoe forming the harbour, the crystals in the sheer bald rock of Fort George glistened like pieces of glass in a cement wall. Normally the rock face was green from the ferns and fungi that grew on it. But they'd withered and had been swept away by the sea breeze, leaving the naked crystals to reflect the sun. The sea at its base was emerald. Directly below me, in pockets of soil between the exposed terrace rocks, sisal and giant cacti thrived: scattered dots of green in the expanse of beige, brown, and rock-grey landscape.

From this perch I took what felt like one last look at this sea. I remembered that before I was tall enough to look at it from the window, I'd stand on a chair and stare at it from Grama's bedroom window, sure that it was alive because it sloped up to the level of the window, though away from it. If water in containers was flat, why then was the sea raised, like a cat with arched back, prepared always to strike the land? I'd asked Grama about this. She said people would make a "pappyshow" of me if they heard me say the sea was alive. But I did not believe her, because a short while before there had been a hurricane, and at a point when the wind was resting the waves had struck the rocks with a force that shook the house; and next day we saw that the sea had climbed quite far up the rocks and swallowed up some fishermen's huts before receding. The wind too, I'd felt, was alive but I'd never spoken to Grama about that.

Today was one of those cloudless days when the sea was mostly royal blue under an azure arch; only at the shoreline was the water turquoise, forming something of a transition between water and land. Its swaying hum was barely audible. The islands rising out of it, the Dependencies that stretched south, looked like solidified smoke. There was hardly a ripple anywhere in its surface. At the shoreline was its white beard, but no lace lay scattered about its surface. Flying fish leaped wildly out of it, the light reflecting off their bodies in meteoric flashes against the blue tissue of the sky. The air coming off it smelt cleansed, dust-free, with a slight trace of the surf. My mind went back to a Christmas when I was around seven. Benjy had told me that at sunrise on Christmas morning the sun danced with the moon. I had got up while it was still dark and went to the edge of the plateau and waited as the light turned from dark to grey and the white lace fringe of the waves breaking at the shoreline became quite distinct. But the sky near the sea where the sun rose never turned purple or orange; instead a shower of rain came from inland, and I was thoroughly drenched before I got back indoors and found Grama wondering where I was. For a moment the memory quieted my soul torn between leaving and staying.

Seven years later when I finished at McGill and was sure that my years in Canada had clad me in shit, which only my birthplace could wash off, it was to these memories I wanted to return.

But that day in July 1974, they objectified the waiting unknown and focused my fear that I would soon be without the references that gave meaning to my life.

Late that same evening, Brother Shiloh—he and Mr Sam were the only visitors still remaining—gave me a dark brown leather satchel that went back to the time he was a headmaster. He advised me that when I got to Canada I should remember always why I'd gone there. I wasn't to allow myself to get into trouble with white people. White people had their plans and I had to have mine. "If you fall down, my son, the important thing is to get up and brush off yourself and keep walking. If you get bruises, attend to them before they get infected so they won't hold you back. Even if you must use crutches, keep moving. Stick to getting an education, so that if you want to, you can come back home and help your people."

"What you mean, Shiloh: *if he want to*? I waiting patiently for Pedro to come back home and prescribe medicine for me in me old age."

"Ma Moore," he smiled and shook his head, "the first thing Pedro must do is put his mind to his studies to become whatever he wants: doctor, lawyer, teacher, engineer, accountant, whatever."

Mr Sam sat quietly through all this. His gift to me proved to be haunting. It was at that stage a sealed envelope, roughly six inches by four inches. Smiling, he instructed me not to open it until I got to Canada. Better still I should wait until I was in Canada for about a month or two. Grama looked at Mr Sam, perplexed. Brother Shiloh wrinkled his brow. But neither said anything.

Several people had already dropped by: church sisters from my grandmother's Women's League, church brothers from the Methodist Social Club, Reverend Abrahams, Mr Fraser, Mrs Cameron my English teacher. Even Chauncey and Benjy. They'd brought gifts and good wishes. Mrs Duncan had donated sandwiches, cake and lemonade to feed them. Ishtar had helped prepare them.

When everyone left I sat at the dining table and just looked at Grama, remarking the changes I had noted over the last five years. She was a tall woman (I can't be sure now how tall but she was taller than I at fourteen and I was five-six then). She was of medium build, but her frame was withering. The clothes she had bought several years earlier seemed to be swallowing her. "One morning you not going find me. I going be nothing," she once said, grasping the extra inches in the waist of the dress she was wearing. Nowadays she had to lift herself up slowly if she'd been sitting or bending, and her hands would brace her back for a few seconds before she fully straightened out or began to walk. In the process she'd sometimes close her eyes and take a deep breath. Occasionally too, if the chair did not have an armrest or wasn't beside a table, or if she was sitting on the step, she'd stretch her hand out for me to help her get up. When walking she threw forward her shoulders one at a time in a sort of upright swimming motion. She'd bought herself a metal cane but wasn't using it. I'd told her it was useless. She said it wouldn't be if I misbehaved. Her flesh followed the pull of gravity. It would hang loosely from her arm when she raised it and would shift on her calves whenever she moved her legs. She was often out of breath.

She had an unroasted coffee-bean complexion crisscrossed by shallow wrinkles. Her aquiline nose ended with a slight hook; her eyes were almond shaped and their whites contrasted vividly against her dark skin. When light shone into them a tinge of milky blue was visible around the edges of their amber irises. With some difficulty she could still thread her own needle. She had all her teeth, probably because she cleaned them with salt and baking soda first thing in the morning and last thing at night and always chewed a hibiscus stick right after lunch. Her gargle was a mixture of vinegar—which she made herself from fermented golden apples—salt and lime juice. When she was puzzled her facial skin converged towards her eyes and nose, forming deep ruts. Two folds of loose skin hung from behind her pointed chin. Tiny hairs grew on her upper lip. This evening she was wearing one of her many headscarves, an indigo-burgundy plaid one that Mrs Linton had given her the Christmas before. She never went out into the open air without wearing a head scarf, unless it was to church, at which time she wore one of her many hats decorated with plastic or wax flowers.

Tonight she and I sat at the opposite ends of the dining table for a long time in silence. I was afraid that if I spoke I'd cry. Between ages six and eight I'd often wondered what would become of me if she died. Once she'd had bronchitis for about a month and Mrs Duncan took over her washing and my care, and I was worried that Grama would die. Mrs Duncan was too, because she'd asked me if I would like to live with her. I always knew that she liked me; she gave me socks and shirts at Christmas and on my birthday and was always finding something delicious in her fridge to give me.

I had taken for granted that I would be there to care for Grama when she became bedridden, the way she'd cared for me. In spite of Brother Shiloh's assurances, I was afraid she'd pine away and quickly die. I was leaving her when she needed me most.

"Time for go to bed," Grama interrupted my thinking. "You got a big day tomorrow. But before you go I ha' one last thing for say to you." She told me then all she was prepared to tell me about my father. And anticipating what my reaction would be when I found out the full truth, she advised me that people had to create secret places in themselves to put the things others did not need to know about them. She called hers her secret bag; Mrs Duncan called hers her dark cupboard. I began wondering what was in Grama's secret bag. I must have given her a perturbing look, for she lowered her head, wrinkled her brows, and said, "I clean out my secret bag a long time ago." She slapped a mosquito that had settled on her wrist. "And you have to be careful; not everything that you want for keep secret will stay in yo' secret bag. Sometimes it just ups without warning and announce itself to the whole world, 'cause some things we think is secrets not supposed for be secrets."

She was silent for a while, and I could see she was doing her best not to cry. But she didn't succeed. The tears already glistening in her eyes, she said, "It hard for see you go. I raise you from the time you born. It hard. The old mustn' hold back the young, just like the dead mustn' hold back the living. I will miss you, but I been living with adversity since Bertie go to war. Thank God he leave me with good memories for sweeten me life in the midst o' bitterness. O Pedro, that is something you must know, that you is likely fo' find Canada lonely. Carry yo' memories from here, the sweet ones. Keep them like a jar o' honey and when times get hard or things get bitter take a spoonful, and when the jar run out, come right back here and get more." Her last words that night were: "When you get to Canada, you must obey your mother. You is just fourteen, a bird that don' have feathers yet. Don' try for fly before yo' time or else you will get lost, or fall flat on your face and hurt or kill yourself. Obey yo' mother. She older than you and got experience that you don' got. And is yo' duty to obey her. The Bible say, 'Honour thy father and yo' mother that yo' days will be long in the land which the Lord thy God giveth thee.' You don' got no father so all the honour due to yo' mother. In due time, darling, God willing, you will get yo' own wings, strong wings"—she smiled—"and fly of yo' own accord, but don' try fo' fly before yo' get them."

Wings.

8

IT WAS MY FIRST TRIP on an airplane. I had never paid more than passing interest in airplanes. From the top of Mount Olivet, they looked like giant birds asleep on the tarmac below. Now, inside this one, I was inside a bullet: a flying, winged, giant bullet. I sat rigidly in my seat as the bullet hurled along imperceptibly.

They served strange white chicken in a white sauce. No colouring, as if they hadn't been taught to cook properly. There was cake filled with cream. The woman in the aisle seat beside me wolfed hers down—I could hear her gulps—and even licked off some cream that got on her fingers, but I could not eat it. I was nervous and prayed for a safe passage as I thought of the plane crashes that the news sometimes reported, and relaxed only when I realized that the passengers were quite at ease. I was astonished at how smooth the ride was. I'd expected it to be like a car moving over a bumpy surface. And the clouds below me seemed solid, like floating islands or pneumatic tubes on water. I wondered about the technology required to keep a 737 in the air. I remembered Grama's story about a sexton of the Methodist Church who'd put a tub of oats in front of the first car the Methodist manse had bought and had expected the car to eat it. Asked why he'd done so, he said that after such a long journey, all the way to the country and back, the car had to be hungry. When he was told the car was not an animal, he'd pointed to the head lamps and the radiator and asked if they were not its eyes and nostrils.

The white woman sitting beside me said she was from Montreal. She was extremely thin. Her long, sun-tanned arms hung like limp twigs from her lime-green tank top. When she removed her shades to wipe them I saw that there were deep wrinkles in her sun-bronzed face. She said she was a social worker, and her clients were mostly Haitians, who didn't understand Canada and had many problems. "For one thing, nobody understands their French." She wanted to know how come my English was so good, and told me I would have to learn French.

"Do you speak Creole?" I asked her. Reverend Abrahams had told us that the Bible had been translated into Haitian Creole.

Her forehead creased, and after a pause of about ten seconds she said no. She asked me when last I had seen my mother. I told her ten years and she replied, with a smile that wasn't really a smile even though her laugh lines deepened, that I mustn't be surprised if Ma and I didn't get along. It was none of her business, I felt, and we said very little to each other after that. When the plane landed at Dorval she wished me well.

A woman immigration officer stamped my passport and welcomed me to Canada. When she handed back my passport, I told her I wasn't sure I would recognize my mother. She showed me a seat and told me to wait there. I waited, listening to the faint hum of the fluorescent ceiling lights and staring at the white walls and the bodies streaming past the immigration wickets. There was nothing familiar. Above the earth, even if I was in a bullet, there had been the sense of space, but once I entered the terminal building I'd entered what seemed like a lighted corridor in a universe of darkness. I have come to see over the years that the corridor has merely widened.

I'd needed, I know now, to be with someone whose love and affection had been proven over and over—someone like Grama. She should have accompanied me; she should have been there as a go-between during those first weeks when my mother was getting to know me and I her, and was retrieving her mothering skills from wherever she had put them; at the very least some sort of ritual handing over should have taken place before I was categorically given to her.

I heard my mother's name announced along with the message that she should report to the nearest security desk. It was another fifteen minutes before she appeared. Although I had seen photographs of her, except for the fact that she was black I wouldn't have recognized her in the crowd.

She examined me quickly from head to toe. "Hmm! You's a lot bigger than I thought. Good thing I didn' waste money buying clothes for you." Her tone was dismissive, impatient, as if I'd broken into her privacy. I expected her to hug and kiss me. She didn't. I felt cold suddenly, clenched my teeth and folded my arms and pressed them against my stomach, which had begun to churn violently. As we waited for my luggage to appear on the carousel I looked closely at my mother. She wore a well-fitting, glittering yellow dress and a black dynel wig. She was shorter than me. She was forty-four; she'd had me at thirty. It was a sin, I distinctly remembered hearing her tell Grama in one of their quarrels, to be a virgin past thirty, and I had wanted to know what a virgin was. Her face was round but un-gentle; she had Grama's unroasted coffee-bean complexion but not her symmetrical nose. Hers was flat like mine, and the spaces between it and her eye sockets looked like half saucers. At some point she put on a smile—grotesque, gauzelike, stretched, it seemed, over some sorrow it could not hide, and it disappeared and reappeared, like a curtain that rose and fell by some mysterious manipulation, depend-ing on whether she was looking at me. And suddenly it was gone. She was fat and, therefore, "prosperous." In Mount Olivet, "Rawny bone no sickness," but fat people were "prosperous." Thin visitors returning from abroad were said to be "having it hard"; when they were female and children weren't around, observers pronounced with certitude on what was missing in their lives. But Ma's was not the fat that brought the flirtatious compliments of Mount Olivet men. It hadn't the smooth roundness, the inner radiance, none of the bounciness that made men look past or around the person they were speaking to—or stop speaking altogether—that made them promise women to do the jobs their husbands wouldn't, that made them say, "Dou-dou darling, I shutting me eyes before I embarrass meself." The best she'd have elicited, from the most generous of the men, would have been, "Sis, le' me help you sweat out a lil' o' tha' stiffness." I guess every boy wants a mother who'll turn heads.

Once Ma and I boarded the Murray Hill bus, she dropped into a deep silence and lines settled into her face with a transmogrifying swiftness. I became momentarily enthralled by the speed with which the bus was travelling. Our roads—in places wide enough for only one vehicle, full of hairpin curves, snaking up and down valleys, built at points on the brinks of precipices without guardrails—did not permit speeding. Before we disembarked in front of what used to be the Mount Royal Hotel to take the Metro and later another bus, I knew I was unwelcome.

Baffled by the sea of lights around me, fascinated by the Metro, with my arms pressed close to my body, I observed an almost entirely white, silent population. At fourteen all I knew about North American whites was that they had murdered Martin Luther King because he'd been fighting for the rights of black people. The churches on Isabella Island had held a big service in Queen Elizabeth Park the day Martin Luther King was buried. Grampa's conscription, the denial of Grampa's pension to Grama, white men who forced their black servants to have sex with them, white people who threw out bones black people fought for—this was what I'd heard about white people. Mrs Cameron was the exception.

"I miss the bus stop," my mother said as she rang the bell and positioned herself to get off the bus. We walked under what I came to learn was an overpass, did a couple of quick left turns and walked for a short distance. "This where we live: De Courtrai," my mother said. "Get the name right in case you lose yo' way when you go out."

In a few minutes we turned into a doorway full of the smells of people's cooking. The light bulb in the entrance was burned out, but Ma found the keyhole easily. I followed her down the stairs. Underground, I could not help thinking, since basements were nonexistent on Isabella Island.

The apartment stank. Its last occupant must have been incontinent. The air-freshener Ma had sprayed in it mixed with the other odours to create a nauseous, sweetish vegetable rot. The entire apartment was a bed-sitting room, kitchenette and bathroom. In the main room there were a sofa and an armchair, both of them old and shabby. On an armrest of the sofa something darker than the already deep brown fabric had left a glaring stain. The floor was carpeted with a tangerine shag rug that was worn bare in places. I sat on the sofa and raised a cloud of dust that set me sneezing. A wobbly, scratched-up, walnut-stained coffee table, a small round kitchen table with two chairs, all with metal legs, and a floor lamp with a burlap shade completed the furnishings.

"I just start furnishing it," my mother said testily.

But just as I began wondering why she was so edgy, a loud noise from what was obviously a car with a damaged muffler jolted me and I smelt exhaust fumes. *A garage! We are sharing a garage with cars coming and going.*

"I still have for look around for a desk for you and a lamp," Ma resumed in an accusatory tone. "But I too tired on my days off to do more than this. I getting the telephone on Monday."

At that point the doorbell rang.

"That must be Agnes. She say she will check me out. God help me! I don't want her for get too friendly. Pastor Draine had no business praying for me open like that, telling them my business, and now they all butting in."

The footsteps were loud, the rapping louder. Ma looked through the peephole and opened the door. She introduced Sister Agnes as a good friend. Agnes's bright eyes seemed to be popping out of their sockets with curiosity. She was a short cheese-coloured, "rawny-bone" woman wearing a red pantssuit and an Afro wig; Mount Olivetans would have called her dry (perhaps the comparison was to brittle firewood, the sort women easily broke across their knees; perhaps to something less polite. When I got to know her, she was more like a spur, an invincible thorn—she'd have said *maca*—one was wise not to tamper with; if wood, it was the kind that broke the breaker's knee).

Sister Agnes squeezed my hand, examined me the way I imagine butchers do steers before buying them, and said, "Lawd, the bwoy done reach man. When you tell me him fourteen, I did think you was talking 'bout somebody thisya high." She raised her hand just above her right breast. "But him is big man; soon him gwine feather him own nest."

Ma smiled scornfully. "He better not start thinking 'bout feathering no nest. Before it come to that I will feather his behind."

"If you teach him for walk in the straight and narrer, Sister, him will be all right. Now, if Margaret did start training her pickney-them right, her big bwoy wouldn' be in jail, and the other two wouldn' be heading there."

"That is God, Sister, punishing she for turning her back on Him," Ma said.

"Did you see the youngest one 'pon television? Mug some black 'oman on Goyer. The 'oman say she knock him down and sit on him 'til the police and the television people-them come," Sister Agnes continued, loud and excited.

"Train up a child" — Ma chimed in.

"'—in the way in which he ought to grow, and when he is old he will not depart from it.' Amen!" she and Sister Agnes parroted.

Looking at me, her facial muscles set rigidly, Ma declaimed theatrically, "I hope you taking all this in. I done make up my mind that if you don' follow my rules and regulations, it will be the grave for you and the gallows for me. I not one for spare the rod and spoil the child."

"Him just arrive, Sister Milly, him just arrive. You have plenty o' time for read 'im the riot act. Bwoy, how you enjoy yo' flight? You ever been 'pon a plane before?"

Ma went into the kitchen. Sister Agnes handed me an envelope. "Is a liklow something for you. I didn' know yo' fit so I giving you the money so you can buy yo'self a liklow something."

I thanked her.

"Seek ye first the kingdom of heaven and its righteousness and all things shall be added unto you.' And he promised never to leave us nor forsake us. That is God holy word and it bound for be true. You mus' trust God, you know. You save yet?"

I grinned, wondering if all my mother's friends were this eccentric.

"You mus' lissen to yo' mother, you know. When the young people-them come here, them think them know how the lie o' the land stay; some o' them even think is them what own it, and 'fore you can say bullcow, is jail them reach, and when them get in trouble is we the parents what have for do all the running around. I have one. Is like when she hear the name o' the Lord is Satan she see. But otherwise I is proud o' she. She going to university and on the honour roll and all kindo' thing. Only thing she ungrateful. She think that if she did follow my advice for walk in the footsteps o' the Lawd she wouldn' be in university. God will surely put 'im 'and on 'er, if she don' watch out and 'umble 'erself. I hask 'er, who give 'er 'ealth and strength and hintelligence, if not de Lawd? And whose sparing mercy keeping 'er going heveryday, hif not de Lawd? Take care, I tell 'er, 'moon a run till day catch um,' and don' feeget, 'the wheels o' God turn slow but them grind f-i-ine.'" She was enjoying herself.

The apartment was stifling. Ma knocked around pots and pans. Sister Agnes went into the kitchen to help her. The air was heavy and steamy with the odour of cooking chicken and stale piss and air freshener. It entered and left my lungs with the heaviness of water. I went to the bathroom and saw the roaches scampering. On Isabella Island they were several sizes bigger. I examined the shower and felt relieved that I wouldn't have to shower outdoors as I'd been doing at home. I turned on the water taps. The hot water surprised me. At home, only the wealthy had hot water. The cost of electricity made it unaffordable. The thought of having a hot shower excited me. I decided it was the thing I most wanted to do then. My mother couldn't be as poor as she made out in her letters.

Back in the main room, Ma, wearing a dungaree apron tied at her waist and neck, and Sister Agnes were putting the food on the table (a card table, I later found out). There was a big plastic bowl of salad, a platter heaped with fried chicken, rice and peas, plantain and dasheen. I didn't know plantain and dasheen were available here. She turned the grace into a long prayer, begging God to bless us and keep us "in the rays of your guiding light, and to receive us into your kingdom on the last day."

Sister Agnes and I sat at the table. Ma heaped a plate for herself and ate sitting on the sofa with the plate on her lap.

It was around eleven pm when we accompanied Sister Agnes home. She lived on Goyer, a few streets away. Ma said the neighbourhood wasn't safe. "Too many black people." It was altogether about a twenty-minute walk.

When we got back to the apartment, she pulled off her wig. Her scant hair, more than fifty percent grey, was braided in corn rows.

Her face now looked naked, the face of someone afraid, vulnerable.

She gave me a set of keys, saying that I would need them since I was going to be on my own most of the time. The size of the apartment shouldn't bother me, I told myself. Many Isabellan families lived in single rooms, even in Hanovertown, and as many as thirteen to a room on the large Isabellan plantations. *But they weren't obliged to spend most of their waking life indoors.*

Ma handed me a blue dressing gown and a pair of burgundy pyjamas. She showed me how to operate the shower and ordered me to hurry up because we had to be up for church at 7 o'clock the next morning.

When I returned to the main room, I saw through the steam-laden air that the sofa and the armchair had been pulled out into beds. The armchair bed was mine, the sofabed hers.

"Did you say yo' prayers?" she asked, seeing me in bed when she came out of the bathroom.

"Yes," I lied.

She hesitated. "I want this to be a Christian home. The devil always busy."

She herself knelt down and prayed unendingly to impress me, I was sure. Part of her prayer was silent, and I thought, now, wouldn't that be something if she fell asleep on her knees! But she didn't.

That night, awake for several hours because of the day's excitement, the heaviness of the air and the choking dust in my bed, not to mention the grating, noisy garage fan and the traffic in and out of the garage—so unlike the sea's rocking sway that for fourteen years had patterned my sleep—I knew I wouldn't get along with my mother. She hadn't even embraced me—after not seeing me for almost ten years—and seemed afraid of me. Grama would have held me and spun me around and questioned me and held me again and spun me around some more, and planted kisses all over my forehead. That's what she'd done the previous August when I returned from a two-week Youth Fellowship camp on Baleine Island. That night I wanted to be in Mount Olivet, in my own bedroom, cooled by breezes full of the sea's goodness, knowing that next morning I would awaken with the sun shining through the window and on my bed; later, shining on the dining table when it was setting; at dusk fireflies filling the air with sparkling emeralds, the air perfumed by jasmine and the gentle body odour of sea surf; nearby, the Caribbean Sea breathing like a baby in its sleep. I didn't want to be living underground, inhaling car exhaust. My mother snored away. I would ask her to let me spend the rest of the summer with her and return to Grama at the end of August.

Next morning we awoke at five and got ready for church, which turned out to be half of an old warehouse the congregation was renting on Saint Patrick Street. Inside was hot—all the women had brought fans—because, I later saw, the outside skin of the building was of tin, and the windows were closed to prevent the heavy traffic on Saint Patrick Street from drowning out what the pastor was saying. The floor was of pressed wood, with pieces of carpet spread on the platform altar and in front of it. The seats were uncomfortable white plastic chairs. Outside the window, I saw water and later found out it was the Lachine Canal. Of the forty or so people present, everyone, except the pastor and his wife, was black.

At one point in the service, the pastor asked all the young people —we were about twelve—to stand and sing:

Saviour, while my heart is tender,
I will yield that heart to thee,
All my joys to thee surrender,
Thine and only thine to be...

After that, he prayed and asked God to send the Holy Spirit to "afflict their youthful hearts with heavenly power so that they will not only sing obedience to God's will but surrender unto it." I smiled.

When the service ended, Ma introduced me to almost everyone who came by, women mostly, most wearing bright floral prints and straw hats; a few black, grey, or brown suits; and Sunday bests. At times she was forced to shout because of the heavy traffic zooming by in both directions. The faces cancelled one another out. I kept waiting to hear her say, Sister Louisa from Mount Olivet, but she didn't. In a tone that had suggested that Grama ought to feel flattered, Mrs Manley had told Grama that Louisa and Isis attended the same church. But she did not say which church it was. I was sure now both Grama and she thought it was a Methodist Church in Montreal.

"Sonny," a tar-black, beady-eyed, heavy woman wearing white gloves and a charcoal suit said, "you must keep to the straight and narrow way."

"Amen!" said a short man with bulging belly, rectangular, jowly face and oily forehead walking towards her. His eye sockets rose out of his forehead like mountain ridges. He seemed to be peeping out from behind thick glasses that magnified his eyes and moved as if every step were a painful, consciously executed limp; his arms were bent at the elbows and held stiffly in front of him. The lime-green polyester suit he had on was too big, his shirt was frayed at the cuffs and collar, and the tie badly knotted.

"Him promise for make the crooked smooth and the rough straight," the man continued. He drooled slightly and spat involuntarily.

"Brother Carlton, what stupidness you is telling the young man?" the white-gloved woman asked, a slight smirk on her face. "You mean make the *crooked straight* and the *rough smooth*."

"Is no' that me say? Him know what me mean."

Ma smiled. "Sister Andrews, leave Brother Carlton alone. Pedro knows what he means."

Compared to Hanovertown Methodists, they were freaks. I wondered whether to laugh at them or pity them. I did not want to get to know them, let alone become one of them.

We could not leave immediately because Pastor Draine, whose preaching I had found amusing, wanted to speak to me. We waited until Draine had shaken all the hands and said what ministers say to their departing congregations. He finally came to talk to us. He was about six-five, with sky-blue eyes, glossy auburn hair, broad shoulders, and a stomach that pushed out the vest of his three-piece suit.

"A most wonderful commencement, Sister Millicent." His voice was like a sonic boom, as I imagined God's would be on judgment day. He beckoned us to follow him into his office, a small partitioned-off space, in which he kept a bookshelf, a desk and two plastic chairs. There we knelt close together because of the cramped space while Draine asked God to guide me, to help me seek his saving mercy soon, and put my feet in his footsteps. "Lord, you know it's not easy to be a single parent in this city. Give Sister Millicent a double portion of your wisdom and your strength and your guidance. Your will be done. Amen."

Ma pulled at my arm impatiently. Outside the church, the Andrewses (the white-gloved woman and her dumpling of a husband) were waiting for us. Ma and I were to have brunch with them.

The Andrewses occupied a lower duplex in LaSalle, the second-to-last one on Thierry Street, near Cordner Street. The land just beyond their house was vacant for a great distance and covered with weeds, grass and young wild saplings. Plastic bags and paper were scattered about it. My mother asked whether the upstairs tenants had paid off the back rent, so I knew that they owned it. The smell of smoked herring announced what we were going to eat, and I knew it would probably upset my stomach. Plastic flowers were on all the side tables; and three-foot high plastic philodendrons, dusted and oiled, were in every corner of the living and dining rooms. Their high-backed sofa and armchair were upholstered in beige vinyl, and a wall-to-wall burgundy rug covered the entire floor. Scattered about the walls were the usual plaster of paris plaques with a border of roses or some such framing statements like "Christ is the master of this house . . ." and "For God so loved the world." A fan painted in glowing gold whirred noisily above the white arborite dining table. A white melamine china closet with a mirror backing and turned-on light invited us to examine its insides, mostly cheap dishes, glasses, and made-in-Taiwan souvenirs.

Basil, the older Andrews boy, was finishing high school. He was tall, sinewy, and very black, like his parents. He was an army cadet. His darting, shark eyes fascinated me. Langley, who was my age and was entering grade nine that September, looked sheeplike, was a trifle paler than his parents, wore thick glasses for his near-sight-

83

edness, and had his father's round, dumplinglike shoulders. They hadn't come to church.

After grace, Basil winked at me, reached over and seized the dish of shredded smoked herring, cucumber and raw onions and raked what he wanted onto his plate. The Andrews boys ate fast and noisily, with their forks and fingers, which they licked periodically. Knife and fork suspended, Ma stared at me hard, relaxing only when she was sure I was not going to use my fingers. Basil finished before everyone else, got up, burped, patted his belly, went down into the basement, and turned up the television—loud.

When Ma and Sister Andrews began to clear the table, I followed Langley down into the basement. He headed into his bedroom. I stood beside the couch on which Basil's long self was stretched out watching a football game. There were no other seats. Without taking his eyes from the TV screen he said, "Don' make them full up yo' head with stupid religion. They alright, but they afraid o' life, so they hide from it inside their church."

After standing there in silence for another ten minutes, I realized that they were not interested in me, so I ascended the stairs and went to stand on the porch. A building that turned out to be a school called Terre des Jeunes blocked the southern view. I sat there on a porch chair, facing the north, the sun striking my back, and stared at the vacant land beyond Cordner Street, wondering where this adventure I was on was headed.

Just before we left, Basil borrowed ten dollars from his mother and left. Brother Andrews told him if he wasn't back before nine he would not let him in.

Hmm, I said to myself. A month later I learned from one of Sister Agnes's put-downs of Sister Andrews that Basil was already the father of a two-year-old.

9

"HOW YOU LIKE THE CHURCH?" Ma asked. We were on the bus heading up Côte des Neiges hill on our way home from the Andrewses.

"I don't know. It's too soon to tell." I felt as if a lump of putty had stuck in my gut. I belched and tasted the cucumber and smoked herring I'd eaten earlier.

"Well you better start liking it, 'cause you don't got no other choice." She said it with a barbed grin that made her cheeks pucker.

We'll see. I didn't come to Canada to become a Wayfarian. I felt sorry that my mother had gone backwards. The rest of the trip was taken up with thoughts of home and periodic belching.

At home she invited me to sit with her at the table. "You listen to what I telling you. I reading you the riot act." I was eager to hear it. She outlined to me her weekly earnings and the apartment, telephone, electricity, and transportation costs. Her total costs amounted to one and a half times her salary, so she must have lied about her salary or the costs or both or had forgotten how to add. She estimated that ten dollars per week was all she could spend on food. "This not Isabella Island. Every penny you make you have to spend. Sometimes things cost more than you make. Soon as you get for know Montreal, you will have for get a little job, 'cause, as I show you, the expenses more than what I make."

"I don't understand," I told her, thinking of the hundreds of emigrant Isabellans who returned almost annually and gave away clothing and money.

She stared at me with incredulity.

"I thought everybody in Canada was rich," I told her, as a sharp pain rippled in my gut and sent a spasm all the way to my bowel. I dashed to the bathroom.

"You only think so because you see the niggers-them coming back home and showing off," Ma picked up when I returned. "Lying to people! That is what they doing. Showing off! Most o' them credit the things they share away, and is borrow they borrow the money to pay they passage. One big farce! And when them come back is slave them have for slave for pay it back."

I didn't believe her.

"Lemme tell you right off, a lot o' the clothes you going be wearing going be second-hand."

My stomach tightened and I counted three painful spasms as I got up to return to the bathroom. *People's hand-me-downs!* I hoped I never met anybody I knew. The practice carried a very bad stigma in Isabella Island.

"You used to send me new clothes," I told her when I got back.

"That's 'cause I used to buy them on sale for little and nothing in the fall when they had clearance. And them days I didn' have apartment rent for pay.

"Another thing, I work all the way out on the West Island, and it take me two full hours for go and two full hours for come from here to there." She stared at the floor and her voice quavered while she told me this. "I have for get breakfast ready for Mr Wilton for him catch the seven o'clock morning train. And 'sides all that, I can't pay for this apartment and pay bus fare too."

So I was a problem, a burden. I remembered her letter to Grama about my coming.

"You mean I'm going to have to stay here alone?"

"I going be here on my days off—Thursday and Sunday."

What would Grama say to this? She would object. "But I will be alone most of the time! I don't know anyone here! I don't even know you!" My eyes began to fill. I was overwhelmed with contending emotions. I clenched my teeth to hold back the tears.

"You better wipe them eyes!" Her voice was a terror-filled shriek, like a gust of wind in a bamboo grove. "This ain't no country for no sofie-sofie body. When you out there, you have for fend for yo'self. Don' think where I is in Baie d'Urfé I going leave my job for come look after you. You will sink or swim on yo' own. I need somebody to look after me, let alone looking after somebody. Dry up! Dry up yo' tears! Right now! SH-U-T UP!"

My tears froze.

Later, she showed me that the fridge was full of food, much of it already cooked. I was to remain inside at all times, she said. If anyone rang the doorbell, I was not to answer. Under no circumstance was I to get friendly with the neighbours. She wagged her finger at me to emphasize this. "If you bring trash inside here, I will put you out with it. If any of them question you, don' tell them nothing. I don' know any of them, and that is how I want it to stay. You hearing me?"

I was too stunned to answer.

"I say, ARE YOU HEARING ME?"

"Yes!"

"Yes who? None o' yo' damn freshness! No damn freshness from you!"

"Yes, Ma." I heard myself thinking, *There must be a full moon. Isis!*

"Well you better show me some respect. I won't take no nonsense from you."

Eventually she calmed down.

Later I asked her about her friends from home.

"Friends! Is better to keep away from black people. They chat too much. If you making poopoo in the bush and you see a nigger coming, sit on it, else the world will know you been making poopoo in the bush."

I stared at her, amused.

"I associate with the people in the church, 'cause I don' have no choice. I only see them on a Sunday, thank God, 'cause it too far for travel during the week."

"Everyone calls you Sister Millicent. Is that the name you always use?"

She looked at me as if I'd struck her, then collected herself, sucked in her cheeks, compressed her lips to a spike which she moved from left to right and back again, rubbed her hands, and said, "You will see what name I use around certain people, and that is the name you is to use. If you not sure ask me."

"Be serious!" *Hello. Ma? A man here wants to know what your name is. Which one should I tell him?* "What about Louisa Manley?"

"What you want to know about her?" her voice acid.

"Mrs Manley wanted me to bring something for her. Grama told her I couldn't bring it. I had too many things to bring. She said I should create room because Louisa had lodged you and helped you find a job when you came to Montreal. Grama didn't tell her what you wrote: 'Don't let Pedro bring nothing for nobody, else I will put it in the garbage.'"

"She put me up, yes. A long time ago. I don' want to have nothing much—nothing at all—to do with her. What in the goat bound for be in the kid."

"Not you too, Ma! All that stuff is superstition."

"Superstition! If she did suck your blood, it wouldn't o' been superstition."

"You must show me Sister Louisa."

"You see her this morning. She was the brown-skin woman in the yellow dress sitting in the front row where she can stare at Pastor Draine crotch." Her hand went to her mouth, and I laughed.

"You shut up!" she said, embarrassed. "But Pastor Draine not going give up his wife for a . . . like her."

I remembered the woman.

"Why you didn't introduce her?"

"That's for me to know and you to find out. I not in court and you is not a judge. I have for rest up before I leave for Baie d'Urfé." She opened up the sofa bed and lay down.

She snored away. I sat quietly, not wanting to disturb her. The few books I'd brought were still in my mostly unpacked luggage. I was too anxious for sleep. I sat at the table, mystified by the mother I'd come to.

Before leaving she showed me where the telephone should go and said that a church brother would drop off a television sometime the next day. She'd kept an old radio Mrs Wilton was throwing away because it made too much static. She would bring it for me on Wednesday night.

"Aren't you going to give me the telephone number where you work?"

She didn't answer.

And then she was gone.

I recalled a night I'd dreamt someone was in my room trying to kill me, and Grama took me into her bed, and I slept there with my head in the cleft of her breasts, inhaling her lemony odour, her arm solidly girding me. Chilled to the bone despite the heat, I pulled out my armchair-bed, too battered to be bothered by the dust in it, and lay on it and sobbed.

10

LONG BEFORE SIX AM Monday I was awake to escape my nightmares. Anxiety made me alternately sweaty and chilly and the tightening in my stomach was constant and the diarrhea persisted. I remained stretched out on the armchair-bed, fleeing my anxiety with scenes from Grama's house, paying attention to it for probably the first time: its walls painted grass green; the picture of Christ on the partition wall, his open mouth, radiant head, intense pale blue eyes, golden hair and beard, brown toga; his hand grasping a shepherd's crook, telling those looking at him to feed his lambs. On the seaward wall a Methodist church calendar with a group picture of the ministers of the Southern Caribbean Synod. On the western wall a picture of the Last Supper, and a clock in a rectangular case of polished ebony. It had stopped at ten to noon or ten to midnight, I often wondered which. Grama said she always knew the time from her inside clock, so she did not need to repair it. The living-room furniture consisted of one two-seat and two single-seat Morris chairs with moss-green cushions arranged around a circular dark mahogany table. Almost against the wall that divided the living room from the kitchen were Grama's mahogany dining table and four chairs: her "inheritance"—all her mother left when she died. The floor was covered with linoleum in alternating squares of green and red. The curtains were of white lace. Ma had sent them in one of the barrels. They were tied to hooks on each side of the window because of the strong sea breeze that blew through the house. Those in my bedroom were always tied back because I liked to awaken with the sun shining on my bed.

I revisited the terraced drop that began about a hundred yards from Grama's house, and less than fifty from Ishtar and Saul's, down to the sea. I smelled the sea's surf and tasted its salt on my lips when it was boisterous. And I recalled those nights I'd awaken and hear it kissing the shore or thumping it if the wind was strong.

Here in Montreal, the sill of the tiny window—about twelve by eighteen inches—was level with the ground outside: we were at grave depth.

As early as six in the morning, heavy vehicles rumbled outside, vibrating the walls and emitting piercing siren sounds. Intermittently all day, the metallic monsters came and went, shaking the building and blasting the air, like lions warning strays away from their territory. At seven, a clanging, rolling noise heavier than the others shook the building, but from the back. I got up and tried to peer through the window but I could see nothing. Then the insistent blowing of a whistle made me know it was a train. The process was repeated every half hour, and I discovered there were train tracks behind us. Later I would see the vine-covered, chainlink fence separating the apartment building from the tracks, and still later I would know it was because of the train tracks that we were living there: the rent was cheaper, this was an apartment better-off Canadians would not want.

At nine o'clock I got up. The telephone had to be installed that day. I placed the bed in its armchair position and put away the bed-clothes on the top shelf of the coat cupboard. There was a thick piece of roughly cut, unfinished, unpainted plywood screwed into the gyprock at its base. Soot had created a feathery frame around its edges. I had to pull the clothes toward me when I pushed them; otherwise the wood blocked them. I wondered what it concealed. It emitted the smell of dust, grime, and urine. Maybe it was just above the sewer.

The telephone installer came around eleven.

It was mid July and hot inside the apartment. Little light came through the tiny window. I stared at it, thought of how the fierce raindrops from the Isabella Island downpours flattened out against the window panes and streamed down the side of Grama's house, how they sounded like gravel falling on our galvanized roof and washed the trees and air of dust in the dry season; the ruts they made where our yard sloped; I'd sprained my ankle in one. In the hole I was now in, unless the sewers backed up, I'd never know it was raining.

I had to go outside. It was that or hang myself. Ma could not control me if she wasn't around. I remembered limping Miss Haynes taking care of her grandson Allan, who was my age. His mother was in England. When Allan should have been in school he'd be roaming the wharf. Miss Haynes was always beating him for coming in late or skipping school. One day last year she came after him with a pigeon pea switch. He did not run, as he used to. He stood still, letting his grandmother close in on him. He dodged her blow. It set her off balance and she fell and rolled over, a tree trunk on the bank preventing her from falling onto the highway. Allan took the switch from her and helped her to her feet; and when he was certain she hadn't broken any bones, he said, "Grama, you is ol' an' weak, and is my turn to look after you. From now on, if anybody round here going to get beat, is you." Ma had better pass laws she could enforce. The television set had to be delivered before I could whip—or try to whip—my mother.

The telephone rang at one pm. It was she. "How did you know the number?"

"Stop being a *coonoomoonoo!* Ain't I must know the number o' the phone I paying for? Did you sleep good last night?"

"No."

"Did you eat?"

"No."

"How come?"

"I don't know."

"Well when you eat make sure you wash up the dishes. Don' leave dirty things lying around—the place done full with cockroaches."

"You needn't worry about that, and, please, don't scream, I can hear you."

"Brother Solomon bring the television?"

"No."

"I was hoping he done bring it so you can watch something to keep yo' mind occupied. I have to go now. I will call you later."

So she'd got the telephone to keep checking up on me. I thought of Grama's ruses to make me come home right after school.

Brother Solomon came with the television around half past five. He stood a full head above me. He was in his fifties. His dungaree overalls and blue T-shirt gave him a relaxed look. A round-shouldered, elephantine, red-eyed man, with a head of thick steel-grey hair, a bumpy, gleaming forehead and coal-black skin, he looked very strong, though a lot of what had been muscle was now fat, evident in the way his belly sagged.

"You must feel lonesome lock up all by yo'self in here?" His voice was kind and surprisingly soft.

I didn't answer.

"Yo' mother trying she best." His eyes roved around the apartment. "This country hard. And you have for meet hardness with hardness." He sounded as if he was talking to someone faraway.

I stared at him, puzzled. Had my mother sent him to bamboozle me into accepting her ways?

He pulled out his wallet, extracted a twenty-dollar bill and gave it to me.

I thanked him.

"Yo' mother tell me you comes first in school. This country got opportunity fo' bright black people. My oldest boy him in university, in engineering at McGill, and the other two-them following in his footsteps." He paused, glanced around the apartment again. "If you feel lonely here of a days, you can come down to the house and visit my boys. This week and next week I is on holidays. But after that the younger boys-them there in the afternoon when them come in from summer school."

"Is it near here?"

His brow furrowed.

"Can I walk to your house?"

"No, No. I live in Verdun. You take three buses, or two buses and the Metro for get there."

"Brother Solomon, if I want to get somebody's telephone number what do I do?"

He told me, then said, "Seeing that you is here by yourself, why you don' come home and eat with us? You can phone yo' mother when she get in and tell her where you is. I will drop you home afterwards."

He drove a rusting, noisy Country Squire with a dent on the driver's side; the back seat springs protruded. His apartment was in a brick building that extended an entire block. The rooms were big, especially the kitchen. The floor was of polished wood. All three of his boys were home. Harry, the oldest, merely nodded at me; the other two grinned and ignored me. Two of them weren't as dark as Brother Solomon. Joe, the middle one, was darkest. But they all had his bulbous nose, roundish features, and heavy lips. Two of them were taller than their father; Joe was about an inch shorter. I felt short in their presence.

Brother Solomon had cooked a big pot of boileen with green bananas, circular corn dumplings the size of hamburger rolls, pigeon peas, okra, West Indian vegetables and pickled pig tails. It was on the stove and everybody served himself until he'd had enough. After my first helping I sat with my empty plate in front of me, conscious of Grama's instructions "when you in people place."

Brother Solomon took my plate, held me with his other hand, led me to the stove, handed me the ladle, and said, "Help yo'self. Eat all you want."

His sons laughed at my embarrassment, Joe choking himself in the process and setting the others laughing at him.

While I was serving myself, the telephone rang, and as I was taking the food to the table, Brother Solomon told me it was for me. Ma had phoned the apartment to check up on me and was verifying whether I was at Brother Solomon's. "Behave yo'self now. Don' do nothing for cause me for hang me head in shame."

Joe washed the dishes, Maurice dried them, and Harry put them in the cupboard. I looked on, impressed by what it was to have brothers. There was none of the claustrophobia and tension I'd felt at Cousin Lucy's place. It was more relaxed than at the Andrewses. Brother Solomon's love for his children and their love of him filled the apartment. I felt happy there.

After supper we played scrabble. I didn't know the game but

learned it very quickly. After the second game, Harry began to play his guitar, Joe went off to his bedroom, and Maurice and I continued to play. It was around 10.30 when Brother Solomon took me back to De Courtrai.

I was already asleep when the telephone rang. She wanted to know whether I'd returned. "Brother Solomon is a good man, but I don' want for be beholden to him. In this place favours don' come free. That is what Miss Wilton always say. And if you want for know what happening in the sea you have for ask the turtle."

Next morning I woke up feeling happy. After eating I turned on the television. I didn't like anything on it. At home I used to watch the National Geographic Specials on Saturdays and the news on weekdays. Homework or reading novels from the Public Library or the books Mrs Cameron lent me took up my time.

I decided to try to get the phone number where my mother worked. I opened the telephone directory left by the telephone installer and looked for Wiltons in Baie D'Urfé. Around one o'clock I summoned up enough courage to phone the first name on the list. Ma answered the telephone. I replaced the receiver.

At three Brother Solomon phoned to say he was coming to pick me up. It was after hanging up that I remembered the card in my suitcase from Mr Sam. He'd said to wait a month or two. I opened it. In the envelope were two East Caribbean five-dollar bills and a card-size piece of Bristol board on which someone, Mr Sam probably, had drawn a picture that was framed by a rainbow. One end of the rainbow ended in a serpent's head and the other in its tail. At the centre of the picture was a palm tree—brown trunk and green fronds in a pale yellow halo that suggested sunlight—located on a tiny island coloured dark chocolate, an island, just big enough to hold the palm tree, surrounded by a dark blue sea.

On the back of the Bristol board were the words, written in a tremulous hand:

Pedro, the son Shango denied me,
find the tree of truth and climb it
to Africa and further. Be as good as you can. Pardon others.

You will need their pardon. Misfortune is half of life.
Feast him and fete him, or you will be his feast.
Find out your obligations to the ancestors and fulfill them.
And learn everything I didn't have your chance to know.

While waiting for Brother Solomon to arrive, I mulled over Mr Sam's words. They touched me even if I felt I should resist them. He'd called me his son. He wanted me to find the tree of truth and climb it. I loved him for that. I did not know he could read and write, let alone in standard English. He probably did it all in his bedroom, out of sight. Either that or he'd got one of his literate confreres to do it, but I preferred to think that it was he, that he never exhibited his talents unnecessarily. But the rest of his words to me were related to his Shango beliefs. The Shango stories he'd told me meant little more than the Doum-Doum stories Chauncey told. When Brother Solomon arrived, I replaced the two five-dollar bills and the card in the envelope and left them in the suitcase where I forgot about them until I got Grama's letter a month later telling me that Mr Sam had died.

Ma didn't phone Brother Solomon's house that evening. But when I was back at the apartment, she phoned and told me that the next time Brother Solomon invited me down to his place, I was to say I had to have her permission first.

"How will I do that if I don't have your telephone number?"

"That is it. You don' have my permission."

Harry had promised to drive me around the city the next day. I decided I would not tell her.

Next day Harry took me to St Joseph's Oratory, then to Mount Royal Park and finally to La Ronde, where we spent the remainder of the day. Brother Solomon had given him the money to pay for my rides. I'd never been to an entertainment park before though I'd seen one in a film. I made a complete fool of myself and enjoyed it all—screaming along with everyone else in the 360-degree cinema when it seemed as if I was about to plunge into the Grand Canyon; throwing darts that nearly always hit the bullseye; having my fortune read by a prunewrinkled white woman dressed in an Indian sari with a blood-red rhinestone the size of a quarter on her forehead, and told that I would become a millionaire and live to a ripe old age; descending to hell to meet the devil. My fear of heights made the cable car and roller coaster rides more torture than fun and cured me of any wish to ride the Ferris wheel. On the way home, when the euphoria had subsided, I realized how costly my day had been for Harry, and I wished I had been more disciplined. Grama would have been angry with me, would have said I'd dived without know if the water was deep. Harry took me straight to Brother Solomon's, where I ate. Brother Solomon beamed when he saw me. I must have been beaming too, for I knew Brother Solomon liked me. I understood then what it meant to have a real, loving, providing and present father. In the things that matter to an adolescent male, Brother Solomon was more important to me then than my mother.

When I got home Ma was there, stiff as if she'd been ordered to stand at attention. She was still dressed in her travelling clothes and had on her wig. She left work on Wednesday evening for her Thursday off.

"Where you coming from?" she screamed.

"Brother Solomon's place."

"What I tell you last night?"

I looked away. The slap she gave me stung and echoed. "By hook or crook you will obey me. You will get what I can afford. And what I can' give you, you will do without." She was breathing audibly and when she resumed talking, she was out of breath. "By God, I plan to pull on the bit, apply the reins and dig in the spurs."

Horses can kick and bite and even run away.

She had brought food from her workplace. I couldn't eat it because I wasn't hungry but I preferred to let her think it was from surliness.

I was hurt, confused, and frightened. I'd hoped to broach the subject of going back home with her then, but in her vindictive mood she would have surely said no. That night I wrote Grama my second letter, telling her I was sorry I'd come to Canada. I was a burden to my mother. She seemed always angry with me. She could not afford to look after me. She didn't want me to talk to other people, and she had me in an apartment all by myself. "Please, ask Ma to send me back to you. I can't live with her."

Next day she took me to the immigration and manpower office to get application forms for children's allowance, a social insurance number and a Medicare card. I stuffed my pockets with one of every pamphlet in the office. Afterwards she took me shopping in the Bay basement. I didn't tell her about the money Brother Solomon had given me. With the money from Sister Agnes, she bought me a pair of shoes.

When we got back to the apartment, she emptied two shopping bags of clothing she had brought the previous evening. She'd modified the hems and the waistlines of Mr Wilton's clothes so that I could wear them. She went on about what good quality clothes they were; poor people couldn't afford such "nice things."

If they're so nice why didn't the Wiltons keep them? I clenched my teeth.

"You not even showing any appreciation?"

I walked away, pretending to go to the bathroom.

"Pedro!" It came out with venom.

"Yes."

"Yes who? Come back here!"

I returned to stand about two feet from where she was sitting on the sofa bed.

"Understand one thing. You wear what I give you to wear, you hear. When you start earning your own money you can do what you like with it. But so long as you is not paying, you will eat what I provide—whether you is pleased or not; and you will wear what I can afford—whether it suit you or not."

"Yes, ma'am!" I replied, turning away from her.

When I looked at her again, she was staring intently into space, her forehead deeply creased, her cane-rowed half-grey hair framing her face; she looked especially vulnerable. I felt a twinge of guilt. I didn't want to hurt her feelings. It was just that . . . I couldn't complete the thought. I had no words for it. We said nothing to each other for the rest of that day. Her banging things around, even her singing, irritated me, and her cooking added sultriness to the apartment's already stifling stink.

Eventually I summoned up the courage to ask her, would it bother her if I returned to Isabella Island. She was standing at the sink, wiping perspiration from her face with one end of her dungaree apron.

She did not answer immediately, nor did she turn to look at me standing in the entranceway to the kitchen, staring at her. "Why you want to go back?" She was wiping both hands in her apron now.

"Because you're like a grenade waiting for me to stumble on your pin."

"Good. Then keep out o' of my way, if you don' want to get blow up." She fell silent.

"You didn't answer my question."

"What question?"

"Would it bother you if I returned to Isabella Island?"

She turned around now, looked at me, then at the patterns of black and white squares in the linoleum covering the kitchen floor. She reached for the mop in a corner between the counter and the fridge and mopped up some water that had spilled near the sink. She put back the mop and straightened herself to her fullest.

"Bother *me!*" Her voice registering fake nonchalance, but an octave above her normal speaking range. "Oh no! But you will have for pay yo' own passage. Go out and buy a newspaper and see what job you can find and put aside the money for pay yo' fare home. You don' even have for tell me when you leaving, just give the key to the janitor with a note." She paused. "But listen to my crosses? Where you get all this mannishness from? And, listen to me, who you think will feed and clothes you when you go back home?"

"Shouldn't you have known all that before you had me?" I paraphrased Grama's statement to that effect.

"And all the pickney-them that people drop behind them when they go overseas and never look back on? You think I can't do that too? I is human just like them."

I smiled, shocked to hear myself thinking, *I should have known you're a heartless bitch.*

"What you smiling 'bout?" She took two steps toward me.

"I eat your food and live in the apartment you pay rent for, but it doesn't entitle you to my thoughts," I said slowly with deliberate cheek.

She stared at me open-eyed, took a deep breath, turned and went back to the kitchen sink, where she stood muttering to herself and opening and closing her fingers as if she were dry-washing them, or trying to restore the circulation in them.

I was relieved when she took her customary nap before getting ready to take the Baie d'Urfé bus.

On Friday and Saturday I had a lot of time to reflect. I hoped Grama would do as I asked. I'd spend the rest of the summer—I couldn't endure longer than that—and leave at the end of August. Brother Solomon was great but the rest of Canada I could have done without. There was certainly lots of food, as Benjy had said, but I was no glutton. Would Grama be able to send me the fare? I would go back without even telling my mother. Or Mrs Duncan? *No, not Mrs Duncan.* I would wait to hear Grama's response to what I'd told her about Ma.

On Friday I explored the neighbourhood and saw that the northern side of the street, the side on which we lived, was really one long block—bounded by Victoria on the west and Côte des Neiges on the east—of warehouses, depots for goods unloaded from or to be loaded onto the freight trains that stopped there. There were few apartment buildings on our side, and all but the one I lived in abutted on the sidewalk. In contrast to the northern side the entire southern side of the street was tree-lined. It had a couple of warehouses but it was mostly residential. One apartment building at the Victoria end had a large, very green lawn and a circular fenced garden of flowers, many of whose names I did not know. *Why couldn't we have lived in that one?* Almost all the houses on this side of the street had gardens and window boxes. I thought of Mrs Duncan.

Next I went to Côte des Neiges Plaza. There were a few Blacks, East Indians, and the occasional Chinese person scattered among the throngs of Whites in the Plaza. I ventured into Steinberg's and could not believe how cheap food was. A tin of cocoa for which Grama would have paid nine dollars sold for a dollar seventy-nine. And the price of meat! In Isabella Island there were no cuts for under $4 per pound, and at that price it was usually a lot of bone and fat. I wondered if Ma told the truth about the cost of things and I understood why there had been so much fried chicken on the table the night I arrived. Affordability, not welcome.

For an hour I loitered in the main aisle of the shopping centre, watching the human traffic. I saw that people rarely spoke to one another. They were as indifferent as the Andrewses boys. There were a few Blacks my age. I wished they'd recognize me as a stranger and be curious. In Isabella Island, I'd have done that, though not as easily as others. When I looked at them, however, they turned their heads away.

When I got back to De Courtrai, a man was mowing the yard-wide strip of grass fronting the apartment building I lived in. A couple of flower boxes placed against the building contained weeds. If flowers had been planted in them, they were long dead. On the steps sat two black teenage boys, smoking and tapping their feet and rocking to reggae that came from a boombox placed one step above the step they sat on. This was what we saw of black Americans on Isabella Island TV. Consequently, shiftless Isabellan males strapped themselves to their boomboxes, sported dark glasses, smoked cigarettes with gangster antics, and affected a menacing, undulating, catlike style of walking. Near them you felt as if trespassing onto their property. Grama looked at them askance, at anyone who didn't attend church. On the day of judgment, church bells will bear witness against them " 'cause they call them loud and clear to come and praise God; and the wind will testify against them 'cause I hear it all the time in the trees whistling praises to the Maker."

The boys stared at me fixedly when they realized that I was headed for their building.

As I reached them, one who was wearing a green, gold and red beret said, "Bwoy, is here yo' live?"

I didn't answer.

"Ratid! Him mus' be can' talk! Or him dotish-no-bombo-clart!" he continued. They both laughed.

I quickened my pace.

11

THE NEXT EVENING, SATURDAY, when my mother arrived, she asked, her face ugly with irony, if I'd found a job, or would I like her to help me find one? It was too much: overload. It would just have to spill.

When we went to church the next day, I sat with Brother Solomon and Maurice three rows in front of Ma.

It was definitely a Wayfarian congregation—no doubt about it—like those that had held "services" each weekday evening at the Mount Olivet Crossroad. "Wayfarians," Grama called them. "Always starting out hot-hot. Say them done stop sinning—like if a body can stop doing that. And the time you take for blow yo' nose them belly start swelling. And no husband! Backslide long time!" Once, teasing a woman who lived further up the hill from us, a little distance in from the highway, and whose voice we sometimes heard proclaiming "the wonders the Lord have done for me"—Grama asked her, her lower lip heavy with irony, her eyes fixed on the woman's face, "Darling, like religion getting you fat?"

"Go 'long, Ma Moore, you tease people too much. You know is backslide, I done backslide."

"Honey, take it from a' ol' horse like me: slide on yo' foot, yo' belly will stay flat."

Every year, between December and March, as many as a dozen itinerant healers came to Isabella Island. They'd rent the sports stadium. Mostly they'd charge five dollars for admission but sometimes it was free. People attended in the thousands, carrying their mongoloid and paralyzed children as well as their quadriplegic or paraplegic, blind or senile parents to be healed. The taxi and bus industry loved the increased business. The daughter of a quadriplegic

Methodist would wipe the tears from her eyes whenever she recounted to Grama how her mother had leaped from her wheelchair at one such session, but for spite had resumed her paralysis, all because she enjoyed being a burden.

"Spiteful, Ma Moore! She could o' been on her own two feet today and I would o' been off somewhere, in Canada or the States, enjoying myself."

"Take it to the Lord in prayer, dear," Grama would console her.

What would Grama say if she found out Ma was Wayfarian? That she hoped she doesn't slide on her back? Maybe I should tell her that. I had every expectation of arriving one Sunday and finding the traffic blocked and a river of wheelchairs and stretchers heading onto the asphalt in front of the warehouse while in the background the congregation shouted and swayed and prayed, my mother's and Agnes's theatrics overpowering them. There was a story in the news then about a statue of the Virgin Mary crying tears and sick people being taken to the site to be healed. The tears turned out to be drops of pork fat the church sexton had put on the Virgin's face. It felt good to be in a society where "sacred claims" were not taken at face value. Today the bells of their tambourines were ringing up a holy tempest. Did the constant slapping not callus the skin on their thighs? Metal and larynxes trilled and bodies swayed to the tramping beat of "Oh Come to the Church in the Wildwood." "A Mighty Fortress Is Our God" came from their throats and off their tambourines, a pulsing heart throb. Reggaed. They made the most of their services, I suppose, since every pleasurable act, even nonprocreative sex, was a satanic snare.

"Testifying" came just before the sermon. Pastor Draine called on them to testify to the wonders the Lord accomplished in their lives. It wasn't a time for confession, he'd remind them. Wasted breath.

"I was a sinner," I heard Ma saying.

I turned to look at her and held my breath.

"Yes, you was. Sister, you sure was."

"Lost in the forest of damnation. And Jesus came to me."

"He came, Sister. He sure did."

"He said, 'Millicent!' I didn't answer. 'Millicent!' he said, a second time louder."

"*Wrassle with her, Lord! Wrassle with her!*" Their eyes were closed, their bodies rocked, the women fanned away.

"The third time he said, 'MILLICENT!' I start to tremble, and I say, 'Lord I too unclean.'"

"*Jesus can wash you clean. Sister. Whiter than snow! Hallelujah!*"

"I commit all manner of sin. I unclean. Lord, I shame to come in yo' presence. The Lord says to me, 'Get down on your knees and beg fo'giveness.'"

"*Bless Jesus! Bless Jesus! Praise our redeemer.*"

"And I do that, and I feel His warm blood wash over me, from the mould o' my head down to my foot bottom, and a' inner peace fill me. And I come like a newborn baby."

"*Praise God!*"

"And then I know I save."

"*Hallelujah!*"

"And I not turning back."

"*Bless you, Sister! Keep to the track.*"

"And for nine long years, I been leaning on His arm."

"*Lean, Sister, lean!*"

I let out my breath.

As if on cue, "Leaning, Leaning, Leaning on the everlasting arm . . ." Pastor Draine began to sing and the congregation joined in. I knew all their hymns. Every Wayfarian sect that came to Isabella Island invariably sang them at Crossroad.

Ma was really in deep. At Crossroad a woman had said, "I can tell you all with confidence that I throw away two pickney, and God so merciful, he done forgive me." Needless to say it was talked about for weeks.

"Did you hear?"

"Calamity!"

"Lord, she bold face eh!"

"Comess for last!"

"No born-again talk going save she from the fire."

And the woman, constantly assailed by whistles and howls and shouts of: "Pickney-eater!" "Fire! Fire!" "Brimstone and fire!" or people singing a calypso popular at the time, "Fire! Fire! in me wire,

wire" whenever they saw her, grew tired of being a prisoner in her home and fled to Trinidad. And her American pastor compiled a list of unmentionable sins.

Saul had joined a Wayfarian church, and it was the talk of Mount Olivet for weeks, until one night we heard him beating Ishtar. "Hey, Tomcat," Mrs Duncan called to him next day, "you perfectly right for backslide. Don' make the word o' God turn you into a eunuch. You did miss all that beating you put 'pon poor Ishtar, eh?" He told her to go push her hand . . . Grama gave a piercing shriek and clapped her hands over my ears. "People like them is low, Pedro, low! On the very brink o' hell itself," she said when she removed her hands from my ears.

Duncan was still alive and he was home. He never got involved in his wife's quarrels. The villagers couldn't understand why he'd given her so much freedom and would ask him about it. He'd pretend not hear or suck his teeth and move on.

"What you smiling 'bout?" my mother's question interrupted my reverie and I became aware that the bus was moving alongside Côte des Neiges Cemetery.

"Nothing," I replied as my eyes readjusted to the scenery around me.

"Nothing!"

Then a thought I knew would rile her flashed into my mind. "You remember Cousin Mavis?"

"Why you asking me that?"

"Nothing."

"Ain't she still in the madhouse?"

"Yes. On account of her religion," I said it slowly.

"What you implying?" Her face began to twitch and she opened and closed her fingers rapidly.

"I hope I didn't say anything to make you so upset?"

She turned and stared out the window.

12

BACK AT THE APARTMENT, in spite of the earlier "witnessing," singing, and shouting, Ma was tense. She cooked in the early afternoon, singing through the entire process. While we were eating—rice, pork stew and fried eggplant—I told her I wanted to know my father's name and to have an idea of what he looked like. Did she have a picture of him? She said nothing but her hands began to sweat and to tremble so badly that she had trouble keeping the food on her fork. "I know he went to live in Trinidad when I was three months old."

"You know a lot. Put a ad in a Trinidad paper: 'Pedro Moore, heart-broken from Isabella Island, looking for his father.'" She forced a laugh. It looked like a grimace.

"I am serious!"

"Don't you scream at me in here! You not paying the rent for here!"

Instinctively, I struck the table with both hands and snarled. The plates heaved, spilled food, some of it onto the floor. I got up, my eyes dark, staggered toward the apartment door, and went to sit on the stoop outside. I stayed there for about forty minutes until I was calm. When I reentered the apartment, Ma was dressed to leave, a full two hours before her usual departure time.

She'd escaped this time. She couldn't escape always. Bored, I took up my copy of *The Rubaiyat of Omar Khayyam*—the Methodist Youth Fellowship had given it to me as a parting gift—and began to read through it. I read for several hours, visualizing the open desert stretching away from the oasis and a clear blue sky. This vision of an absurd universe frightened me. "And that inverted bowl we call the sky/ where under cooped we live or die / Look not to it for help/ For it as impotently moves as you or I." I'd never felt such loneliness.

My thoughts turned to sex. When my voice changed, Grama asked Brother Shiloh to counsel me. He said, "Your grandmother is a poor but respectable woman. Your mother is in Canada trying to better her condition. You have to help them lift the family up. Your grandmother has always been a respectable woman. Your mother made a mistake with you, but we can overlook that. You have to keep a straight path. If you start giving in to your desires to have sex with women, you will soon end up being a father. The trouble is you will want to have sex so badly you will have it with girls you don't respect and will never marry. The children you will leave them with will come to haunt you. It is better not to start." It sounded so much like a prepared speech, but I understood what Brother Shiloh meant. I'd wondered many times why Cousin Lucy had allowed herself to have so many children, knowing that she lived in a single room and couldn't feed those she already had.

Mr Sam had been more forthright. His tone would have scandalized Grama.

"What the name o' that girl you always looking at in school and getting a hard-on?"

"Who?" I asked, embarrassed.

"What you mean *who*? Don' tell me you get yo' hard-on watching boys? All boys yo' age get a hard-on when they look at girls with firm breasts and full lips and round tight bottoms." He winked, a conspiratorial wink. "Watch out, you don't pull her in the toilet. Pedro, sex at yo' age not easy to deal with. At yo' age, son, that thing dangling between your thighs want action. But leave people gal pickney alone 'til you ready for get married. Do what all boys yo' age do."

My ears and cheeks got hot.

He laughed. "Just don' talk 'bout it."

But such advice didn't prevent my many fantasies to be naked with a woman. Occasionally I'd dream about some girl I'd been observing and have a wet dream. Sometimes I couldn't wait until I was asleep. Once too I awoke frightened. I'd dreamt that Chauncey and I had been in bed naked, that Chauncey had kissed me and I liked it and ejaculated.

Putting the book on the floor in front of me, I wondered what difference it would make even if I found out who my father was. It would change absolutely nothing. I couldn't go to him with my problems. I couldn't even write to him. Maybe that was how my mother felt. Why did she give her body to such human garbage? Was it really such a big deal to know his name? One thing was sure: it would change nothing in my present existence; perhaps that was what my mother was trying to show me. And maybe, just maybe, I would not like what I'd find.

I remembered then the pamphlets I had brought back from the immigration and manpower office. One of them was a map along with an explanation of the Montreal Transit system. Another was a map of Montreal showing the cultural facilities and giving directions to them.

Next day I decided to test myself to see whether I could get to Man and His World without getting lost. It was a cinch. I didn't go in.

When I returned home, my mother phoned. She had phoned Brother Solomon and he hadn't seen me. I should stay indoors. I didn't know the city.

"If you want me to stay in," I blurted out, "you are going to have to be here to keep me in." There was silence for about fifteen seconds and she hung up. She didn't call back for the rest of the day.

That evening I watched the news on CBC. It was followed by a programme on child abuse. A man interviewed in prison said he was there because he felt a need to beat up on all women for the way his mother used to beat up on him. He said he didn't want to get out of jail because being there kept him from beating up on women. His psychologist said that he was an extreme case, the damage was usually subtler. There were additional stories from children, whose faces were blanked out, and adults who said they had been abused.

I had been taught that God, the Bible, had ordered parents to beat children. Even illiterates could quote the passage. And some, like Miss Haynes, demonstrated their holiness by the severe beatings they gave their children. Now I learned a long list of things that could go wrong with me, because I was being abused: verbally and emotionally; moreover, I was constantly threatened with physical abuse. I could not wait for my mother to arrive on Wednesday.

"What you said to me on Monday?" she asked me as soon as she had changed from her travelling clothes and taken off her wig. I had forgotten and looked at her puzzled. She came toward me menacingly.

"Don't touch me, you child abuser! I will call!"—

She froze momentarily. "You will *what?*" She asked slowly, shrill as a heat-crazed cat. And then she pounced on me. The blows fell fast, mostly on my arms as I tried to fend them off. She gasped as she beat me, "I work day and night, take abuse. For what? For see you get ahead. And you going call the police for me! Well, you have something to call the police for. Call the police! Call the police! Call the police!" With each statement a fresh blow.

The outburst exhausted her, and she sank into the couch, her chest heaving, her breathing laboured.

I was determined that she wouldn't get away with it. I remembered the single slap during the fourteen years with my grandmother—that time when I'd told her I was hungry—and the liberties *this stranger* had just taken on me appeared more outrageous. The psychiatrist on TV had said, "Many parents are clueless about the needs of children. It's a miracle society produces so few misfits."

Standing beside the door I said to her, "You're not fit to be a mother. You're a child yourself." Before she could respond I'd fled. From a phone booth, I called Brother Solomon and told him what had happened. He told me to wait near the phone booth. He arrived about twenty-five minutes later and accompanied me home.

Secure in his presence, I poured forth and didn't stop until I felt empty. I spilled almost everything: that in Isabella Island she had never paid me any mind; she never thought she owed me more than food and shelter; I repeated what she'd told me on the night of my arrival; what she'd said about my going to his place; I told her then about the money he had given me, that I was using it for prison leave; finally, to crown it all, I said that she had left me to sleep in the apartment all by myself the second night after my arrival and had refused to give me the telephone number where she worked; and since then she expected me to stay alone in the apartment five days a week. The only thing I held back, deliberately, was the fact that she'd refused to let me know who my father was.

Her shock gave way to heaving sobs.

"All that he just said is true?" Brother Solomon asked, incredulous, his eyes bulging with fear, his mouth agape, as he waited for her answer. It never came. He continued, "You is setting this boy up for destruction. I don' want to interfere, but, Sister Millicent, as a father of three boys what I raising myself, I can tell you that nothing in this whole affair smell right."

"I want to go back to Isabella Island. I don' care what Canada has. That's what I already told her."

"Calm yo'self!" he said sternly.

Not getting a word out of my mother, he waited around until her sobbing stopped. "I taking him home to sleep by me."

She nodded.

I shared Maurice's bed that night. The rest of the summer saw me backwards and forwards between the De Courtrai apartment and Brother Solomon's place.

Not long afterwards I reminded her of why I had come to Canada, and told her, if she wasn't willing to send me back to Isabella Island, we had to find some way of living peacefully together. When she didn't answer I turned to verbal jabbing. "You're not perfect, you know. You said that God called you Millicent. You don't think that God should know your real name is Isis?"

I was on the sofa bed. She was sitting at the table, her head half turned to me. She had on one of Miss Wilton's castoff grey dresses; the sleeves reached down to her elbow. I looked at her wigless head and laughed, but it did not stall her.

"You think after you did done strip me naked, disgrace me, expose all my faults to Brother Solomon, I would o' run and buy yo' ticket for send you back home. Well think again." She stopped, pulled a loose thread from her left sleeve, rolled it into a ball, and placed it on the table. "You young people, all you think all you is steel saw and we the older heads is rotten wood. Well *you* will break before *I* fall."

"Oh, Ma, admit it: you're upset because I know God didn't hold any conversation with you. You made that story up. How often do you hear voices? Next thing I know some voice will be telling you to sacrifice me the way Abraham tried to sacrifice Isaac."

"Stop it!" Her face began to twitch and her body shook as if she had ague.

13

ALL OF JULY AND the early part of August, she agonized over which school she would send me to. Côte des Neiges Comprehensive was out. "Too much niggers going there. Sister Agnes had a niece what was going there. An' she get pregnant at fifteen. An' I learn long time the less you have to do with coloured people the better off you is," she'd say looking at me with a ping-pong rhythm, as if her statements were balls I should hit.

" I need glasses," I told her with fake seriousness.

"What for?"

"I'm not seeing colours right. I see black when it's white! Aren't you white?"

"Dry up! Niggers is my race but not my taste! When I come here, I lend a Vincentian woman $500 to put in the bank to get her stay. She and I was sweet-sweet before. Soon after, she stop phoning me. When I call she, operator tell me, 'This number has been changed to a confidential one.' That thief done unlist her number so I can't ask her for my money. One Thursday I meet her in Eaton's. Soon as she see me, she make up she face like a thunderhead. When I go up to she, she say, 'Hi, I been meaning for call you for gi'e you me new number. Excuse me a minute; I goin' to the washroom. Wait here for me.' I wait fo' she upwards of a hour and she never show up. Disappear like smoke. That thief!"

"So which school you intend to send me to?"

"To General Wolfe."

The following Wednesday (she was home on a week's vacation), she took me to General James Wolfe High School: a long, rectangular, three-storey building with a grey stone facade—English Renaissance style—two hundred and seventy-five feet long from east to

west and eighty feet wide. Fronting the main structure were steps
that led up on three sides to an arched stone walkway supported by
fluted columns, two on either side and a third pair that was partly
embedded in the main structure of the building. Two stone eagles,
each with its beak clasped around the throat of a snake whose tail
merged with the stone work of the spandrel, emerged at a forty-five
degree angle from the corners of the front spandrel. One of the eagles
had lost half a wing but it did not lessen the ardour with which it
clasped its serpent. In the middle of the spandrel and occupying
twice as much surface as the eagles, the heads of three bulldogs with
colossal jowls and bared teeth looked down at Ma and me. Below the
bulldogs, stencilled in gothic script, were the words arranged around
a Rosicrucian cross:

> *eruditio*

> *sapientia*   *disciplina*

> *officium*

They were repeated in a straight line on the eastern and western sides
of the arch. We mounted these stairs, went under the arch, opened the
middle one of three doors and entered a vaulted entranceway before
finding ourselves in a foyer with a grey marble floor. The foyer was
three storeys high and at least fifty feet by thirty feet wide. It was
awash with light from three storeys of windows. In the middle of
the foyer directly below a domed skylight, was a marble, life-size
statue of General Wolfe. A two-foot-high wrought-iron fence some
six feet in diameter encircled it. Along the length of the wall at the
first floor level were hundreds of framed portraits with the names of
the people below them and GWG in parentheses (which I learned
later meant that they were alumni of General Wolfe). A sign on a
carved door in the middle of this wall said *AUDITORIUM*, and directly above the door were two portraits, larger than all the others, of
Queen Victoria and Queen Elizabeth II.

    Ma seemed bewildered. At that point I saw the sign saying *OFFICE*
with an indicating arrow, and so we headed there.

A storklike woman, in a sleeveless avocado dress, received us and escorted us down a flight of stairs and along a long corridor to the office of Mrs Black, who said she was a guidance counselor. Mrs Black had short feathery blond hair, large brown teeth and bulging, watery grey, red-rimmed eyes—as if a cartoonist had highlighted them with a thin red line. She was wrinkled all over. She was heavy. Her flesh shook whenever she moved and dangled in places. The leer she proffered for a smile unsettled me (later I found out that the students had renamed her the Gargoyle). Her sleeveless blouse exposed large areas of dried out potato skin. I needed to go to the bathroom. I tried to hold it in, but would have wet myself if I didn't go.

When I returned, Mrs Black said, "I've examined your school record and I'm impressed, but kids from the islands are always behind, so we'll try you out first in secondary-three general. Normally we test the children when they first come, but since your marks are good and your teachers say nice things about you, I won't test you. What do we say? Secondary-three general?" She paused, looked at us fleetingly, then fixed her eye on something behind us before saying, "If you can handle it, we'll put you in regular. General is a lot easier than regular." She looked at my mother a little longer this time, then yawned and excused herself, saying it was a hot day. It wasn't.

Ma looked at me and then sought refuge in space.

"What is secondary-three?"

"It's the third year of high school."

"That's too low for me! I have already completed three years of high school. And I was first in my class."

She was silent for a few seconds. She removed her hands from her lap and placed them on her desk, and looking away from me, to her left, she said, "As I've just told you, children from the West Indies are *always* behind." She paused, then repeated with greater emphasis: "Always!"

"I was a Grammar School student!"

"Grammar school! Did you say grammar school?" her voice becoming a high-pitched whine.

"Look at my record. It says Boys Grammar School."

"In that case, I will have to test you." Her leer disappeared; her face turned sickly beige. "Can you come back tomorrow?"

"Yes," I told her before Ma could answer.

When we returned to the foyer, I saw the full splendour of the windowed wall. With a little imagination it became a luminous waterfall. Encrusted in its eastern corner were three slabs of black marble, in the shape of arched tombstones arranged one above the other. The names of General Wolfe alumni who died in the Boer War, World War I, and World War II (a plaque for each war) were etched in them in gilded lettering. All three ended with the inevitable *Dulce et decorum est pro patria mori*. Turning from it to the opposite inner wall, I observed, at the second storey level, a gigantic mural of what I knew was St George slaying the dragon. Its bloody redness filled me with dread, though I could not tell why.

"You coming or you staying?" Ma asked impatiently.

"Just a minute." I couldn't help looking on. Only the Anglican cathedral on Isabella Island had architecture remotely resembling this (it was only when I visited the New York Public Library some years later and beheld all that marble and wood paneling that my awe was surpassed). Awe gave way to intimidation and intimidation gave way to fear, I could not understand why. (I remembered these feelings vividly almost two years later when a student spray-painted General Wolfe's face black. That foyer was intended as subliminal instruction, to tell me I was nothing, that learning decreed by the powerful was everything. But I would only know this when, at university, I took a course on meaning in art and architecture.)

Later on, when I learned about the school's history, I found out why my mother had been told to send me there. It had been built in 1801 on fifty-one acres of land. The arch was not a part of the original structure (it did seem like an excrescence). It was added in 1938, a gift from the Hudson Bay Company, to commemorate King George VI's visit to Montreal in 1939. The King had cut the ribbon and had been the first person to walk under the finished arch—at least that was what the school history said. General Wolfe had been for a long time a residential school for boys. In fact, the places where the old fireplaces had been filled in with concrete were quite noticeable. It used to be a privately endowed academy, but it fell on hard times.

Eventually most of the land was sold to keep it going, but in nineteen fifty-two it was on the verge of bankruptcy, and the trustees decided to turn it over to a public school commission. One of the conditions was that it would continue to function like a private school. Up to 1960 (when a South Asian parent whose child had been refused admittance won a discrimination suit against it) it had selected its students according to its own criteria. This fact was not included in the booklet describing the school's history. But Mr Erskine (my science teacher) made sure that we all knew about it. It wasn't until 1968 that Blacks began attending the school in significant numbers—when they were displaced from Little Burgundy because of the construction of the Ville-Marie Expressway and relocated in large numbers in Notre-Dame-de-Grâce.

Despite the land sale, General Wolfe had an immense playground—about six acres of playing fields and woods at the back. At the front it was only about half an acre. In fact, within twenty feet of the building to the east were bungalows, and at about the same distance to the west were apartment buildings. Across the street from the front (to the north) was the parking lot of a shopping centre. It is still there exactly as it used to be the first day I arrived there.

Next day I walked three blocks north from the apartment building and took a bus from there to the school. Mrs Black put me in a windowless basement room hardly bigger than a walk-in closet and gave me the test. It asked several questions in math and logic, English and general knowledge. There were questions about Wendy's, Burger King and McDonald's, and about television cartoon characters. One of the questions in the logic section was: "Wheat is to the American what rice is to (a) Australia, (b) South America, (c) the Soviet Union, (d) India". Mrs Cameron, my English teacher in Isabella Island, would have underlined *American with red and written "parallel structure" above it (perhaps Mrs Black had prepared the test herself). I knew the answer was India, though coming from the West Indies, I could easily have put South America. Isabella Island imported rice from Guyana. I'd been taught that the major staple in the North American diet was the potato. The test asked questions about John A MacDonald and Lester B*

Pearson, and whether Washington or New York was the capital of the United States, and about the Declaration of Independence (whose?). I finished the test before the allotted time. Mrs Black then asked me some questions that I could see were intended to make a fool of me, and I was determined that she would not.

When the test was over she left me in the room and went to grade it. She returned exclaiming, "Something's wrong. Something's definitely wrong! You said you were in grammar school, didn't you?"

I looked at her, intrigued as much by her ugliness as by her question.

"Do you have a learning disability, dyslexia or something? Do you see double when you read? Do you see *was* when the word is *saw*?"

I shook my head.

She was agitated. "Spell privilege."

" P-r-i-v-i-l-e-g-e."

For a moment she was like a statue—her grin gone, her pupils pin-pricks of light, her face a bag of wrinkled flesh. It was as if I had hit her or had pushed my hand under her dress, and she was overcoming shock before crying *rape!* or *help!* "You are too bright to be in gram-mar school," she finally mumbled, her head bowed, her gaze fixed on her desk.

"But, Miss, on Isabella Island the brightest male students are divided evenly between Boys Grammar School and Hanovertown Academy."

"What do people do when they graduate from grammar school?"

"Some teach, some work in the civil service, and some go away to university."

She hit her forehead with the palm of her right hand and hissed through her teeth, "I thought you were retarded and they had you in the early grades of elementary school. That happens in many countries, you know. What did you do in math?"

"In algebra the last things we did were simultaneous equations and graphs. In geometry we left off at the Pythagoras theorem. In arithmetic . . . compound interest. In . . ."

"I get the picture. You shouldn't have trouble handling the work in secondary-three. You scored in the top ten percent. The first student from the Islands to do that. I'm even prepared to put you in regular."

"I have completed secondary-three."

"Well, we'll try you out in three regular—academic, not general and see if you can handle it."

I shook my head. "From the time I was eight I have been first, occasionally second, in most of my classes."

She stared at me with mocking irony, her lips hanging, her eyes like a mongoose's (what I now call the "who-does-this-nigger-think-he-is-kidding" look). "I better call the vice-principal. Our policy is to put the students coming from the islands back a year—and they *always* need it. Some need two, some even more; some haven't even learned to read. Your age makes you just right for secondary-three, gives you time to catch up." She picked up the telephone and spoke into it.

Five minutes later a diminutive, squinting, bespectacled man, dressed in a blue suit, came and stood in the doorway to her office. Mrs Black said his name was Mr Johnston and that he was the vice-principal. He asked what the problem was. Mrs Black told him, "This gentleman refuses to be put in grade nine."

"You got no choice in the matter," Johnston said. "Mrs Black says grade nine and grade nine it will be. Any more questions?"

I gritted my teeth. Mr Johnston left almost as quickly as he had come.

On the bus on my way home after the test I remembered that the papers in Isabella Island had said today was the day Patrick Percy would be executed. I'd wondered off and on whether he was my uncle. I spent the next couple of hours feeling sorry for myself, thinking that coming to Canada to study was a mistake, and it still wasn't too late to convince Ma to let me go back home. If this was to be my first encounter with Misfortune, I wasn't going to fete him or feast him. I would fight him. Damn him!

Ma wasn't home. She'd left her handbag on the sofabed. I decided to rummage through it. A small photograph album caught my attention. There were six snapshots in it. One was of Grama cut out from a larger photograph, another was of me a few years earlier, the third was a miniature of the photograph that Grama had of Grampa. The fourth was the photograph of a man who looked familiar. I turned it over and read,

To Icesis My hunny
From Your luvver boy
Patrick Percy

I dropped the photograph and all the heat flowed out of my body. The photo paper had greyed and was brittle. *Patrick Percy!* I did a quick calculation. From fifteen years ago. He looked different in the picture in the *Trinidad Guardian*. I moved from shock to anger. I could not wait for Ma to arrive. To think how she and Grama had deceived me! I was sure now that he was my father. I thought of the conversation Grama and Mrs Duncan had carried on in whispers on the day the murder was announced, of Grama's behaviour at the dining table. What did they think I needed to be protected from? I looked at the photograph again, doubt overtaking me this time. Even if he had been my mother's boyfriend it didn't mean he was my father. Sweat began to pour from my hands and down my armpits. I could not stay still. I paced up and down the apartment until she entered.

"Come sit here beside me," I told her, trying to sound as calm as possible.

A look of fear came into her eyes. She hesitated before saying, "What's this? You're giving me orders?"

With the palm of my hand I tapped the place on the sofa where I expected her to sit. She came forward cautiously and sat.

"Who's this?" I pushed the picture towards her. She stared at it and the skin on her face gathered as if a knotted thread were pleating it; her hands pressed forcefully on the sofa bed.

"What you was doing in my purse?"

I saw her hand raising in a striking pose. I shook my head. "Oh no! Not today. You and Grama have made a fool of me. Not today. Touch me and you will be a dead woman. Lower your hand. *We* are going to talk."

Her hand dropped heavily, her chest heaved. "No use getting all het up. That man made a fool o' me but he not yo' father."

"Who is my father?"

"I am. Yo' grandmother is. Especially yo' grandmother. The people who raise yo' and take care o' you is yo' parents. Stop all this foolish talk 'bout yo' father."

"Why can't you tell me his name?"

"Because I don't want to. You understand? And you can't make me." She'd regained control of the situation

She sat for a while longer, then I heard her sobbing and blowing her nose.

"You might as well cry because the papers at home said he would be electrocuted at six am today," I shouted above her sobs.

She got up and went to the bathroom and remained there for some thirty minutes.

When she returned to the room her eyes were red and puffy. She pulled out the ironing board and began to iron and sing:

My Lord's a rock; in Him I hide:
A shelter in a time of storm—
Secure, whatever ill betides:
A shelter in a time of storm.

Her voice swelled in volume, triumphant, as she sang the refrain:

Jesus is the rock in a weary land,
A weary land, a weary land;
Jesus is the rock in a weary land:
A shelter in a time of storm.

While she ironed and sang I remained seated on the sofa bed, numb, feeling betrayed, hating Grama, Ma, Mrs Duncan—everyone who had conspired to keep me ignorant of my father's identity. *Secret bags.* To hell with them! But before I got up from the sofa bed I realized I was relieved by my mother's statement that Patrick Percy was not my father. Maybe I was wrong to be pestering my mother about it. Maybe my father was someone as bad or worse than Patrick Percy.

The next day Grama's letter telling me of Mr Sam's death arrived. He was found dead in his house. His hernia had ruptured. I told my mother and then left the apartment. I needed a quiet place to sit in and think. I walked for a long time, up Côte des Neiges, all the way to Mount Royal Park, and sat under a willow fronting Beaver Lake, and thought about him and tried to gauge the influence he'd had on me. I thought of the advice he'd written for me, his goals for me, the stories he'd told me. I'd written to him and thanked him for his gift and advice. He'd not had time to reply. Misfortune had had the last word. Did he die in pain? Did he welcome death? Would he have considered death to be the same as Misfortune? Where had his soul gone?

14

THE TUESDAY AFTER Labour Day, Ma phoned to make sure I would not oversleep. Half an hour later, dressed in Mr Wilton's sweater and trousers (she'd done a good job altering the waist and hems but the crotch extended almost halfway down my thigh) and trench coat (darned at the right elbow) because it was already chilly, I went to the school cafeteria: it hummed with the dammed-up talk and laughter of over 1500 students, who looked like flowers and butterflies in a garden of orange table tops. So different from the white shirts and grey trousers of my three hundred schoolmates and me. We would have been scattered outdoors under the cedar and almond trees of the playground until summoned indoors by the assembly bell.

I was shepherded to my home room teacher by an enormous, puffy-eyed, pale, blond girl with "glitter" in her hair and a pink rosette on her left breast. Her green satin dress swished and rustled as she led us up the stairs and along the corridor to Ms Mackenzie in Room 316—a dark room with dirty beige walls, as if the dirt on them had soiled the paint. Despite the small half-open window the room was musty and too small for the number of desks in it; soon it would acquire the stench of our breath, genitalia, armpits, flesh—so unlike my Grammar School classrooms in and out of whose open windows swift breezes blew. All the classrooms I went to were like this or worse, excepting the cafeteria and gym, which had been added to the back of the first floor in 1965.

Ma, in trying to keep me away from Blacks, had got her facts scrambled. One in every five General Wolfe students was black. But in my home room class there were only two other Blacks. One was a plank-bottomed, stumpy girl with thick glasses and bugshitbespotted beige skin that looked like whole wheat bread minus the holes. Her hair was a coarse Afro the colour of corn tassels. The other student was a midgetlike, syrup-brown boy. Ms. Mackenzie called our names. The girl's was Agatha and the boy's Edouardo.

"Eddy!" he snapped. "Don't you be calling me no funny names! You hear?" He wagged his head, extended his arms well above his head, shook his fingers, and wiggled his torso. Monkey antics.

Ms Mackenzie fascinated me. She wore a charcoal suit, a pale cream blouse, and black patent leather shoes with one-inch heels. She had to be in her forties, was over six feet tall with a maternal bosom and square shoulders. Because of her big bones she appeared overweight, but she wasn't. She had a pug nose, something of an ivory complexion, hazel eyes that could in an instant burn you or comfort you, and flaxen hair cut very short. She spoke in a rich, resonant contralto, and had an air of what I would now retrospectively term invincibility. She lectured us on punctuality, homework, and politeness, handed out the locker numbers, and read a bulletin from Mr Bellamy the principal that said loitering in the foyer was forbidden. Under no circumstances were we to use the front door. The foyer was to be used only on ceremonial occasions or if we had to cross it to come to the office, change classes, or enter the auditorium from the front.

I didn't know what a locker was, never had nor needed one in Isabella Island. When home room ended Agatha and Eddy moved towards each other and began talking. I noticed that his left shoulder was considerably lower than his right and he dipped slightly to the left when he walked. I pushed my way through the students to catch up with them. "I'm Pedro," I said.

"We know," they both replied and laughed.

"What's a locker?"

"He for real?" Eddy said, gesturing disdainfully at me with his thumb. "Ain't he like som'n out o' the dark ages? Man, where you found that coat? At the Sally Ann bargain basement?" He spoke as if shooting rapid-fire from his larynx.

"No," Agatha said with an unmistakable English accent. "He found it on the curb." She had on a pink windbreaker with metal rings and straps. Her perfume was strong. She wore green eye shadow, false eyelashes, and carmine lipstick.

Eddy wore a tan leather jacket. (How deceiving looks were! That was probably the only week he came to school clean. He'd also probably borrowed the jacket.)

They both laughed again at some silent joke. Eddy, fluttering his froglike eyelids, his caramel eyes bulging, did a little hopscotch dance. It was the quaintest thing I'd ever seen.

I turned to the closest white student, a short, plump girl with large breasts, prominent cheek bones, golden hair, wide haunches and long legs. "Can you show me where the lockers are?"

"Just follow us."

I stayed at her side. We were almost there when I asked her.

"What number you got?"

I told her and she showed me where it was. "You have to get a combination lock. You will want to buy Master, else they'll break it before you can say Jack Rabbit. Don't let nobody know your combination . . . You new here?"

"Yes."

"You would want to be mighty careful. Watch what we do and do like we do. You like sucking up to teachers?"

"What you mean?"

"You're a brownnoser?"

"What's a brownnoser?"

"Did you say you're from Mars? Zachary!" she shouted.

A boy about ten feet away looked at her. "What?"

"Come here!"

Zachary came over. "Pedro doesn't know what a brownnoser is."

"That's 'cause he's one."

"How did you know my name?"

"Easy. See, like we was all in the same class last year and stuff. You dig? You'r the new kid on the block. See. No sweat."

"What's *your* name?"

She paused, lowered her eyes. "Hilda."

Zachary, a string bean of a fellow with a pimply, hatchet face, and an uncooked noodle complexion, shouted, "That's a new one, *Ellen D Chasseur!* Hi-Hilda-Brumhilda, a-pumpin'-me-dilda. Don't listen to her. It's B J Bertha." Some students guffawed, others clapped, and he backed away, barely missing the swing she took at him.

"Cocksucker!" she exclaimed.

I gasped.

Everyone laughed—at me.

"Man, where you from? Jupiter?"

"Bet you he still a virgin," Eddy said, shrill as a squealing pig.

Laughter again.

I left quickly.

My first class next day was English. Ms Mackenzie gave me some lined paper and three essay topics: "Negotiating My School Environment," "Dreams versus Reality," and "Being One's Self in the Crowd," and told me to choose one and write an essay on it in the library. I chose the second topic and recounted what my expectations of Canada had been and what I had so far encountered, including my experience with the guidance counsellor.

When I got back Zachary was standing outside the closed classroom door. "The bitch kicked me out," he said. "She'd like you. She likes suckers. Fucking dyke! I should lean her up against this locker and dryfuck her." He was laughing.

I froze. No one dared speak this way in Isabellan schools. We'd have been sent home for good. And thrown out of one school, we couldn't get into another. Our relatives relied on us for "respectability," for the white-collar jobs we were expected to hold when we finished school. It was better to be tarred and feathered than to be expelled and live through the put downs afterward.

When I returned to class, Ms Mackenzie was explaining how she wanted compositions organized. Eddy was asleep with his head on his desk. Three girls a couple of desks to my right had turned their backs to her and were carrying on a conversation with two others behind them.

Ms Mackenzie's voice rose over theirs. I gave her the composition; she told me to return to see her at three.

French class was the worst. My classmates circulated a drawing of a bespectacled frog tied to strings upon string of eggs. They labeled it *La Grenouille*, their nickname for the French teacher, Mme

Montcalm. Someone had scribbled, *Elle fait de bonnes pipes.* It was the last class of the day, and before it ended paper planes were flying across the room.

I got to Ms Mackenzie's room at 3.20. She questioned me about the English I'd done and the books I'd studied.

She smiled. "I see. You're too advanced for the class you're in. I'll get you transferred into my secondary-four enriched English. I knew some brilliant West Indians at Edinburgh." She stared into my eyes with a warm smile. I left her room floating, happy I'd begun to prove Mrs Black wrong.

The next day I joined Tim Chang as the only other non-white student in the grade ten advanced English class.

That first week of school Ma was frantic. She said my school supplies had emptied her bank account. "What they want all those things for? When I was little all you did need was a slate and a reader." The supplies had come to sixty dollars, and I'd not yet bought everything. "How come you can't get them for give you yo' school supplies for nothing? I hear them have some kind o' fund for aid poor children. What you got tongue in yo' head for? Tell them I not working! Tell them I on welfare."

"I thought I wasn't supposed to tell lies."

"Don't contradict me! Why you must always have a plaster for every sore? God know if poor people don' tell lies sometimes, they won' eat."

I said nothing. She was sitting on the sofa looking pensive. After a while she began to hum. Then she went into the bathroom and leaned over the tub to wash my clothes, which she'd left soaking there.

It was my second full day of classes. I wanted to talk to her about it. But I did not want to hear threats and biblical citations in lieu of advice. At recess I'd been wandering around in the front yard. The students were in groups, eating snacks and horsing around. Some were tuned into their Walkmans. Others were kicking a soccer ball. Most were just hanging out. There weren't more than a dozen black students altogether scattered among these groups. None of them noticed me. I walked around aimlessly. At one point I found myself in the middle of a group of about fifteen white boys. They were eyeing me. A stocky one with freckles, shoulder-length blond hair, wearing jeans and a jean jacket more faded than the others, said mockingly, "Monn, is you a Jamaican, monn?" There was something odd about his face. (He had no eyebrows, no eyelashes; the shoulder-length hair too, I discovered later, was a wig.)

The others laughed.

"Like hell, man! He's a deaffie."

I stopped walking and stared at them.

"You got any dough?" the stocky one asked, his eyes a glassy, morning-glory blue.

A third one I couldn't see said, "Now what kind o' foolish question is that, Dreyfuss? You ever see a rich nigger yet, unless he's a pusher or got long fingers or something?"

"You sure you in the right century, man?" another asked.

"Look like you been on the Crusades and got lost," Dreyfuss said, inspecting me from head to toe. His voice was deep, gravelly, ominous. "Where's your Matchlock, man? Lost yer cathopurse?"

They all laughed, elbowing one another and pointing to my tweed trousers with narrow legs and my canvas sneakers. They wore bell-bottom jeans and platform shoes, and leather or jean jackets.

When I was about to turn to go around the school, Dreyfuss stepped up in front of me. Trembling, I looked back to see whether the other groups of students were watching what was taking place. They were completely absorbed in their own affairs.

"Don't say a word. Do like I say and we won't do you nothing, see," Dreyfuss mocked, his eyes luminous sapphires, his face granite pink.

I tried to pass him, turned my head to look for an alternate route, and realized they'd encircled me.

"What you trying to run away from us for? Like you don't like us or what? We got horns or something? Tell us if you see horns growing out of our ears," Dreyfuss said, laughing. A few of them in back of me chuckled.

"You know who we are, man? Ask yer nigger brothers who Nations is, man, and watch them shit their pants. I have a mind to take you in the john and make you suck me off." His eyes flamed.

"Bet you he'll like it too," one behind me said. "Got the right size lips."

"See that big, round ass on him? Bet you he gettin' it in the ass," another voice said.

At that point, the one nearest the chain-link fence separating the school from the nearby apartment buildings tossed his head to indicate the middle of the schoolyard. Magically, they all began moving nonchalantly towards the centre of the schoolyard, I with them. Within seconds three black boys wearing black leather jackets came around the corner of the building. I broke out of the circle and followed the black boys until I got to a side entrance, ran up the steps, and reentered the building. I was breathing rapidly, aware for the first time how frightened I was.

It was the same week that the school bussing issue exploded in Boston. I'd watched it on TV and wondered if something like it could happen here.

Throughout the third period my fingers shook. The first exercise was an auditory French comprehension test. A tape recorder played a dialogue in French; this was followed by questions, the answers to which I was to circle on a sheet in front of me. I deciphered three words in all that was said. For three years I had studied French. I twirled my pencil between my thumb and forefinger.

Looking bonier and crueller, with her copper hair and jade-green, dead eyes—today she didn't wear her humungous burgundy frame glasses—Madame Montcalm observed us *sans emotion*. I never once saw her change that expression in this class—it was as if she had a face of plaster.

Mme Montcalm said something in French. I didn't understand. The other students took out their workbooks. When she spoke next I understood "pages 11 to 14." It was verb conjugation. I'd already learned all the basic tenses; French was one of the four subjects I had always got the highest grades in. Mme Montcalm came to my desk, picked up my test paper, and examined it. She spoke to me in French. I understood not a word. She hesitated.

The students beside me looked up. With her forefinger she motioned for me to follow her. Seated at her desk, she wrote something and, in a whisper too low for the class to hear, said, "Your compray'enshun of zee French eez no good. I am zending you to zee guidance to shange you." She motioned to Eddy, who rose and told me to follow him.

In the corridor, Eddy asked whether I was from Jamaica.

"No. Why?"

"'Cause, man . . ."

"'Cause what?"

"Y'all eat monkeys. That's what. Y'all eat your own family."

"What are you talking about?"

"You talk funny, you know that?"

I'd stopped listening to him. I watched, out of the corner of my right eye, his left leg for the first time. It angled outwards while the right one was straight and his weight fell on the inner length of his left foot, not the sole, explaining why his left shoulder was lower and why with every step he dipped to the left like a poorly ballasted ship.

By this time we were at the Guidance Office.

"In there's where you go. Good luck, man. You got any voodoo stuff on you? Don't leave the doom room in more than one piece. When the Gargoyle grins pick up her hand and kiss it." He winked. "I'll bring your books if you not back in time."

Six students were waiting. When Mrs Black saw me, it was almost lunch. She read the note. A grin deepened her wrinkles and exposed her big, brown teeth. The walnut dress she had on, along with her hair, white at the roots and blond elsewhere, and the liver spots on her arm, reminded me of the dry fields Isabellan farmers burned to kill off insect larvae. "Well, I told you so. Never fails. Never! I've programmed enough Jamaicans in my time to know. I'm putting you in vocational French. If you get tutoring—it's fifteen dollars per session, two sessions per week—I'll move you up in January."

I listened to my mother washing away, washing away. She came out of the bathroom.

"You should learn to wash yo' own clothes, but I ain't got money for you go to the laundromat. You could wash them by hand." She paused, measured her words. "But if down the road you turn out funny, is me they will blame, say I start you off wrong."

Not you too! I buried my head in my hands.

I had homework to do, but my head throbbed. I pulled out my armchair-bed and went to sleep, telling myself I would wake up at three next morning and do it.

I was awakened before three. Ma was up, heading to the bathroom, and she stumbled against my bed and awakened me. She went into the kitchen and remained there.

"Ma, you're all right?"

She didn't answer.

"Ma, anything wrong?"

"Don't aggravate me."

She was moving things around. I went to check. She was in a red flannel bathrobe, her hair dishevelled. Her back was to the counter; she stared, at nothing.

"What's wrong?" I asked, a plea that she should share her pain with me.

"How you know it not 'bout you? And then what you will do? Disappear?"

My face must have told her something, for she quickly said, "No, I just saying that; it not about you, is about a nightmare I just had." She was silent.

"Aren't you going to talk about it?"

She looked at me and squinted. "All right, since you want to know. I dream I was in a pool of blood and I couldn' swim and I couldn' get out. And I was saying to myself, 'How come I in all this blood and where it coming from?' Then I heard you crying in your baby voice. And I see the blood was coming from you, and I heard Mama saying, 'Isis, you will heng for this.' 'I didn' touch him,' I say. She say, 'Tell the judge that.' Then I hear you turning in yo' bed and I wake up."

"It's all those hymns you sing in Church. They affect you when you're sleeping."

"What hymns?"

"'Wash me in the blood of the lamb. All those fountains of blood you all plunge in."

"You better plunge in the blood o' the Lamb yourself! 'When I see the blood I will pass over you.' I don' want God to call me to no

129

reckoning over yo' soul."

Even so I remembered how she'd shaken when I taunted her about voices that might tell her to sacrifice me as Abraham had sought to sacrifice Isaac. Had my caprice caused her nightmare? In any event, her nightmare disturbed me.

On her deathbed, eleven years later, she told me where it had originated.

15

THURSDAY AT RECESS I headed straight for the rear schoolyard. Crowded around a boom box on a picnic table near the centre of the paved portion of the yard were some twenty mostly black students. Eddy, Agatha and Ellen were with them. Those sitting tapped their feet or rocked; a few of those standing snapped their fingers and danced for real; most only hummed or sang along. *Common class behaviour!* Grama's voice echoed in my head. People wouldn't distinguish me from them.

I stood a short distance away, observing them. Elsewhere there were several groups—some mixed, some unmixed—of Chinese, Whites, Blacks, Indians; one group of Indians all wore turbans. Most of the students were within twenty feet of the building. Only a few students were off under the trees.

A member of the dancing group stood out. His face seemed familiar. He was jet black, obsidian smooth, half *dougla*, with an oval face, an aquiline nose, even white teeth, glowing light brown eyes, glossy black hair with big curls which he wore as a bushy Afro. Very good looking! He had on reflective dark glasses; a pair of plantation-green, skin-tight trousers; and a red shirt. A blue face cloth protruded from his back pocket. He gave me a long, scrutinizing stare. Several of his friends wore red, green, and yellow berets, suggesting a uniform.

The boom box changed to "Jah-Jah Children," a Bob Marley song I knew and liked. I realized then why the *dougla* fellow looked familiar. He was with the Jamaican boy I'd passed on the step the first week I came to Montreal. The boom box was probably his.

The boom box stopped, and someone said to the *dougla*, "Hollis, gi'e we a number."

"Yes, yes!" the cries multiplied.

"What a fellar is to say, except le' we spread joy, yes," Hollis said. He stretched out his arms like a condor. "I just make this up. All you lis'en good. All you gon' like it."

PP No-Lolo
find he mudder
doing fikky-fikky
with a fat snake
in the canebrake.

He signaled to them and they joined in, some singing the words, others furnishing a drumbeat—

dumma dumma dumma
dumma dumma dumma

His voice was deep and melodious, his singing perfect, even if the lyrics were asinine.

"Hollis, who PP No-Lolo is?" the fellow who'd asked for the song inquired when the singing ended.

"Look him over there." He pointed at me. "He name Pedro."

They laughed! They laughed! Every last one of them. Some even wiped their eyes. I felt like the rags used in Isabellan outhouses.

"Gro' Lo' is a better name," a long-haired boy, who looked Indian and who stood a little distance from them, said.

Another boy put in, "Try thisya one, Hollis: 'Pedro Gro' Lo' done lose him tolo.'"

The group shook with laughter again. I felt soiled and returned inside before they stopped.

When recess ended, I went looking for my new French class. It took me some ten minutes because the room number wasn't on the door. As soon as I entered the room, I heard, "Unna look! Unna look, Pedro Gro' Lo' without him tolo!"

I recognized about twelve of the laughing faces. At the back of the class, a student seemed asleep, his arms on the desk under his head serving as a pillow.

I handed the teacher the slip of paper from Mrs Black. "I'm Ms Skrapper," the teacher said.

"La Crappe, for short," someone in the back whispered. A few students chuckled.

Ms Skrapper's voice hissed, as if she had a lisp. Later Hollis said it was because she'd had "hoof n' mouth disease" and had to remove her teeth and put in false ones and hadn't yet learned to speak properly. She looked like a stout pencil with a small eraser for a head; a few inches more and she'd have passed for Ichabod Crane's sister. Her bottle-green eyes peered out from behind big horn-rimmed glasses, her face was narrow with bulged-out cheeks, and her skin was like paper that had been uncrumpled. She wore a beige shirt—there was the barest hint of breasts—dark green, masculine-style polyester trousers, and a broad brown leather belt with a silver buckle.

"Class, we have a new student. His name is Pedro Moore."

"No, Miss, is Gro' Lo'," Hollis interrupted.

"We want Pedro to think we're a class of hardworking students. Don't we, now?"

Several students sucked their teeth.

She removed a white boy sitting beside a black boy whose thick beard and sideburns made him look adult; he had a kidney-shaped head and fierce-looking, dark eyes. His hair was closely cropped; one of the few black boys without an Afro. She gave me the vacated seat. The older boy turned out to be Mervyn, the leader of the boom box group.

Ms Skrapper handed me a copy of *Le Français International Book I* and a copy of the accompanying workbook, saying, "If you're polite, we'll get along. You can tell me anything so long as you say it nicely. I don't send students to the office," her bottle-green eyes glinting with pride, her false, even teeth exposed.

It was true. Three weeks later she tried to rouse a sleeping student so he would do his test, and he called her a pus bag. Several students told him to apologize. Instead he stood up, his eyes beady, his face like boiled conch, and lumbered out of the room. He returned shortly after, said he was sorry, and stayed awake for the rest of the period.

On the blackboard Ms Skrapper had conjugated *être* in the present indicative.

"Repeat after me," she said in English. We repeated after her.

She told us to do the first exercise in the workbook. The date was written on the blackboard: "Septembre 7, 1974."

"Ms Skrapper," a student behind me asked, "when're we going to learn real French?"

"What do you mean?"

"I mean, like this is English, this ain't French. You don't even know to write the date properly."

The class chuckled. The questioner switched to the indecipherable sounds I'd heard on the tape the day before.

Ms. Skrapper said, "Jay na compran pas."

"You're a French teacher! You know less French than my Ibo slave ancestors."

"Don' get in trouble, Alfred," Mervyn told him.

Alfred became quiet.

I did the exercise; exactly as I'd done it three years before in Form One. And so I was back at the bottom of the hill I thought I'd already climbed.

That noon, when I got to the cafeteria, Mervyn and several students from the vocational French class were in the food line. I sat down. I had nothing to buy. Six of them came to occupy my table and the nearby one. Mervyn had three containers of juice on his tray. He offered me one.

I shook my head.

"Take it! What you pretending?" Hollis said. He took the drink from Mervyn's tray, unscrewed the top, and put it in front of me.

"Them white boys start fee gee you trouble yet?" Mervyn asked.

I said nothing.

"Well if ever they start, le' we know, oui," Hollis added in his booming voice. "Last year I crack a chain over one o' them fellas head and now when them fellas see me, is clear they clear the space, oui." I loved the richness of his voice.

His friends laughed.

"The other day Dreyfuss run from me. Run, man, " Mervyn said.

"Big Fraid tek him. 'Cause he know if I did catch him he would o' been hung, drawn, and gartered."

Everyone laughed.

"With him own socks."

"If they see you hanging 'round with we, they going leave you alone. But if you is like that Oreo that is president o' the student council, we will le' they whale yo' arse, oui, if you pretend you is better than we," Hollis picked up.

Already there were worry lines on Mervyn's forehead. His protuberant lips hung slightly, leaving his mouth half open; his chin looked like the tapered end of his kidney-shaped head. There were small gaps in his otherwise perfect teeth. (At the time I had overlapping canines.) His flattish nose flared whenever his ire rose. He rarely spoke, except for the odd bantering remark, or when his stare did not stop arguments that verged on violence. He intrigued me even then. Over the two years I observed him at General Wolfe, his mind always seemed far away like a grown man's worrying about his family. Hollis and I were amnesty children. He wasn't. To get landed immigrant status, his mother had paid, he long afterwards told me, a man to marry her. He was certainly our big brother, protector and guide. He forbade us from criticizing our mothers and discouraged conversations about fathers, but he worshipped his maternal grandfather.

He'd had very little elementary education; his grandparents had needed him to take care of livestock; he contracted typhoid and was declared dead at age fifteen, but sat up while the villagers were making his coffin, earning the nickname Lazarus while in Jamaica. He was wary of white people because some Jamaican Whites had robbed his grandfather of fifteen acres of valuable coastal Ocho Rios land.

That lunch hour we talked about Isabella Island, Jamaica and Trinidad. Mostly about whether things found in Jamaica were also found on Isabella Island too. They were eager to know whether Isabellans understood Jamaican "labrish." (On Isabella Island "labrish" means both "vulgar" and "gossip").

Trinidad cows, Hollis said, were blood red, with six-foot horns; they defended their owners like dogs; on mornings they butted on doors to wake their owners up. "Trinidad cattle smart, oui".

"I bet the milk red too," Mervyn said.

"No, it black like you."

"Our cows are green, they blend in with the grass and trees. It's called camouflage," I said, determined not to be put on the fringe as had happened at Grammar School.

But Hollis was onto another topic. "I hear all-you Isabellans eat monkey. Is true?"

Eddy laughed and slapped his thighs.

"Cut it out!" Mervyn growled.

"I ain't saying nothing bad. I just want to know if he eating monkey, oui."

Mervyn's nostrils flared.

"Man," Eddy said, "the man want to know so he can protect hisself."

"Who you calling monkey?" Hollis asked Eddy. "I gon knock out yo' teeth, oui."

The conversation turned to the other classes I was in.

"Him is smart, man. Him no' one o' we," Mervyn said admiringly. He turned on Alfred. "Him smart too, but him sit on it. The boy got more chance than all o' we put together, and is no' throw him throwing them 'way. And his mother is a 'oman with plenty college degree. Alfred, why you so worthless?"

Alfred grinned. He was black, silk-smooth, and "basketball-tall" with a symmetrical face like the work of a Bemba sculptor. "Man, 'cause you got a beard ain't mean you're my father. Dig?"

"You lucky, else I would o' straighten you out long time."

"Lay off Alfred, man. I think he going come out good this time, oui," Hollis said. He extended his palm across the table and Alfred slapped it.

Then Mervyn looked at Eddy and shook his head with pity.

"Go fuck yourself, man!" Eddy said.

I saw them in class everyday for the first term, and when I changed to a more advanced French class, we met in the cafeteria and on the school grounds.

16

ONE FRIDAY, ABOUT A MONTH after I'd been put in vocational French, the vocational students were away on a trip to Ottawa. I didn't belong to their home room. I was sitting in the cafeteria having my lunch: a peanut-butter sandwich, an apple, and a bottle of Koolaid.

Alfred showed up.

"I thought you went to Ottawa."

"A wasted thought. I've been to Ottawa several times. I don't have to wait on teachers to take me places."

I quietly noted the put-down.

"So Gro' Lo', how you spending the winnings?" He sat down. I counted six gold rings on his fingers, one with a large ruby.

"What winnings?"

"You in advanced everything and you don't know what a gro' lo' is?" His bright eyes focused on me; his eyebrows were drawn slightly, his lips, curled somewhere between mockery and astonishment, definitely showed condescension.

"I don't know everything."

"I can teach you a thing or two. It means the big lottery. It's spelt g-r-o-s l-o-t."

I said nothing.

He pulled at my shirtsleeve with a thumb and forefinger, disdainfully. "Ugh!" He wrinkled his nose and let go of the sleeve as if it were a shit rag. "Seriously, you don't think it's time your mother stop decking you out in white people's diapers?" He laughed.

The remark stung. I said nothing.

"I want to discuss a important project with you. Meet me down here after school."

At three we went to the shopping centre and into Zaney's Department Store. "You like these jeans? Let's try on a few," he said, before my hesitation allowed me to answer.

We did and talked while doing so.

"Where you live?"

I told him the house number and the street.

"What apartment?"

I told him, hesitatingly.

"When I get my allowance, I'll buy you a pair o' these jeans."

"My mother won't let me wear them."

While on the bus going home I reflected on the fact that Mr Erskine had warned me two weeks earlier to stay away from people like Alfred. Erskine was Barbadian, mulatto, in his late twenties. On some days his eyes were blue and on others grey. He looked white, whiter than most of my teachers. Only in the curliness of his hair did his African genes show. His bottom was plank-flat, the kind Isabellans made fun of. He was about five-eight and stood straight as a bamboo. His waist couldn't have been more than twenty-five or -six. He looked lean and hungry, but it wasn't because he didn't eat. I'd met with him during a lunch period, and we'd eaten before he began to instruct me. He'd put away several slices of bread, a tin of sardines, a chunk of cheese, two bananas and two apples. Seeing him for the first time you'd have thought he'd either recently lost weight or that he bought his trousers two sizes too big, because he was always pulling them up. His head looked huge, probably because of his turkey neck. When he bent his arms, his elbows were like pickaxe blades. A bottle of soda pills was always on his desk and he popped several during each class.

He asked me why my mother had brought me here before I finished high school. I told him what my geography teacher had said. He laughed and said there was more money here to waste and with a tenth of it he could turn all West Indians into scientists. "The crap they call exams here is plain tomfoolery. Here they ask the students the questions and write the answers down for them. I know something when I can explain it to you from memory. If I want to tell somebody about a chemical, what use is it to me if I have to go to a book to find out what's in it?"

I watched him attentively.

When Erskine shut his mouth, he stared at me for a long time with probing intensity before asking, "How long you been here?"

"Since July." .

"Ms Mackenzie thinks you're super bright. They got traps everywhere you turn here. In Isabella Island, if you're bright, it's certain you'll get somewhere, if you want to. Here, if you're black, most white people will resent your getting anywhere. They're not even aware they do. Black bright people frighten them.

"In 1969 a biology professor at Sir George Williams University decided he would fail all his black students. He knew we wanted to get into medicine. Only a handful of students get into medicine. So every black student who got in would take a place he felt should go to a white student. I was one o' those black students. A Greek classmate copied my lab report. He got A. I got D. We fought back and ended up charged with rioting in the computer centre. Mind you, the police were the ones who damaged the equipment in their attempts to oust us. Some of us went to jail for it. One of the group got expelled from the university even before the computer riot. He'd written a critique of a novel that was head and shoulders above the white students'. The professor said no undergraduate student could write like that and accused him of copying it from somewhere. The university expelled him. The dean refused to let him state his case. Luckily for him, he got into an American university. He's teaching at Howard University now. But a handful of them are okay. Even some Chinese think like them. Yesterday your biology teacher asked me if you're black. I asked her if she hadn't seen you yet.

"And that Ms Mackenzie—even though she's better than the whole parcel o' them—gives the average black students hell. The comments she puts on their compositions! They say she doesn't answer their questions in class." He paused and stared at me briefly before asking, "Why am I telling you all this?"

From his silence I realized the question wasn't rhetorical.

"I don't know."

"You'll find out soon enough. A lot of you black students are ready to become monkeys to get white people's approval." He looked away and took a deep breath.

"Talking about monkeys. About three weeks ago I was going down the escalator in the Guy Metro station and I heard somebody belting out 'Yellow Bird High in Banana Tree' from the foot o' the escalator. When I got there, I see this black man with a monkey mask on, playing away on an accordion and singing like a regular Sambo, without a care on earth. Only thing missing was the straw hat.

"'You blasted, monkey! You fool, you! You don't know white people think we're monkeys already?' I told him. I pulled off his mask and then I see it was a Trinidadian I used to see hanging around Atwater Metro station hassling women."

"'Chill out, man!' the monkey said to me. 'I don't care what they call me. The ones that ride my donkey know I ain't no monkey'.

I laughed.

"'Man, before I had on this mask, I use to clear 'bout fifty dollars every day. Now I clear a hundred and fifty, sometimes two hundred. Make up the hundred a day I gon lose and I go stop wearing it. Man, why you don' get lost? I done lose 'bout twenty dollars since we been talking.' He pulled on his mask and went right on being a monkey."

Erskine shook his head. "Everyday—every blasted, livelong day! —I see black people doing things that make me want to hide my face. I'm telling you all o' this because white people have expectations of you." He waved his arms now, conducting an invisible orchestra, and his eyes turned a clear sky blue. "Two years ago when I came here to teach, one o' the female teachers used to come into the staff room asking us every morning, 'What Beethoven used to say to his wife on mornings? *Ba naa naa naaah!*' One day she said to me—I was the only black teacher on staff then—'And what about you, Trevor? You're always so sulky, like if you never empty your banana?'

"'It's not a chamber pot!'

"Over the next weeks she'd sidle up to me and invite me to this and that with her. One day she exploded: 'Trevor, you're always pushing me off. You're queer or something? Everybody knows black guys are oversexed.' I looked at her and shook my head. She taught *moral and religious education.* She took up with a black teacher who came on staff a term later. His wife came here and beat her over the head with her shoe right in the cafeteria with the students looking on. They had to transfer them both."

"To the same school?"

"Heavens, no. There'd been enough fireworks in this one."

After a pause he continued, "White people expect us to be a thieves. And we don't disappoint them. Each week they catch a couple o' you shoplifting over there." He pointed to the shopping centre. "If you keep company with crooked people and anything dishonest happens, you'll be the first suspect."

He got around to saying that he wanted me in his grade-ten physics and chemistry classes and he'd already spoken to Mrs Black about it. "I'm glad Ms Mackenzie put you in her advanced English class. She worships the student council president. She expects all Blacks to be like you two. He's graduating this year. She'll transfer the adoration to you. You better enjoy it. Lots of black students will pay for it." He stopped speaking and stared into my eyes so hard that I had to avert them, and then he smiled.

"By 'bout next Wednesday, you should be in muh classes. Ef yuh start to feel yuh too big for yuh britches and gi'ing yuh mother trouble, I gon tell she to lemmuh come and cut yer ass for she."

17

AROUND SEVEN PM THE doorbell rang. It rang again. I didn't buzz back. A minute later I heard a loud rapping on the apartment door. I looked through the peephole and saw Alfred.

I let him in.

"You didn't hear me buzzing?" He had his Adidas bag.

"Yes, but my mother told me not to bring anyone here."

"Fuck your mother! You're a fucking sissy or what? Tell her yes and when she's not there do what you fucking well please."

"Do you always talk like this?"

He laughed. "I talk like this to my mother all the time."

"And she lets you!"

"What choice she's got? Anyhow, what's the fuss?" While he spoke he unzipped the Adidas bag. "Look what I brought you?" It was the pair of jeans he'd promised to buy me.

When I collected myself I said, "I thought you said when you got your allowance? And I told you my mother won't let me wear them."

"You here all by yourself?"

"Yes."

"That's far out, man. I wouldn't mind a pad o' my own. I can pay for it too. But my parole worker makes me stay with my mother, see. Otherwise they'll put me in a group home."

"Well, I don't just live alone. My mother—" I stopped.

—"works as a live-in maid and only comes in on her days off."

"How'd you know that?"

"Easy. My mother's writing a book on it. She's a sociology professor at Université de Montréal." His eyes flashed, he smiled pleasantly. I could hear the admiration in his voice; he was proud of his mother despite what he'd said. "She's been interviewing lots o' black maids.

I figured it out when I saw the peanut butter sandwiches, the Koolaid, and your out-o'-style, cutdown clothes. You notice the vocational guys don't tease you about it? That's 'cause they went through the same thing. Now they don't dress like that anymore, and we think it's time you start dressing decent."

"My mother won't let me wear clothes she didn't give me."

"And my mother says, 'Nothing beats a trial but a failure.' I have some plans for me and you. What days your mother's off?"

I stalled. His intensity, the way his eyes darted, his jerky movements, the way he studied my face whenever either of us spoke—unsettled me.

"You still afraid of her, right? It's Thursday and Sunday. My aunt —she got killed in a fire—never went shopping on a Thursday because the store clerks treated you like a maid. Better-class Blacks don't shop on Thursdays."

We both became silent. He stared me nonstop in the eye, and I was forced to drop my gaze from time to time. "I'll be by tomorrow and let you see what I've got cooking."

He left then, leaving the pair of jeans behind. I certainly wanted them. Wherever I went, people's eyes roved my body, sometimes with accompanying smiles, and it wasn't because they desired it. I tried on the jeans again and admired myself in a mirror my mother had recently affixed beside the apartment door.

Alfred arrived around eleven next morning. He brought his books. He had a composition to write and a page of arithmetic to do. "Imagine," he said, "I did all this crap in elementary school. Four years wasted. Man, I want to finish school." He stared at the floor, seemed vulnerable. "I can't do it by myself."

We were silent for a while. "So what you want me to do?"

He didn't answer right away. Then, looking shame-faced, he stared at the floor and in a low voice said, "Help me get through school. I'll help you with your French. I lived in a French area till I was twelve and I took French immersion all through elementary school. If someone bright is with me while I work, I'll do my work. On my own I can't."

"Your mother couldn't . . . ?"

"I won't do anything she tells me. I hate her. I would o' done it, anything, for my aunt, but she's dead."

"So you want me . . . ?"

"*Us*. To work together. You're bright and it makes me jealous. See?" He smiled.

"But you live in Dollard-des-Ormeaux?"

"We could work in the library or the cafeteria."

"Okay." I was elated about the French part.

We began working that day. Alfred wrote his composition, "A Very Special Memory." It was about the day he realized his father wouldn't be coming back. "Mom left him. He ain't nothing but a batty man—a no-count faggot, man! Mom caught him screwing in the basement with his boyfriend. A shit bag, man. Funny thing, she won't divorce him, won't let me say anything bad about him. *He*—bold-faced sonofabitch—told me about it. Imagine? The gall!" He quieted and calmly resumed, "He pays half the mortgage, and anything I want, I just have to pick up the phone and call him. He's a urologist in Boston." Beads of sweat glistened on his forehead. I listened in silence, feeling suddenly fearful, my own hands beginning to sweat. "If you ever repeat this to anyone, I'll kill you! And that's not an idle threat."

He didn't put any of that in his composition: a three-page narrative full of misspelt words, without capital letters, punctuation, or paragraphs. First we corrected the spelling and punctuation errors and then we worked on the paragraphs.

He was less enthusiastic when it came to fulfilling his part of the bargain, and I resolved that whenever we studied together French would be our first subject.

Just before he left, he became very pensive. "I told you kind o' embarrassing stuff about my father, but you didn't tell me shit about yourself. How come?"

I said nothing.

"Where's your ol' man?"

"Dead."

"Oh! Sorry, man, sorry. Must be kindo' hard. Did you know him?"

I shook my head.

"Shit, that's even worse."

A long silence followed and then Alfred left. I thought how easy it was to say my father was dead. Yes, that's what I would tell anyone who asked: dead before I was born. What killed him? He drowned. They never found his body. I wondered what Grama would think of this.

My mother arrived around eight pm. She and I had found a way of saying the bare minimum to each other. "No ship can survive long 'pon stormy sea," Grama used to say. "If storm keep up it have to head for port." She removed her coat, pulled off her wig, and sat down on the sofa bed. She saw the jeans—I had left them there deliberately—turned them over, opened them, looked at the brand name, and wrinkled her forehead. I was sitting at the table, pretending to read.

"Where you get these?"

"I stole them." I paused and watched her panic. "Just kidding."

I explained everything to her, just as it had happened.

"Take them back to your friend. Is steal he done steal them. These is not cheap jeans. No friend o' yours got that kind o' money."

"Ma, I need them."

"What you mean, you *need* them?"

"My classmates laugh at what I wear. These clothes went out of style twenty years ago."

"Well, if that is the way you want it." She stopped speaking.

"What're you talking about?"

"I talking about your allowance." She sneezed. "This place always dusty."

"It stinks too."

She looked at me and cut her eyes angrily. Droplets of phlegm on the tiny hairs of her upper lip reflected the light.

"There's phlegm on your lip."

She reached for her purse, removed a tissue, wiped her lip and fell silent.

"You were saying something about allowances."

"I get the first cheque for you today. Seeing that you is good in school I was going to save it for help out with your education later, but if you not satisfy with the clothes I can afford, then go blow it all on clothes. These jeans musn' be here when I come Wednesday."

On Monday, I told Alfred of my mother's reaction.

"No sweat. Throw them out if you like."

"But you paid for them!"

"Says who?"

I was too shocked to reply.

On Wednesday, when Ma arrived the jeans were still there. She ran her scissors through them and threw them in the garbage. "Tell your friend I cut them up. I will cut you up too, if you bring stolen property in my place. Don't bring trash in here!

"Why you staring at me like that? You want to call Child Protection for me?"

I turned my head away.

She removed her purse from her handbag, counted some dollar bills, and handed the bills to me. "I watching you to see how you spend that money."

I bought a jean jacket and a pair of jeans, the whole costing me less than thirty dollars, and two shirts at ten dollars each. They weren't as modish as my classmates', but I was no longer dressed like Noah's son. I gave Ma the leftover money and told her to save it for me. She took it silently.

That Sunday when we returned from church, she said, "Pedro, you can't always do things because you 'fraid o' what people will say. If I didn' wear Miss Wilton hand-me-downs, I wouldn't o' been able to take care o' you and Mama. I have three good dresses to my name and two pairs of good shoes. Anybody that tired o' seeing me in them can buy me new ones. When I come to this country I discover a new meaning to the saying 'Where a jackass tie is there it have for graze.' We here is like the jackass, and is a limit to how far we can graze. Everybody must find out the length o' his rope."

I wanted to ask her who tied and untied the jackass and chose the pastures; and, remembering Grama's statement, "Wha' sweet nanny goat does gi'e she belly-running," I was tempted to tell her that it was to goats, not jackasses, that Grama likened her. Instead I said,

"Ma, you don't understand."

"What I don't understand?"

"That it's hard to have people making fun of you all the time."

"You think people never make fun o' me? Well, lemme tell you, when I first come here, one day I was on the bus going back to work, and some white boys called to me, 'Hi Mrs Nigger Woman.' When that didn' get them no reaction, they asked me if I like to do it with white men. 'Bout four grownups was on the bus; they never said a word to them. Later a white man come on the bus and he tell the driver to put them off. The driver refuse, and the white boys turn on the man and tell him he taking my side because he like for eat 'nigger pussy'—pardon the expression, but I telling you like it is. That day I wanted to go and pay my passage back to Isabella Island. But I couldn' do that. And what I just tell you ain't the half of it."

We were quiet for a while. "That is how it is. Ain't no use crying. It only leave tear-tracks in yo' makeup and wrinkle yo' face ahead o' time. When it loud, people run from you unless it make them happy to see somebody else in a worse off condition than they self." She stopped talking, seemed to be focusing her thoughts. "And what's the sense o' fighting? Starting a war you know you can't win?" She groaned. "These is things I want you to learn, but I can't put them in words."

"Why you don't talk to me like this all the time, share your experiences here with me?"

"What you mean?"

"You're either threatening me or screaming at me—as if you hate me, as if I'm in your way—goat-mouthing me."

She lowered her head. "I does talk to you like that?" her voice full of surprise. "I don' know how for explain it. Is just that I see what happen to children that come here from home, and I frighten, frighten to death, that the same thing might happen to you."

I remembered her story of Sister Agnes's niece. Now I wondered why Sister Agnes had visited us only once. "Why doesn't Sister Agnes come to visit you?"

"Forget 'bout Agnes. Nobody have time with she. When she start to talk you can put down the phone and go and finish everything you have to do and she won't know."

"Tell me the truth, Ma. You have any friends?"

"Jesus is my portion; / A constant friend is he; / His eye is on the sparrow / And I know he watches over me." She gave off citing and sang the rest of the hymn with deep feeling, wringing from the words every bit of comfort she was able to.

I understood then that my mother was lonely, and I felt sorry for her, and began to wonder what it meant for West Indians who left their communities and friends to come to live in a place where people sometimes abused and insulted them.

Around six pm, a short while before she left for Baie d'Urfé, she said, "You know how things is now. I expect you to do your part."

18

A MONTH LATER SISTER Agnes made national headlines. The church members were split over whether or not to believe her. Sister Elfreda, who was a senior Elder—Sister Andrews called her the "Helephant"—said that Agnes had taken to wearing jewelry, a sure sign that she was backsliding, so even if she wasn't guilty, it was "the Lord roughing her up because she done start for turn her back 'pon Him; and as Jonah can tell you, when the Lord God say 'Move!', I dares you to stand still"—she declaimed pontifically outside the church door the Sunday after the incident, blinding sunlight reflecting off her wire-rimmed glasses, her discolouring black pigtail wig sprouting from her head like a freak tail reaching down to her gargantuan behind. Sister Agnes said she was bald: hypocrisy had caused her hair to fall out. "And might as well she don' bathe 'cause she still smell like cat piss: evil trying for sweat itself out of 'er." Afterwards she would add, "Too much de-fe-do 'mongst we black people. Unno people fee run from."

And Sister Andrews would say of the Helephant, "Unno does see how Pastor does hold him breath when she start for quote scriptures? And is not just 'cause she breath stink. Always turning God word into a rod. One day it will cut she own backside." And once she'd dared to tell Elfreda, instead of Ma and Sister Agnes, that God's word is a two-edged sword. "Not *any-and-any-body* can hangle it."

That Sunday, after Elfreda's declamation, Sister Andrews (her name was Zilla but no one called her Sister Zilla) winked at Ma, who smiled and said to her as soon as Elder Elfreda was out of hearing, "People that don' bathe mustn' tell others they stink."

The unstated rivalry between Zilla and Elfreda was palpable. Zilla was barely literate, quite the opposite of Elfreda—at least so Elfreda believed; she presided over Wednesday evening Bible study. But Zilla could sing. As good as Koko Taylor or Mahalia Jackson. And she knew a thing or two about improvisation. Pastor Draine used her often for "Jesu, Lover of My Soul" and "When We Walk with the Lord." She allowed the congregation to play with the refrains. To her "Trust and obey," they replied, "There is no other way." It was like her sermon to a wayward congregation, her filling presence pressing them, it seemed, against the warehouse's tin walls in a collective purging of shameful will and sinfulness—a purging by the Lord, who was then none other than Zilla Andrews. It easily eclipsed Elfreda's dubious erudition. "If she know so much," the whisper ran, "how come all she can do is operate a hospital elevator?" And Sister Agnes was sure that Elfreda's going up and down in that elevator all day doubled the hospital's hydro bill.

"You all should stay close to Elfreda," I told Ma.

"What you mean?"

"'The person that stays close to an elephant doesn't get wet.'" I'd got it from a book of African proverbs.

Ma nodded appreciatively. "Well Elfreda broad but she short. She wide but she not deep."

Sister Agnes's story, which was broadcast on national television and radio and in every major Canadian newspaper, featured her returning from Jamaica with a carton containing a dozen one-pound tins of Milo. The tins had seemed genuine enough, and the initial query was whether she could bring this many into the country without an import license. But a customs officer inadvertently looked at the bottom of a tin and saw that it had been opened and resoldered. With the exception of a half-inch of Milo at the top, the tins contained densely packed marijuana. "I is a God-fearing Christian 'oman. What I going do with ganja?" a tired-looking Sister Agnes—grease streaks glowing in her powdered face, her copper wig askew—told the television cameras. One of the shots showed her with arm raised and fist balled to hit a reporter who was pushing a microphone in her face. No dumb, compliant sheep was she.

"She must o' been drinking that Milo a long time; no wonder she can't stop chatting," Ma said when the newscaster turned to another story.

Charged with being a drug courier, she said she'd been asked to deliver the carton of Milo to her niece, who owned a hairdressing parlour. The niece said it was all a mix-up; she knew nothing about it. Sister Agnes was set free after three days in police custody. She won her case: the crown could not prove that she had intentionally brought marijuana into Canada. Draine stood behind her, bailing her and finding her a lawyer, which the church paid for.

Sister Agnes! At church she once broke out in spontaneous leaping and singing "By the Rivers of Babylon" (it was popular then, sung by Boney M, I think). How shall we sing the Lord's song in a strange land?

But sing it they did.

She gave as good as she got, with plenty *brawta*. The last Saturday in November, barely two weeks after she got bail, she phoned the house at six pm, again at six-thirty, and at seven, with increased panting each time. The third time she left a message: "Tell Sister Millicent it got de-fe-do 'nough fee bruck down de church. Child, rucktion today! Them catch Louisa thiefing panties in Miracle Mart today and them arrest her. She go in the try-on-clothes place, and she put on six panty and been walking out the store like if she own it when them catch she. I been in the store and I see when them arrest she. She shame till! She hang down she head. I make sure that she see that I see wha' happening and then I go straight to a phone booth and call Pastor Draine. He go with she to the station. I don' know if she get bail.

"I watching fo' hear what the Helephant gwine say 'bout this one. All o' them well wash out them mouth 'pon me. Judging me like if them is God. Now I waiting fo' hear what they have fo' say 'bout *this*. You should o' see Pastor Draine face! Red like poinsetta. Him always saying 'Sister Louisa this and Sister Louisa that'. Like if Sister Louisa doesn' fart like the rest o' we. You would o' think she is the centrepiece o' the church, that it would fall down if Sister Louisa don' hold it up. Me use fo' even wonder if something not going on betwixt and between them. Well, now we ears gwine get a rest 'cause she no' gwine able put she foot back inside the church."

"Sister Agnes? Sister Agnes! I have to go." I hung up the telephone.

Ouf! Sister Agnes was glad that Sister Louisa had been caught shoplifting! I remembered, back on Isabella Island, Brother Solomon's response to a husband-hunting church sister who'd been insisting that a born-again church sister would make him a fine wife. "*Born again!* Darling, what you been drinking? It got a whole heap o' things the blood o' the Lamb don' wash out."

"So who you waiting on, Brother Solomon?"

"The Lord."

"The Lord is a *man*, Brother Solomon!"

When I gave Ma Sister Agnes's message, she said, "That is not news. I stay with her three weeks when I first come here and I see all the expensive jewelry she been bringing home, though she not supposed for wear jewels, and I figure out long time that she thief some o' it. She must be did think she could o' leave the store invisible like her mother when she go out to suck blood. You understand now why I stay 'way from she? A person is known by the company they keeps."

Ma went on to state, with too much relish, that Sister Louisa's first job in Montreal was as a domestic servant—"She who did have servant to wait 'pon she, hand-and-foot. All the same, setting aside looks and the couple dollars they had, she never did have much for brag 'bout. Give her one thing though: she don' look down on people, not like her mother." But she'd failed the entrance exams to Isabella Island's better secondary schools and did not matriculate from the one she'd attended. Around the time she was caught shoplifting she worked as a stitcher in a garment factory.

19

THE DAY BEFORE SCHOOL reopened in January 1975, Erskine phoned to congratulate me on my success. All my courses were now at the grade ten and eleven regular or advanced level. He'd borrowed a tape recorder from the school as well as a level-four French text and passed them on to me. I had got Alfred to read pages of the French text into the tape recorder and I would sit with the text open and listen to Alfred's pronunciation, and after a while try it myself. Sometimes I spent as many as three hours on a single paragraph, by which time I knew it by heart and my pronunciation approximated Alfred's.

"At this rate you're going to be next year's valedictorian," Erskine said to me. "Keep that in mind. Reynolds is definitely getting it this year. You have to get it next year. Two years in a row! We must have it two years in a row. Let the racist buggers choke on that."

Reynolds was definitely special: not just president of the student council—he'd already published poetry and won a ski medal. He was Jamaican. How did Mrs Black take that? She'd obviously not programmed him.

Alfred and I were moved up to grade-ten French. He changed English classes too. He'd been in an all-vocational programme. He'd requested vocational, knowing it would be "no sweat. See, it's like this. If I would o' gone in regular classes with my reform school shit, those guys would o' look down on me. These guys in vocational can't read worth a dime, so they can't put me down. See? If they mention Shawbridge, all I got to do is ask them how come they so illiterate, if they don't have schools in Jamaica, and stuff like that. Get it, man? Now it ain't bothering me like before. See, I'm getting my shit together. Getting it together, man." I was happy to see him happy.

Hollis had also programmed himself into vocational courses. We took the same bus to school and we were in the same phys ed class. He lived on Mackenzie, one block up from me. He came to my place twice.

The first time, he'd hardly got inside the door when he said, "Boy, how come in here smell o' pee so? You still peeing yo' bed?"

Seated on the sofa he'd gone on to say, "School ain't play it easy here, no."

"What you mean?" I didn't find it easy.

"You can pick yo' classes and thing. I go in classes where I don' sweat, oui. The work I doing now, I done do since third grade in Trinidad. Is pure ninety I get in everything. My mother don' spare a chance to tell she friends-them, oui. I bet you, you ain't getting ninety in nothing?"

I didn't answer.

"Them teachers here stupid. Boy, they stupid! They don' even beat the children. How they expect we to obey them?" He blew his nose into his hand and wiped it onto his sweatsuit.

"When I used to go to Côte des Neiges Comprehensive, I had this old dry-up bag for a English teacher. Boy, her classes was boring! You know the calypso 'bout teacher Mildred?"

I nodded.

"I uses to sing it in she class. Every time I get to where 'the lizard run up under she dress,' the schoolchildren-them round me start laughing. One day a white boy ask me where the lizard go. And I tell he, 'In she cunt.' The teacher tell me to leave the class. I ask she what for. Boy, she come over to my desk and is belt I had to belt it out o' there, oui. They expelled me." He looked into my eyes briefly, smiling with a handsomeness that frightened me.

"Man, in this country, you can get away with anything." He paused and looked into my eyes again. "Well, not everything. See, if here was Trinidad I couldn' do that. The principal would o' whale me ass. Here they don' know how to handle students."

Hollis stopped talking for a while and became fidgety.

"You want to hear 'bout the part I ain't get away with?"

I didn't answer.

"Well I don' does do it no more, but when I first come here, I get in with some boys that use to steal. They catch me out at the Plaza. Boy, what them police officers ain't do with me is what they ain't imagine. One o' them push three o' his fingers up me ass. Say he sure I have drugs in there. But I know is bull he did want to bull me."

I laughed.

"You laughing. I don' want no fellar to do that to me, boy. You crazy!"

"So how you got to General Wolfe?"

"My mother threaten to sue the school commission if they didn' take me back, so they tell her to send me to General Wolfe."

"But you're still being suspended?"

"Why not? I don' mind. I still come school. Plenty skippers does be by the shopping centre. Learning ain't my bag. I go 'cause my friends-them does be there. It did have this fellar in Trinidad what uses to always have he head in book all the time. He was a preacher at Tranquillity Methodist Church and all o' that. When you hear the shout, my uncle and some fellars catch he by the Savannah bulling. They tie he to a tree and beat he till he pass out, oui." Hollis looked around the apartment. "What time it is?"

"Five o'clock."

"I don' want miss my programme." He went over to the television and turned it on. "Man, is black and white TV all you got! I gotta go home. Is only colour I watch."

Three days later, a Saturday morning, he came by with a pile of magazines under his arm.

"I bring these to show you. Bet you ain't never see nothin' like this before? You ever get wife?"

The expression was so vulgar, I froze.

"Aye, Aye! Big man like you ain't know wha' wife is! You ever fuck a woman?"

I didn't answer.

"Boy, anywhere it have women to fuck I going. If you put a dress over a couple pieces o' wood, I gon' ha' check it out."

"What about on a clothesline?"

"You not funny. You wan' hear a song I compose?" He cleared his throat, took a deep breath and sang, calypso style:

"Ladies come lemme fill your can.

I am the semen man.

Ewes of every race and taste,

I'm the all-pleasing ram."

"How come you ain' clapping me?" He seemed a trifle hurt.

"You know you can sing. You sing well."

"I know that. I mean the lyrics. You like them?"

"No. They're vulgar." Actually I found them funny.

"Gros Lot, go to hell!"

We were silent for a few seconds. "How old you was when you start fucking?"

I was tempted to lie, but decided not to answer.

"Man, I been fucking steady since I twelve, in Trinidad. A woman who uses to rent two rooms downstairs from my grandmother. She did have a TV and we didn' have one, so I used to go down there and watch TV with she. Her husband use to work evenings. One evening she start feeling up my lolo, just around the time it start getting big. So I le' she. A next night she take off my trousers, so I le' she. A next night she pull me on top o' she. I hoist up she dress and pull down she panties and she spread it for me. Lord, she grabbed me with she tree-trunk legs! I think she would o' break me back. Man, that was the first time I come. After that, man, I used to *watch* TV *every* evening. When my mother send for me she come to the airport to see me off. She cry. Man, she cry, 'cause she know what she gon be missing. I ain't find she replacement yet, but when I find she I going make she pay me, oui. I nearly find one. Meet she sitting on a park bench up Kent Park one day. She keep staring at me and I wink at she. She come over to talk to me, come telling me 'bout how I is a little boy. I tell she little axe does cut down big tree. She tell me how I have for be careful 'cause I good looking and I gon get meself in trouble. Then she tell me she married. I tell she that don't change nutten. I gi'e she me phone number just in case she change she mind. But she never call me." He stopped talking.

We were quiet for about a minute, and Hollis looked as if he didn't know what to do with himself. His eyes darted quickly over every spot of the room. "You want to see something?" He was smiling and his eyes were brighter than usual.

"What?"

"Just say yes."

"Okay."

He stood up and pulled down his trousers. He was wearing a navy blue gym outfit. The trousers lay piled in a bundle around his feet. I waited nervously for him to pull down his jockey shorts. There was a faint smell of unwashed genitals. He pointed to his right thigh, to two capital Ts of scarred tissue, one above the other. The skin covering them was raised like termite tunnels and was a shade paler than his complexion. Hollis's face was enveloped in a big grin. He passed his hand over the T-s as if he were wiping dust from a sports trophy.

"Boy, is wife that gi'e me these. It did have this lil' Indian gal what didn' live far from we. She and me was in the same class at Tranquillity. She uses to always watch me and laugh and wink. Fresh lil' thing, man. Tits too big for the dress she wearing. Fresh like smoke herring ready to roast. To make a long story short, I and she get around to business one Saturday in my grandmother privy. Just as I pull down she panties, the toilet door open and her three brothers was out there. Two o' them was already big men.

"'You leave!' one o' them said to their sister. 'We gon deal with you later.'

"I try to make a dash for the door.

"'Not you, man. We not finish with you. And don' make a sound, else we carrying yo' balls when we leave.'

"Boy, they pin me ass 'gainst the side o' the privy; one o' them take out a razor blade and carve them two letters here on me leg.

"'They mean think twice,' the oldest one tell me. 'You lose yo' balls next time. And if you got sense you keep yo' mouth shut.'

"*Think twice*, huh. Trinidad is a big place, oui. I is the same person that take their sister maid 'bout a month afterwards."

When I caught myself, I realized I was holding my breath.

"You always so quiet? I's the one doing all the talking."

I was sitting on the armchair. Hollis pulled up his trousers and resumed his seat on the sofa; his magazines were beside him. He began leafing through them. "I didn' buy none of these, you know. I uses to go in the store with my school books, and when they not watching I slip a magazine between them." He leafed through them more quickly while he spoke. He got up and brought me a couple.

I perused them. I hadn't yet seen pornographic magazines but knew of their existence as "dirty pictures," and I was a little awed by the frankness of the poses. A lot of the pictures dealt with fellatio. Many of them were of white women doing it with black males who had abnormal penises, the kind racist Whites believe all black men have.

I was so taken up with the pictures that I completely ignored Hollis, until I heard him gasping and saw him shooting semen onto the rug. When Hollis' breathing was again normal he began to gather up his magazines. "You want to keep them until this evening?" he asked.

"No."

"You 'fraid yo' mother going find them?"

"Yes."

"You such a baby! Why you don' do like me? The last time my mother hit me I call the police. She ain't try it again. You know something?" He paused. "I don't know if I should tell you this? Promise me you won't repeat it to nobody."

I said nothing.

"I will kill yo' ass if you ever tell anybody!"

"Tell anybody what?"

Hollis lowered his voice. "One day I skip school and come home early. When I open the door I see my mother on the couch with my magazines spread out around she. I didn' see she do it, but I sure she been playing with sheself."

I couldn't laugh. Mervyn's group, Hollis in the lead, made jokes about women who used vibrators. We'd convinced ourselves that Ms Skrapper had one since we couldn't imagine any man would want to sleep with her. Everyone needed a secret bag, had things to put in it, as Grama said. Hollis should get one.

"If you ever tell anybody 'bout this I going kill yo' ass."

I smiled.

"You and I gon be good friends."

Not really. "Take your magazines with you." *My mother doesn't need them.*

Hollis picked up his magazines. "I live on Mackenzie, just up from here, the third building in on yo' right, apartment 212. You must come home with me one day next week." He left.

I wiped his come out of the rug. It left a lingering odour.

The following Tuesday afternoon Hollis was on the bus. "You coming home with me? We gon' drink a couple o' my mother's beers and watch dirty pictures."

We got off at the same bus stop at the corner of Mackenzie (his street) and Côte des Neiges. "I can't come to your place. I have a lot of homework to do."

"How come you have time for that jailbird and not for me?"

I was surprised to hear him call Alfred that. We suspected that Alfred had resumed tampering with drugs, and sometimes Hollis and he went off together.

"Don't I know you all got something going!"

"I help him with his homework, and he helps me with my French."

"I won' mind watching all yo' lessons. Bet he got a big one, an' you is the one that does lie down on yo' belly. Chicken! Fool! You wasting yo' boy days, oui."

"What you mean?"

"Read all the books and pass all the exams, but we go end up the same place."

"Which is?"

"Unemployment, welfare, or in some factory. Only one certificate they respect here, oui: white skin."

"What?"

"Man, you retarded or what!"

"Look at Mr Erskine!"

"You think Erskine black! He a white man. He don' even need a lil' washing." He laughed. "Man, I tell myself I go do just what life say I go do, yes. In Trinidad we have a saying, 'What is to is, must is.' Is just so I feel, oui." He stopped talking and grinned. When he resumed, he stared at me with a twinkle in his eye and said, "I know one thing. It ain't no schoolwork that going make a woman keep coming back. I know another thing too: if I satisfy she, she go work for me and she."

I headed towards DeCourtrai, thinking that I had been warned by everyone who had my interest at heart to stay away from people like him. As I was about to turn onto DeCourtrai, I looked back and saw him still standing where I'd left him, still staring at me.

I never did go to his place nor did he ever return to mine. At school he continued to speak to me. But in his presence I'd hear Grama's voice echoing in my head: "It easy for run down the hill. If you want gold, you have for dig deep."

20

AROUND THE MIDDLE OF the second term, Mervyn told me, almost within earshot of Alfred, "Be careful." He motioned with his chin that he was referring to Alfred. "He hang 'round with you now 'cause you helping him with his school work, but when he don' need you no more he will plough you up."

The next day Ms Mackenzie asked me why Alfred and I were such close friends. Her question puzzled me. She knew he helped me with my French. Erskine asked me a similar question two days later.

"Why is everybody asking me about Alfred?" I asked Erskine.

"You don't know, eh? Well I hope nothing happens to you before you find out."

That same afternoon, Mervyn asked me if I'd started to take drugs yet. I was annoyed and told him to get off Alfred's back. "I *know* he wants to make good. So you're the one putting ideas in Erskine's head."

"Maybe, but tell 'im if I find out he try for sell drugs to anybody in our group I will buss him head. Tell him jus' like how I tell you."

"Deliver your messages yourself."

One recess, about three weeks after this incident, Alfred told me to come to Room 226 at the beginning of the lunch hour. Room 226 was a small room located in a recessed area at the extreme eastern end of the east-west second floor corridor. It was a room sometimes used for tutorials.

"Why?"

"I'm not telling you. Just come. Don't tell anybody."

I was the first to arrive. Alfred came about three minutes later. He looked nervous. He peeped around the alcove along the corridor every few seconds. "You see Hollis?"

I shook my head.

Hollis and two heavyset girls, one white and one black, both about age fifteen or sixteen, arrived some five minutes later. The girls, I later found out, were students at a high school belonging to another school commission two blocks away. Hollis glared at me, visibly angry. But he said nothing. "Keep a eye out," he told Alfred. We were all standing in the recessed area, out of view.

Alfred stretched his head around the wall and surveyed the corridor. "Coast clear," he said.

Hollis picked the lock with his ID card, and we all entered the room.

Hollis placed his arm around the black girl. Her complexion was like new potatoes. She was buxom and looked a little like over-raised dough. She wore a red dress, and the imprint of her brassiere made it look as if she had four breasts. She looked about her nervously. Hollis quickly joined two desks together. As if on cue, the girl pursed her lips, glanced quickly at the others in the room, lifted her skirt, folded it back, and lay on her back on the joined desks. Her lower legs dangled. Hollis pulled down her panties, spread her legs, and placed a supporting desk under each. Then he dropped his trousers.

When the desks began to creak, Alfred moved in on the white one. She was wearing jeans. Alfred tried to undo them. "Go easy! She told him. "Play with my tits first and kiss me."

The desks Hollis and his lady were using creaked furiously.

My hands began to sweat. I was keenly aware of what would happen if Bellamy caught me in here. But I was fascinated and aroused. *Leave. Get out of here. Every second you stay is dangerous.*

Just as Alfred's girl began to unbutton her blouse, I opened the door quietly and left and headed into the closest bathroom to cool myself down.

Ten minutes before the end-of-lunch bell, Hollis and Alfred showed up in the cafeteria. "Chicken!" Alfred screamed at me. "That's why you still a virgin."

Well, I'd rather be chicken out o' hot water than in it.

Mervyn looked at us with curiosity but said nothing.

Three days later Bellamy caught Hollis and the girls going at it. Bellamy suspended him for a week. Hollis, grinning his self-satisfied grin, proudly told us about his suspension. Mervyn suggested he wear a T-shirt telling everybody he's a prick. *Priapus unlimited!* I thought, emblazoned in black on his red (Hollis's favourite colour) shirt front and back, an inverted penis and a drop of semen for the exclamation.

"Pu," I said in French, absentmindedly.

"What?" Hollis asked.

"It rhymes with *cul*," Vince said.

"*Tu pues de queue!*" Priscilla said.

Several of us laughed.

"All you done gone batty?" Hollis said, twirling a finger around his temple, gesturing insanity.

"You hear that!" Mervyn said, "Him love batty too."

We laughed.

"You all just jealous," Hollis said and began to leave.

"Go long. Gwan!" Priscilla said with a chasing hand gesture. "We ears tired o' yo' one-string violin."

"That's 'cause you ain't vibrate to me music yet."

He stopped walking and began to dance. "Call me the meatman." He closed his eyes, smiled broadly, twirled, stood on tiptoe, and belted out with peacock antics Koko Taylor's off-colour blues song. "I is all those men, see. But just call me Meatman, 'cause I is a sweetman," unaware, no doubt, of the other meanings of sweetman.

"*Sweetman* for sure," Priscilla told him.

She was Jamaican. Her father Black, her mother Chinese. She was bone-thin—bundo—with arms that Hollis said were ropes (to hang him with, she said), twiglike legs, a beautiful, angular face, and bewitching amber eyes. Her long, thick black hair was always combed into two side braids, which she preferred to wear with the tips resting on her chest. Occasionally she joined them into something of a wreath that came to rest on her bosom. Her ties, they became commonplace, noticed only by their absence. She preferred the long, wide ones, in solid earth colours. She was the youngest of three children and the only girl, but her father called her his favourite son. She'd wear a dress only when she wanted to freak us out.

She delighted us. There was never any doubt that Hollis would do battle for her and she for him, that their taunting, except on a few occasions, was mere badinage. We saw her as Mervyn's lieutenant.

She rescued me from Hollis's ridicule one recess while we were sitting around the picnic table at the back of the school. "Gros Lot," he kept jabbing at me, "all learning and no sex make you a killjoy."

"Leave Pedro alone. That's yo' specialty," Mervyn said.

Priscilla, her forefinger and thumb playing with her joined braids, told Hollis, "All sex and no sense make you a toyboy."

Without a comeback, Hollis slouched and grinned, open mouthed, tongue exposed like a dog's releasing excess heat. "Bundo gal," he finally said, "somebody going fix that mouth o' yours. Mark my words."

21

ALFRED AND HOLLIS TEASED me about Ellen (Hilda, Brumhilda, BJ Bertha), the white girl who'd showed me my locker my first school day at General Wolfe. She was in my grade-ten French class, and she'd sometimes look at me and blush. She had wide haunches (more like Daphne's than Helen's) and disproportionately long legs. Whenever she wore her favourite pair of jeans her loose buttocks shook—wiggles interspersed with pauses. Taunts and interdictions. The print of a woman's face, one eye closed in a wink, the tip of the tongue extended over the lower blood-red lip, covered each buttock pocket. She allowed some of the boys, Alfred especially, to pinch her buns. Wriggling her bottom and giggling, her face pink, her eyebrows fluttering, her grey-green eyes glowing, she'd hit them playfully, wag her finger, and say they'd get no further. When in a bad mood, she'd snarl and make mauling gestures. One moment she could wriggle her bottom against your hands or thighs, and the next threaten you with clawing nails and fisticuffs.

She smelt like a puree of overripe apples, bananas, and vinegar which, Alfred said, was her odour to attract men.

When relaxed, her jaws would set in a way that gave her a determined and defiant look. She was broad jawed with bulbous cheeks tapering abruptly to form a short chin. When she wasn't taken up with our clowning, her expression became a sulk.

She never stayed around after school. She was the oldest of six children and looked after her siblings when she got home from school. Once, the anniversary of her father's death, she broke down in tears and had to be sent home. On the few occasions when our class planned a get-together, she took over the planning, drew up a list of what had to be bought, calculated the cost for each student, and assigned the duties.

She did her homework always and got high marks. Before every exam she sighed and signed herself. She signed herself and grinned whenever she answered Madame Montcalm's questions correctly. When her answers were wrong she pounded the desk and swore half audibly.

When walking she pushed her breasts ahead of her the way blind animals extend their feelers. When she laughed her fullest, they'd heave like waves and threaten to burst their bands—when they were in bands—or bounce between her chest and blouse. I'd sit in class and imagine my hands cupping them and playing with the nipples.

(Breasts. At six I was curious about Ishtar's. In one of my dreams she'd slipped her calico dress below her waist, and her breasts had become two bunches of burgundy grapes, which she pushed together with both hands into one large bunch towards my mouth. I ate them, and she became flat-chested like a man; and while I stared, surprised by her transformation, she pushed her hand into my trousers, plucked out my penis, and ate it.)

My classmates fantasized about hips and bums. Bums made for a smooth ride, Hollis said, and he surmised that there was much horsepower in Ellen's haunches. Out of her hearing Alfred called her *donut*; Priscilla: *the highway well*; and Dreyfuss's Nations: *the sewer*. Alfred said she deserved a PhD for BJ-ing, and only then did I understand what Zachary had meant that day in the lockers. The D in her initials, she'd told us, was for Dulcina. Eddy harassed her about it: "Gimme some sugar, sweet Dulcina." It was negative attention but attention, and she wallowed in it. Hollis was the only person who defended her. "You guys lying on her. How come she always telling me to go suck a ice cube when I beg she for a cool-down?"

" 'Cause," Priscilla told him, "she know only yo' mouth hot."

I desired Ellen and hated myself for it; she was so free with my classmates. I knew that what Alfred said about her wasn't true, that it was her loose, unbound body, tumbling over the edges of respectability that sent our imaginations in a gallop. If these had been Victorian times, I supposed the principal might have sent her home to get laced up.

We made a date for the last Saturday in May. I was excited. I was jealous of the adulation Hollis enjoyed though I'd have never admitted it.

I told Alfred. He laughed. "Oh God! You ain't got no class, man. Your first time, right. Make sure you lose your virginity this time. Watch out she don't break your back. For guys without class, she kind o' handy when things tight."

"You ever . . .?"

"Ever what? Fuck her you mean? You can't say *fuck*? Guys like you get fucked: floops!"—he made a thrusting gesture— "Up the ass. No, I never fucked *her*. Never been *that* hardup. 'Sides, man, I got my reputation to protect.'

"Your friends?"

"Get real! *My friends*! We like our women trim, tight, and exclusive. We don't fuck *sluts*."

Like the girl in 226! "Don't call her that."

"What's this? You're in love and she ain't even give it to you yet! You deserve her. *Une saloppe! Bathe with kwellada afterwards.*"

I'd stopped talking, stunned by his cruelty.

She and I met outside the shopping centre around seven. It was drizzling. She'd brought along a duffel army bag, which I took and carried. We walked along a sodden dirt path into a thick cluster of bushes. We had to hang around until it got dark. She led me behind a clump of shrubs, and we began to embrace.

"Your first time, right?" she asked.

"No."

"It's my first time."

I said nothing.

"See?" she said, "I think ahead. I brung a beach towel." She unzipped the bag and took out the beach towel. "We can't undress. The police might come in here. You won't want them to catch us naked." She fumbled with my fly then placed my right hand on her left breast. "You don't know what to do? You don't watch movies and stuff?"

I held her loosely and eased her gently down onto the beach towel. Everything went smoothly from there. I ejaculated in her mouth fifteen seconds after she began licking my penis. She spat out my semen, got up quickly and packed her things. "That's all?" I asked.

"You want me to get pregnant, huh? No sirree!" She tensed, as a bell tolled nine gongs. "Jesus Christ! Mama will kill me. She said to be home before nine." She signed herself, grabbed her bag, and ran out of the bushes toward the street and the bus stop.

At home I visualized myself married to her despite what the guys said. I was sure that once she knew I was serious she'd stop being so free with my classmates.

I wrote her a letter, which I gave her on Monday when no one was watching.

"Did you score?" Alfred asked me as soon as he got a chance to.

"Kind of," I said.

"What you mean, *kind of*?"

I was embarrassed.

"Sucker! I always thought you was a sucker! Why you think we call her Donut?"

"What you mean?"

Alfred stared at me, his face screwed up, and shook his head. "You just born or what? You got a hole in your sense bigger'n her own."

I winced.

When I got out of class that afternoon, Alfred, Hollis, Vince, and Eddy were waiting on the sidewalk. They clapped and laughed and stared at me.

"'Dear Ellen, I cannot get you out of my mind,'" Hollis said.

"'You are such a beautiful girl and I feel as if we are already married,'" Alfred joined in.

Vince continued, "'I would like you to become my steady girl-friend because I can see that you are respectable and don't go too far with boys.'"

Thunderous laughter.

"'You must not allow my classmates to touch your body. They think you are cheap. I am in love with you and I want you to be respectable,'" Eddy picked up while the others laughed.

"'Let me know if you love me too. My heart will break if you don't,'" Alfred mocked.

Hollis capped it with, "Gros Lot, she say she couldn' find yo' *lolo*."

They and the many students who'd begun listening exploded with laughter, which never fully died down until they boarded their buses.

22

OVER THE NEXT FEW DAYS, Hollis and Alfred instructed me on how to "take" sex from women. "Never take no for a answer. Women can't make up their minds. You must help them make it up," Alfred said. "So long as you do a good job, they won't mind."

Agatha was present and she'd listen in silence (she was pregnant at the time but we did not know). Unusual for her. She talked nonstop normally, had earned the nickname Sailmouth from Priscilla, who once told her, "Your mouth always flapping like sail in a wind." Vince's cousin, John, who was a sometime member of our group, was there too, wearing his grease-stained dungaree cap pulled down to the point of covering his eyes. He was studying automotive mechanics. He was less than five feet, had a V-face, curved, narrow shoulders that sloped like a gable roof, and a thin chest. Once Dreyfuss had picked him up by the collar clean off the ground with one hand and shaken him, threatening not to stop until he'd gotten all the shit and hot air out of him. His shoulders curved forwards, and when he walked, his torso rocked back and forth, so that his head was like an upside-down pendulum; his turned-out feet and steel-toe boots stomped the earth. He spoke loudly and threw his arms wildly about. He drove a red patched-up Camaro, each patch a different colour. The muffler spewed thick, stinking, oily smoke at whatever was behind, blackening the road and threatening to poison anyone who ventured close. His official name was Giovanni, but he vowed he'd shoot any teacher who called him that. When anyone upset him, he'd grab his dick and tell the offending person to suck it. He ended every altercation that way. Mostly we ignored him.

"Talking about a good job," John said, his hand on his fly, "me and three pals from Ville D'Anjou had the fuckingest good time ever in

Indian country! Wow! Man, that was some fucking! Like man, that was good fucking. This squaw bitch, man, about my age, man, comes into the bushes where we was and says 'Hi'. My friend Ben winks at me and says, 'Bet you she wants it.' So I went up to her and she didn't run. So I pushed her down and we all took turns. Funny thing, she just lain there with her hands over her eyes and took it. I read somewhere where women like to fantasize about film stars and football players when they're fucking." His eyes were now balls of transparent honey, and his shoulders more concave than ever, he went on, uninterrupted. "I was having my pleasure and I won't deny her hers. Man, by the time the others were done my cock was rock hard, and only a second go would get it down. We all had seconds. Man, even after we finished, she just lain there on the ground, quiet like, waiting for more. Man, what they say is true: no amount of fucking can satisfy some women." He gave his dick one last squeeze.

Next day I had my final exam. When I handed in my paper, I was told to report to the principal's office. Alfred, Hollis, and John-Giovanni were already there. Alfred wiped his mouth when he saw me. They all stared at me.

"What did Giovanni tell you guys at recess yesterday?" Bellamy asked me, his artificial arm on the desk, his good arm stirring the air.

I looked at my schoolmates.

"I'm speaking to you, not them."

At that point something fell. Alfred, who was standing near a shelf of books, had knocked one down, apparently accidentally. In the interim, Hollis, who was closest to me, nudged me and quickly put his finger to his lips before Bellamy turned again to look at me.

"We talked about exams. I don't remember what about them."

"Are you telling the truth?"

"Yes."

"Would you swear upon a Bible?"

I hesitated. "Yes."

"Didn't Giovanni talk about some girl he and his friends raped on the weekend?"

"No, sir. At least not while I was there."

He seemed perplexed, questioned us over and over again and finally told us we could leave. As soon as we got into the corridor we heard Agatha's name announced over the intercom. We yelped and slapped palms.

On June 22 we went to clean out our lockers and, as planned, we met in the McDonald's over in the shopping centre.

"Boy, did I tell Sailmouth off!" John said. "I told that bitch if I ever catch her alone, I'll fuck her with a whisky bottle. I won't dirty my dick in her. Fucken blabbermouth! Condom Nose was with her. Skinning her teeth like a fucken jackass! I told her a couple o' things she ain't likely to forget." He squeezed his dick for emphasis and laughed.

I left them and went home. Within ten minutes of my arrival my mother phoned, saying I was to meet her at the principal's office. When I got there, most of the others were waiting in the general office: Agatha (Sailmouth) and her lightning-eye father (a short intense, round-faced black man in his fifties, who was president of the General Wolfe Parent-Teachers Association), Condom Nose, Hollis, and his mother. John stood trembling beside his father (a pot-bellied florid man, short like John, wearing steel-grey mechanic overalls; he kept shaking his head and saying over and over how sorry he was). Alfred and his worker arrived soon after.

Bellamy had called Agatha a mischief-maker and had suspended her. Stung, she'd got Condom Nose to bring a tape recorder hidden in her bag when she confronted John.

Bellamy said he'd have to turn John over to Youth Protection because rape was involved. John's father broke into genuine tears then; he shook, seemed to wobble, as he pleaded with Bellamy. Bellamy made us apologize to Agatha and gave us a five-day suspension to be served at the beginning of the new school year. We left John and his father in Bellamy's office awaiting the arrival of a Youth Protection Officer.

I didn't hear the end of it from my mother. She had finally got solid proof that I would disgrace her. I didn't have the sense I was born with. Shawbridge was waiting for me. "Maybe you have yo' father..." She cut herself off short. "You better give yo' heart to the Lord. You is surely on the path o' destruction."

Low, Pedro, low! On the very brink o' hell itself. I had failed Grama and Brother Shiloh. What would Mervyn have done if he'd been with us when John told the story? Mr Sam would have reacted differently. He'd have told me to be careful, but would have seen it as part of growing up. That thought comforted me.

The next day Erskine phoned the house. He wanted to talk to me but not over the telephone and definitely not at school. Finally he told me to come by on Sunday and have dinner with him and his wife.

I'd thought he was single.

A sleek woman, several inches taller than Erskine, with sea-green eyes and waist-length golden hair twisted in a pigtail, opened the door. She wore an ankle-length pearl-white dress. Walking with a delicate sashaying of her hips and tiny, leaping dancer's steps, she led me to the living room, where Erskine was seated on a high-backed burgundy upholstered sofa fronting an oval mahogany table spread with magazines and the Sunday paper. A large window was at the back of the couch, its sheer curtains tied to one side. In one wall there was a fireplace. There were several African sculptures on the marble mantelpiece. Erskine was dressed in a grey suit, a white shirt, black tie, and gleaming black shoes. It seemed as if they had arrived from somewhere or were ready to depart. Mrs Erskine pointed me to an armchair to the right of her husband and motioned for me to sit. Up till then she hadn't spoken to me, not even to return my greeting.

"Vat is your name?" Her voice was deep, almost like a man's.

I told her.

"Pedro, no zinner zhere is. I don't vant my life vith my husband to vrap up vith school. So I am going out." She picked up her handbag, checked the contents, and left.

All this time Erskine had said nothing. "My wife's peeved because I didn't give her any warning about your coming. Forget about her. I'll order a pizza."

I hated pizza.

Erskine talked, jumping from topic to topic with characteristic nervous energy, finally settling on how black children were disgracing him.

"I see my plan didn't work."

"What plan?"

"Never mind. Why're you suspended for a week at the beginning of school?"

I explained what had happened.

"I knew it! I knew it! What's new? If you hang around with drug dealers and psychopaths this is only the start."

"You mean Alfred?"

"Oh, so you know he's a drug dealer and you still keep company with him! Where do you all shoot up?"

Was the guy sane! "I don't shoot up with anybody!" I said, screwing up my face, so he'd see I was upset.

"That's what you want me to believe. What white people say about the curse of Ham must be true. Sometimes I swear to God I'm ashamed o' the black blood in me."

You can pass for a dirty white man.

(Hollis loved to tell that story:

"Few years back, at Côte des Neiges Comprehensive, they say it did have this malatta what didn' want people to know he malatta. One day he tried to get inside this white gal drawers and she didn' want him nohow."

"I don't fuck niggers," she tell him.

"I ain't no nigger," he tell she; "I is just a dirty white man.")

"You have to stop keeping company with Alfred. Forthwith! That's an order!"

I have to stay black and die, kid. I was on the verge of vomiting up his pizza.

"But Mr Erskine . . ."

"Don't you *but* me!"

I wanted to tell him that if I could speak some French and was in a regular French class, it was because of the arrangement I'd had with Alfred. He knew that. It was he who'd borrowed the tape recorder for me. I was choking with emotion, and the excess spilled out of my eyes.

"Oh God! You not for these parts! You crying 'cause I want to find out if you doing drugs or not? Yuh mu'err be'er send yuh back tuh the West Indies."

"I'm crying because you won't let me explain myself," I said angrily, almost shouting.

"Now I see you got a little spunk in you."

Confusion filled me again. "Forget it. Can I go now?"

"Go where? We ain't even started."

He'd been well informed. He recounted what had gone on between Ellen and me. He knew I had been in the room while Hollis and Alfred were having sex with the girls from the other high school. "If somebody as bright as you don't have the willpower to keep away from filth, what will become of the race?" He looked away from me as he said this, his face covered in a frown. "God, help us."

He got up from his seat and came to stand over me. He grabbed my left ear and began to pull it. "For God's sake, what you think you got ears for? I want you to listen! Listen! Dammit! And use this!" He held my nose and twisted it. "Can't you smell? Most of what's around is pus. Open your nostrils! Goddamit! And run! Run like hell before disease infects you. You intend to stay away from such foolishness?"

I didn't answer.

His hand was again on my ear, pulling it. "Yes, Mr Erskine. I promise." I needed my ear.

Erskine sat down and in a quieter voice gave me a long lecture on VD. Again he ordered me not to hang around with Alfred and Hollis. "What's wrong with Mervyn? When you're away from Mervyn keep far from those two. Mervyn, now, there's a fine lad. If only that boy had a chance. now there's a race builder. That boy works in a warehouse three nights o' week. None o' you know that, because he won't tell you. And keeps his own counsel. White people can't get anywhere with him." *Would he have said this if his wife were present?* "He goes to Union Church every Sunday, but he'll outgrow that.

"Come September, I want you to keep away from those corbeaus. If French is the problem, I'll get you a tutor and pay for it."

Even if I'm getting zero, your money will stay in your pocket. You're not going to own me. For spite Alfred and I will become even closer friends. You'll swallow it, buddy, or choke. Go to hell, Erskine!

When I got home, Hollis phoned to tell me John-Giovanni had made up the story, but Bellamy was not lifting our suspensions because we'd lied.

23

ON THE FIRST WEDNESDAY in September the first full school day of the '75-'76 school year, Erskine phoned me around five pm to tell me to come to his house to pick up my new textbooks and school assignments. I had to go again on Thursday and on Friday to get the homework.

John did not return to school. Vince said his father had him working at his garage. Agatha did not return either. She would give birth anytime soon, Ellen informed us. She was going to be the baby's godmother, she told us, excited. We asked Vince if it was his. He grinned, embarrassed, and said he'd never done anything to make her pregnant. Hollis sucked his teeth in disgust.

We had one and a half new black teachers. The one was Mrs Henry. A real black woman, with an Afro, West African black skin, African nose—no sign of white blood anywhere. She was from Antigua. She taught grade eleven world history, and I was in her class. She also taught a course in black studies, which all the academic black students avoided, saying it was a booby class, because only vocational and remedial students took it. The half was Maynes. He taught phys ed, or was supposed to.

Alfred was promoted to grade eleven remedial classes. They were a notch above vocational. When he caught up with me in the cafeteria, he said, "That sonofabitch John let the principal bring in Youth Protection and even made the police do a investigation in Kahnawake, and all the time he made up the whole fucking story that got us suspended. Can you beat that? That dumb mother-fucker! That's why they didn't put me in regular classes, man. And I promised my mother, and she was so looking forward to it. Bellamy said no dice. No fucking dice! I feel like throwing the towel in. Setting fire to the whole fucking school! I don't give a fuck if I spend my whole life in jail!"

"Don't talk like that."

"Man, it's grade eleven booby classes I'm in. All through elementary school I was on the principal's honour roll. Can you beat that? All the work you and I did where's it? Gone up in smoke, all because of that dumb motherfucker."

We were silent for a while.

"And I'm not hanging around with Mervyn's group no more. *Grampa!*" He said it with venom. "You guys're his pups; he sure keeps you all on a leash."

"Why're you saying this?"

"Quit being so damn naive! You for real, man? Sides, I just told you, I ain't no puppy dog! Man, I'm trying to tell you. Let's just say I have commitments. It's my life, man!" His eyes were glassy, and I wondered why.

"*Commitments?*"

"Keep up the good work. You're heading for university and stuff. We'll catch up from time to time." He left.

Erskine's praise of Mervyn had dampened my feelings for him. I felt it was he who informed Erskine about me. I wondered whether his "exemplary conduct" wasn't just adult orders he carried out because he couldn't think for himself. Anansi stories were plentiful in Jamaica, so it wasn't for want of hearing them that he couldn't put holes in the wool and see without being seen. I went to church with my mother but spent my time observing the congregation, imagining their lives from their prayers. Before Sister Louisa left the church in disgrace, I'd notice Draine staring at her longer than he should. She was beautiful—no sweat forsaking the cross for a piece o' that ass, as Chauncey would have put it. Who could blame him? His thin-haired wife, bulging bluish bags under her eyes, buck teeth her lips couldn't cover, with short, thick, water-logged legs, in her sacklike chocolate-brown frocks! "Pastor Draine cross," Sister Agnes called her and was sure he'd married her for her money.

Why, I asked Ma once, didn't she use some of her wealth to improve her appearance: straighten her teeth, for example. The upper ones slanted outwards awfully, were spaced like spread fingers and rested visibly on her lower lip when she tried to close her mouth. She might have dyed her salt-and-pepper hair, which was so thin her scalp was visible. Ma said that to alter one's appearance was to show dissatisfaction with God's "handiwork," it was a sin; Pastor Draine was the "head" and he and his wife had to lead by example. "*You,* don' study Sister Draine—you hear me? She happy in Christ. Her looks don' bother her."

"So all the wigs you people wear are sinful?"

She gave a sheepish, embarrassed grin.

"Maybe her looks drove her into the arms of Christ. And Christ gave her Draine in reward for her righteousness. Not a bad recompense. For her, at any rate."

"I don' like this conversation."

"And I know why."

"Why?"

"Because you joined Saints Militants hoping for a lot o' things." I was smiling with pressed lips, so she'd see the mischief in me. *A loving, hard-working, providing husband especially.* "But, poor Ma, you got nothing except a promise of life after death. At least Sister Draine got Pastor Draine."

After a long pensive stare, she said, "Pedro, why you say things to hurt me? Why you talk 'bout things you know nothing 'bout? Why you throw stones in the dark and don' think who they might hit? Well, lemme tell you something: Sister Draine know the body is jus' a container, a jug—you understand—and no matter how you pretify it, if it empty it going stay empty. A lot o' people too frighten fo' look inside, so them put all the focus prettying up the outside. Them is what Christ call 'Whited sepulchres.'"

"Well, I'm glad you're not one of them."

She wrinkled her brow and fell silent.

The Sunday following this conversation, Draine preached that sex should be engaged in for procreation only. I came to suspect that preachers flog the sins they have trouble resisting. He needed dogma to justify his marriage to Sister Draine. But it was the hormonal man that stared at Sister Louisa, a fact that Agnes, and Brother Solomon, no doubt, knew.

From that fall until I finished school in June, I encountered one problem after another.

In October, I'd had to contend with Erskine. He wanted me to run for president of the student council because the fellow we'd elected in the spring had moved to Toronto. Sitting in the lab, which was also his office, he held me with his gaze. "You have to do it, for the Black Cause." For Erskine black students were always competing against white students.

I was silent. Eventually I told him to give me a day or two to think about it. I knew I wasn't going to. Around 3.10 that afternoon, heading to the bus stop, I saw Alfred a few feet ahead of me. I called out to him. He waited.

"I'm honoured!"

"What do you mean?"

"Oh come on! Don't play the innocent!" He was wearing a black turtleneck sweater and his black leather jacket was open (he had at least four leather jackets). A horn-shaped pendant on a thick gold chain rested on his chest. "I'm not sucking up to you any more; get that in your bright head."

"I need your opinion on something."

"I'm honoured—Pedro Moore! You mean you don't know *everything!*" His eyes glowed with sarcasm; he looked even more handsome.

"Remember, you taught me to speak French."

"It's nice to be reminded."

"Erskine wants me to run for president of the student council."

"Go on and run. Be a suck. You're quite a suck as it is."

"What do you mean?"

He smiled. "You're in Ms Mackenzie's English class. Only sucks take advanced English. Regular folks take regular. But you want to put on airs, prove you can write better than us and read bigger books and use words that tie up a normal body's tongue."

"You have to give me a better reason than that."

"I got to do two things: eat and shit."

"No you got to pee too and fart and other stuff."

I began walking away. He came after me, pulled me around to face him, and said, "Now you know how I feel."

Really! I didn't.

"The administration use school council presidents to control the students. Remember last year the Oreo gave us a speech against graffiti, that we should be proud of our school? Shit like that? Remember what we did?"

"You guys booed him."

"You fucking right, we booed him. We boo sucks. All student council presidents are sucks. But you're already a suck. Why'd you bother to ask me?"

That night I dreamed that Erskine and I were standing on the ramparts overhanging the sea at Fort George, and I pushed him off and watched him fall into the water below. But as I was thinking of fleeing the scene, I heard him behind me, saying, "You tried to murder me, huh?"

Vince became student council president. His campaign speech was an hour long and contained examples of various things he intended to do. He even talked about making the administration respect the students. Almost everyone voted for him.

He'd always got the highest marks in Erskine's chemistry class and was almost always first in physics. He spoke with an Italian accent; that and his walnut brown hair, which reached down to his shoulders, made me know he wasn't native Indian. His face was round, his eyes were clearest amber; his teeth, exposed by his constant grin, were absolutely even. We were the same height, but he was chubbier. He worshipped Erskine. Then he dated a black girl who was not in our group. One recess the previous October, Priscilla and Agatha had almost come to blows over him (the fathers of both were on the executive of General Wolfe's Parent-Teachers' Association). In the back school yard Priscilla had pulled off her tie and tossed it onto the ground and rushed Agatha with a piece of steel pipe she'd concealed in a shopping bag. Mervyn and I restrained her while Vince wrestled the pipe out of her hand. "I will peel off yo' skin wha' you take off a' night. Heg! You ain't nothing but a heg!" she screamed at Agatha as she tried to wriggle out of our grasp.

"Don' be so selfish. Share Vince," Hollis told her. "You is the best-lookingest one, so you get the waist." He turned to face Agatha, "You take the head. But bring a pillow case to hide yo' face." At that point Ellen cut her eyes in anger at Hollis, and took Agatha by the arm and led her indoors.

"Whore! You whore just coming off the night shift!" Priscilla screamed, a loud, desperate, stretched-out cry, as Agatha disappeared inside the school doors. Then she went limp. Mervyn and I supported her back into the school building. Eddy picked up the tie from where she had thrown it and gave it to her at lunch.

Few trifled with Priscilla. Once when she was ignoring Hollis's sex banter, he told her that his mother said every woman ends up being a whore one way or the other.

"Bet she never tell you how much she charged your father, and bet she don' know who he is?" Priscilla shot back.

She and Hollis were always duelling. One time he said she should make him her pigeon; he'd coo to her all day long. "And make me work the streets all night," she added. Sometimes she'd drag an end of her tie across his cheeks and seductively call him loverboy.

"See," he would say, "you always mamaguying me." She would smile coyly and wink at the other members of the group. He would continue, "If was in a place where we could o' get down to real business, bet you wouldn't o' been doing this!" "Loverboy," she would say again and rub the tie again against his cheek. On one such occasion he said to her, "I better keep me ass quiet. Yo' go bruise me." Winking to us, she replied, "See ya' though. This bway getting bright."

I was sure Vince was sometimes mistaken for a South Asian, and I suspected that was his real reason for hanging around in our group. Once Eddy asked him, "Italian boy, how come you be hanging 'round us? You're too black for the rest o' them Italian guys, or what?"

"He's a dirty white man," Ellen said, studying our reaction to see if she had ventured into unsafe territory.

"Is we girls-them he can't keep 'way from," Mervyn added.

It made sense that he was Erskine's next best candidate.

He and Mervyn never joined in our joking about Erskine. None of the females too, come to think of it. Once Erskine had overheard one of Hollis's lewd remarks and told him, "You're a nuisance. They should castrate you."

When he left, Hollis joked that La Crappe and he should hook up and make "crapplettes."

"Toothpick offspring!" Eddy said, slapping his thighs, giggling.

"They'll catch fire before they come," I said.

"'Cause will be bone rubbing 'gainst bone," Hollis ended.

The first Sunday of December, my mother got home from church two hours late. (I'd found an excuse not to go with her.) She slumped onto the sofa without bothering to take off her church coat—a bear-brown fake fur affair—her winter boots, or her wig. Her yellow scarf was all she removed, listlessly, letting it fall onto the rug. "Brother Carlton box Pastor Draine in the jaw in church today."

I suppressed my laughter. "Did he break it?"

She gave me a reprimanding look.

"Why?"

"Who knows? The devil don't advertise his intentions. We had communion and some of us was still kneeling down praying, and we heard brudu-dup-dup! brudu-dup-dup! with a beat to it. And we all looked up, and there was Carlton up in front of the altar jumping. First we think was the spirit, but he was carrying on like a bull with his eyes open and only the whites you could see. Then he start to go faster and faster, so we all know something was wrong. He used to take pills to control his craziness but he stopped a few months back, saying God grace is all he need to stay well.

"Pastor Draine come down off the pulpit and he called to Carlton in a calming voice like. And then Pastor Draine approach him and tap him 'pon the shoulder. And Carlton turn and stare Pastor Draine trembling like if Pastor Draine was a lion ready for spring on him. Some of us start to move up to the front, in case he get violent. When Carlton see this he give Pastor Draine *one* box in the jaw. Pastor Draine fall to the floor, and then Carlton start to swing his arms and to make for the door. I was in his way and he pushed me down. I get a bad bruise on my left elbow. He gallop out the front door, no coat on.

"Two o' the brothers and a couple sisters went to aid Pastor Draine, and some others put their coats on and went after Carlton, but they didn't find him. Pastor Draine not hurt, only a little shake up." She grew quiet and so did I.

The police picked up Carlton later that day and took him to Douglas Hospital.

On Wednesday evening when Ma came home for her Thursday off, she said, "I don' know what to think about Elfreda. That woman is sure crazy."

"You mean 'the Helephant'!"

"You not supposed to call her that. Let that be on Agnes and Sister Andrews account. I don't like it."

"So what is it about Elder Elfreda? Who is she badmouthing now?"

"Carlton. She saying that Carlton violate the temple of the living God. She say Carlton stop purifying his body like Paul say we must do. And when he put holy wine into his unclean body it was like putting new wine into old bottles, so he exploded."

"Oh, Ma, I wonder where you people get your theology."

"Not *you people*! Elfreda. She got a plaster for everybody sore but none for her own."

"Next time she starts judging people, pull off her wig. Oops! Sorry about that," I said when I saw the intensity of her stare.

She went on as if she hadn't been interrupted. "But we agree with her it was a sign" (the *we* most likely meaning herself and Sister Andrews). "A trial at least. The devil trying us or else is a sign that we not supposed to try and fool God."

"How you know Carlton was trying to fool God?"

She paused a long while before replying. "I don' know. Jesus tell me I musn' judge nobody. I leave God to judge Carlton. But I know the Bible say, 'Seek ye first the kingdom of heaven and its righteousness and all things shall be added unto you.' He send the Comforter for comfort us. Is like the hymn says," and she began to sing:

In shady green pastures so rich and so sweet,

God leads His dear children along.
Where the cool flow of water bathes the weary one's feet,
God leads His dear children along.

Some through the water and some through the flood.
Some through the fire but all through the blood.
Some through great sorrow, but God gives a song
In the night season and all the day long.

There was nothing to say. Theirs was "the way, the truth and the light." All others were damned. Without friends, my mother needed her religion: its rituals of self-valorization, its sedation of her fears of a society that needed her to clean its dirt but saw her as dirt. She and the rest of the congregation were hungry for salvation and had no interest in examining what they were fed.

They'd come to Canada looking for green pastures beside still waters; the Lachine Canal bordering their warehouse church was still enough. But the Lord their shepherd had delegated the responsibility without the know-how to Draine, who couldn't multiply loaves and fishes but could tell stories: about Job, about Abraham with the knife at Isaac's throat, about Paul purifying his body "as gold is tried in fire," about Stephen dying under a shower of stones. Christ had borne their cross and yet they had to carry it, "Till death shall set us free, / And then go home, a crown to wear—/ A crown of victory." And at times they wondered why it was so heavy, why day in, day out they had to reenact the crucifixion and tried to find in their hymns cushioning to stack their fragile contradictions.

In shady green pastures so rich and so sweet.

Faith that they dearly hoped would one day move mountains.

Heavily laden they certainly were, within—for Zilla and Elfreda, also without—and in labour, but the promised deliverance and rest unto their weary souls proved elusive. Perhaps this was why they clung to their "home" superstitions, didn't fully trust the promises of biblical religion. Ma hid her nail clippings and broken bits of hair from imaginary enemies who might work witchcraft on her; Elder Elfreda carried garlic in her purse; Sister Agnes and Sister Andrews wore *maljeu* strings.

Carlton's drama was positive in some ways. The bruise on Ma's arm turned black; she developed a fever. Draine came to see her. I was home, it was the first day of the Christmas holidays. Roasting with fever, Ma nevertheless insisted that I go out and buy a cake so she could entertain Draine with tea.

He arrived sometime around four and seemed to me to be gossiping. They talked about "a fine Sunday-school teacher, quite promising in the Lord's ministry," into whose "gills" Satan had got his hooks. "Many are called but few are chosen," Ma quoted.

Seated on one of the dining chairs, I listened attentively. Draine was on the armchair, Ma on the sofa. I was conscious of how dingy our place was, of the ugliness of the tangerine rug, threadbare at the front door and also at the entrance to the kitchen and bathroom. I no longer smelled the apartment but I was sure Draine could.

"Pedro is quite a big fellow," Draine said, turning to look at me, his jolly pink face contrasting against his black shirt and white ministerial collar. "How old is he, Sister Millicent?"

"He going be sixteen January coming, Pastor Draine."

"Pedro, don't you have any stirrings—any kind of workings up in the pit of your stomach? Any desire to give your heart to the Lord?"

I prefer to keep it for myself. In reception classes, Reverend Abrahams had told us to tell proselytizers (I'd learned the word from him) that "the Lord expects humans to live human and humane lives and, above all, to be forgiving and kind. The rest would take care of itself."

"Your Lord's too cruel for my liking!"

"Shame on you!" Draine replied. "With a name like Pedro you could become the church's very foundation. 'Thou art Peter and upon this rock I will build my church.'"

And with a name like yours you could be its sewer. Aloud I said, "I am not rock, Pastor Draine." All the contempt I felt for my mother's religion was ready to spew. It was probably, too, because I was annoyed with her: there she was roasting with fever and yet worrying about offering Pastor Draine tea. There was a surreal quality to what was happening. Draine sensed it and stopped speaking.

"Pedro! Apologize to Pastor Draine for your rudeness."

"Over my dead body!" I could not believe I'd said that.

"I say you will apologize."

"And I say I will not."

She got up from the sofa, feebly, to come over to me.

"Why don't you stay quiet? Aren't you sick?" I told her.

"Sit down, Sister Millicent. It's all right. It's the adolescent in him. Most adolescents are like that, rebellious."

He disarmed me. I was primed to go. I wanted somebody to fight with, but he was a far smarter man than I thought.

"You will burn in hell fire for this," Ma said.

"And so will you—for a lot more than this."

"Peace, Sister Millicent."

"I'm going out," I told her, knowing she was depending on me to make tea for Pastor Draine. If looks were bullets, I'd have been shot.

When I got back she lay on her sofa bed covered in sweat. "Take a look at this arm. It hurting me to death."

Her arm was swollen even more and the black spot was spreading. I suspected gangrene. "Get dressed. I'm taking you to the hospital." I called a cab, and we went to the Emergency at the Jewish General. The nurse at the reception took her temperature, examined her arm, and called the doctor. He admitted her right away. She stayed in hospital until December 27. They lacerated the infection and gave her anti biotics intravenously through her good arm. She found out then that she was diabetic. I never asked her if that was a punishment from God.

On December 31, the day she returned to work, Mrs Wilton fired her. She said her children were grown and she no longer needed household help. She gave Ma two weeks of paid vacation, took her into the garage, where she kept things she hadn't got around to discarding, and told her to have her pick. "All the time the woman was taking me for some sort o' buzzard!"

I remembered the empty Ovaltine tins Mrs Manley had given Grama and I wondered if the wealthy everywhere behaved like this.

A week later Ma found fulltime work with the agency that Sister Andrews worked for as a daily cleaning woman. She was assigned homes in Hampstead. Now she was home every day. There wasn't space in that basement apartment for the two of us. I stayed out as long as I could, at the school library and at the Côte des Neiges Public Library.

I continued to go to the Sunday morning services with her, but only when I felt like it. On occasion, though, I teased her. "Ma, if Lucifer had won the war in heaven, guess who would have been the Devil?"

She stared at me, dumbfounded. "Pedro, you musn' say things like that."

"But it's true, Ma. If the Devil had won, his supporters would have written the Bible, and they'd have called God a tyrant, and you'd be singing hymns to the Devil."

She blanched, took a deep breath, and finally shook her head. "I just have to pray for you some more."

Once she fought back—at least that's what I thought. "See, how you fresh? Good thing I didn' breast-feed you. If you was a girl it might o' been different. All you men do is break we hearts, and you all crawl over us from the time you born, and think we's at your disposal." She spoke staring at the floor, her face twitching slightly.

One time I pushed her to admit that she did not know the meaning of the word Pastor. After telling her it meant shepherd, I added that she was therefore sheep whose wool was regularly sheared. She picked up the broom and threatened to hit me with the handle. But I ignored her and told her that that was what her tithe was. Pastor Draine lived in Mount Royal, most likely in a house paid for by his wife. But it was more fun to think it had been bought with his congregation's tithes. I said other things too, capriciously. She would remind me of some of them while she lay dying.

I hadn't come to these opinions all by myself. Mrs Mackenzie was fond of Mark Twain. "To the Person Sitting in Darkness" was one of the pieces we'd had to do a long essay on. We'd also analyzed "Letter to the Earth" and "A War Prayer," and she'd pushed us to reflect on why people pray and whether there was any truth to how Twain portrayed prayer. Thereafter, I could not listen to my mother's congregation praying without seeing it as a wish list, and whenever the young people were made to stand up and sing *Saviour While My Heart Is Tender*, I stood (meeting my mother halfway was how I saw it) but I did not sing.

24

FROM THE TIME MAYNES came on staff in September 1975 he had problems. He was a melon-coloured Barbadian in his late fifties, with spindly legs and atrophied hips. His gigantesque gut counterpoised by a huge behind made him grotesquely symmetrical. He was pregnant back and front, we said, and wondered if he could walk down a steep hill without keeling over. With a few feathers in his behind, ducks would check him out—this from Hollis. The fat on his chest had configured into two prominent tits, and Hollis insisted that if Maynes were still there the following Christmas—we were sure he wouldn't last—we should collect money and buy him a bra. Within a week we'd renamed him Pumpkin. (Today our adolescent cruelty embarrasses me—and not because I have much that's unpleasant to look at. Fate's imprecise hand has botched us all, some more visibly than others, those flawed inside the worst botched. I understand now what Ma meant by the body being a mere container and why she was mostly silent when Agnes and Zilla joked about Elfreda's weight.)

Pumpkin wore grey tweed blazers, navy-blue or black slacks, white shirts, black ties. His gleaming (always black) leather shoes resounded all over the gym. Except for the odd occasion when he removed his jacket, he conducted his gym classes dressed that way. Whenever he mounted the platform where his desk was, he wheezed like an asthmatic horse. During his first lesson, he held the lectern firmly with both arms, steadying himself, and read a prepared text, proclaiming, "Based on my animadversions I affirm emphatically that men in contemporary society are effeminate, deficient in manly discipline and virtue. I'm sure most of you boys are unfamiliar with what it is to have a man in your life—"

We laughed.

"I mean masculine influence. To be a man is to be disciplined, to bear pain without complaining, to be stoic, to be ascetic, to be able to will strenuous work from an exhausted body.

"I will make men of you. No fifteen sit-ups for me—you will do thirty. I will double *all* your exercises. Triple them even. In your peregrinations along life's tortuous road you will with unfailing gratitude remember me."

"Will we have to come back after school?" I asked, smiling. Everyone else was too.

"Why?"

"'Cause there ain't enough time, *stupid!*" Eddy said, softening the last word so that only those nearest to him heard.

"I will find a way! Trust me," Maynes retorted.

"You could do with a little exercise yourself," Dreyfuss muttered. Everyone laughed.

"Unless I can share the joke, you will be doing sixty sit-ups. I would eliminate the humour if I were you!"

A few of us cleared our throats and set off a throat-clearing cacophony, complete with swallowing and hand gestures. But Maynes didn't take our bait, chose not to spout any more foolishness.

Hollis, Eddy, and Vince were the members of Mervyn's group in my phys ed class. In the cafeteria, Hollis said, "I sure Maynes torturing we to keep we weight down. He ain't want we fellars to gi'e he no competition."

We had Maynes's class on Tuesdays, Thursdays, and Fridays. The first Thursday with him, I could not go beyond twenty sit-ups. Wearing a lurid, disfiguring smile that exposed the wide gaps between his incisors, he made us move in time to the raising and lowering of his arm. The pace was brutal.

"Moore"—he called us all by our surnames—"who authorized you to stop? Return here at lunch."

On my way to the gym, I met Hollis. Pumpkin was punishing him because he'd told Pumpkin to get real: "One sit-up and, man, they'll carry you out on a stretcher. And you want me to do thirty!"

When we entered the gym, Pumpkin mounted his pedestal, waited for his wheezing to subside, and ordered, "Okay, Brathwaite, for your insolence, you will do sixty push-ups."

"Not a solitary one!" Hollis said, staring straight into Pumpkin's reddish eyes.

"Now you will have to do ninety," Pumpkin countered.

Hollis sucked his teeth. "You don't have the right to keep us in at lunch."

"I make the rules!"

"No, you don't."

"Oh! Swallow your tongue! You dolt!"

"You hear what he call me! You hear what he call me!"

"And do you think you're Einstein? You're in vocational classes!"

"You ain't exactly a candle," Hollis countered, shaking his head and beckoning to me. "Come!" Hollis began heading towards the door. "And, you," he threatened, turning to wag his finger at Pumpkin, "my mother will sue you. You jackass!"

I hadn't moved.

"Go!" Pumpkin shouted at me with a dismissive hand wave. "LEAVE! BEAT IT! You black children are blighted. All of you! GET OUT!"

Outside, Hollis laughed. "My mother say to ignore he, yes. He another one o' those half-white pompous jackass; they turn foolish 'cause they didn' expect to get this far. I sure he mother was a whore and he father a sailor man she whored with."

Next day, I had Pumpkin last period. He made us do fifteen sit-ups, and acted as if nothing had gone amiss the previous day, as if he were an amnesiac.

Eddy, even though he hung out with us, was always trying to prove he was superior to us. He was different from West Indians, he said, because he was Canadian: "Born here." All other Blacks were Jamaicans and "fucken dummies" who talked funny, ate monkeys, and couldn't "tell shit from silage."

"Now, is that a way to talk about your breakfast cereal?" Hollis teased him.

He lunged at Hollis. But Mervyn grabbed his arms and held them behind his back and lectured him about his temper.

He didn't look like anybody's child. Often his clothes were torn or filthy or crumpled as if they'd been fished out from discarded things. His hair was uncombed and multicoloured from lint. His threats to kick in teeth, break heads, or rip out guts were constant. No one took them seriously.

He took a mixture of regular and general classes because he never did homework. We tended to go easy on him, because it was clear that something was wrong: his temper, his dirty, dishevelled clothes, his frequent absence, not to mention his foul language. Even so, sparks often flew between Hollis and him. "I sure is yo' mother that break yo' left leg to slow you down," Hollis once told him. "But it ain't work. Keep going like you doing and see if somebody don' break the right one too."

Once Maynes told Eddy to "move that left leg!" And Eddy replied, "Up your ass!" All activity stopped. After a thirty-second pause, Maynes ordered us to carry on with our exercises. That day he dismissed us five minutes early and kept back Eddy. In the shower three days later—he'd been absent the previous two—Eddy said, "Good thing he 'pologized! Shit-coloured sonofabitch! My mother would o' kicked his yellow ass to a yellow pulp!"

"Your mother?" I asked.

"Go straighten your fucken chin, man! A fucken pig's yours, if you ask me! Look at your fucken mouth, man! Like a pig's snout. And look at your skin! Go soak in bleach, man! Fuck you!"

He behaved as if his malformed leg gave him the right to taunt others with impunity. In Maynes's class, when we were not working out, we sat on the floor with our legs tucked under us. If we had to take notes, we supported the notebooks on our laps. Vince sat behind Dreyfuss, Eddy beside Vince, Hollis beside Eddy, and I beside Hollis. Often Hollis would stealthily pick up a few strands of hair from Dreyfuss's wig and make a yanking gesture with his other hand. We'd watch intently and call him chicken under our breaths. He in turn would gesture to Eddy and me that we should yank off Dreyfuss's wig. Once I went through the motion, and Hollis grabbed my arm in an attempt to complete the task, but I managed only to hit Dreyfuss, who turned to see Hollis looking as if he were completely absorbed by whatever Maynes was writing on the board. One Tuesday morning Eddy accepted the dare and the next thing we saw was the whole mess of blond hair in Vince's lap. A shocked Dreyfuss—teeth bared, pate bare and reddening rapidly, eyes turned to brimstones, arms and fingers in a strangling pose—turned to face Vince, who shouted, "Don't look at me; I didn't pull off your wig." The class exploded in laughter. Maynes, who probably didn't know that Dreyfuss was bald, began to laugh too, a high-pitched whinny, which we found equally comic. Eddy got up and said, "Sir, I have to go to the bathroom," and hop-dropped it out of there. We didn't see him again until the following Monday. A week later, he was telling Dreyfuss, "Man, if you ain't got sense enough to keep that wig from falling off, attach it with a elastic under your chin. He-he-he!"

Pumpkin loved to pick on the clumsy among us. The week following his showdown with Hollis, he told Tim Chang to, "get those chopsticks moving."

"Moore, put energy in those legs; too much stored in your behind." *Melt some o' the lard in your gut!*

The big explosion came the third week of the second semester—a Tuesday, the period before lunch. Maynes was at the board writing down information about thigh and calf muscles. We were squatted on the floor half-listening to him. Apart from the sound of the chalk on the board the only sound was the hum of the fluorescent lamps. Only Vince and a couple of other students cared enough to take notes. Eddy held a feather behind Vince's neck. Vince jumped. We laughed.

Maynes suspected Eddy. "Come here!" he said, beckoning to Eddy.

Eddy remained seated.

"You bonny clabber . . . , I said come here!"

"Oh! Oh!" some of us let out. Maynes had stopped short of calling Eddy "a bonny clabber nigger." It was the usual put-down for "half-whites" who fled from their blackness; the description didn't quite fit Eddy.

"You fucken tub o' guts! You barrel o' lard!" Eddy exploded. "You heap o' dog shit!"

"Get out!" Maynes said, just loud enough for the class to hear.

"Make me!" Eddy said inversely loud. "I'm going home for my knife. I'm gon cut off your fucken dried-out balls! Fuck you, man! FUCK YOU! FUCK YOU! FUCK YOU!" The veins stood out on his forehead, and he brandished clenched fists and bared his teeth as each Fuck you! detonated. The last one resounded from every corner of the gym.

Spit was at the corners of his mouth and on his chin.

Maynes came towards him.

"Don't fucken touch me!" he told Maynes.

Eddy made his way out of the group and began to leave the gym. When he got to the door, he picked up a chair there and hurled it against the wall. It fragmented. The rest I did not witness.

Mr Goering's shop was next door. He'd heard the commotion and was headed toward the gym. He met Eddy at the door. He asked Eddy what happened, and Eddy told him to get the fuck out of his way. Goering tried to prevent him from moving on, and Eddy began swinging his arms. Then Goering landed a blow to Eddy's jaw that sent him spinning and eventually down on the floor.

We got out of the gym in time to see Eddy flat on his back, blood on the front of his shirt and trickling down his chin, and groaning. Body-builder Goering stood trembling over him. We were sure Eddy was playing it up for what it was worth; it lacked only the TV camera. But his lower jaw had been fractured.

Students, white and black, confirmed Eddy's story. A teacher, who hadn't been present, contradicted their testimony. She said that Eddy had taken aim at Goering, and Goering had hit him to protect himself. We speculated about what went on between her and Goering after school, or, for that matter, during.

Eddy was suspended indefinitely. He was past sixteen and could therefore be expelled. Both Goering and Maynes showed up at school the next morning.

"You see the muscles on Goering?" Mervyn stated his thoughts aloud. "What he want to box Eddy for?"

I didn't have Goering for a teacher, but seven of the guys in our group did. He treated his students to fried chicken and french fries every end of term. He was "jokify, but wacky." He kept posters of pigs on the walls of his shop and a pet pig at home, because pigs were "superior to human beings."

A week earlier, the senior history teacher, Saltzer, who never missed a chance to tell us he'd been a member of the Green Berets, had hit Priscilla. I had got the highest mark in his grade-ten history class, but many black students felt he was racist. Priscilla had asked him why there was no mention of Blacks in our history text.

"Simple," he said. "You people just started arriving here a few years ago. People have to do important things to get mentioned in history."

"What about the all-black regiment that served in World War I?"

"Who cares?"

"And the Chinese," Priscilla taunted him—"'they were imported to do manual work on the railways,' right? How come the book doesn't say white people didn't let them vote or practise any profession?"

"When you become a historian, you'll correct it."

"You call yourself a *historian*? What you know 'bout history? Bet if is Jews they'd left out, you wouldn't answer the same way?" There was disagreement over whether she called him a schmuck or a skunk, but none over what happened next. He ordered her out of the class. She remained seated. He yanked her to her feet. She pushed him, he kicked her, and she slapped him.

Bellamy suspended Priscilla for a week, but no action that we knew of was taken against Saltzer.

During lunch Vince told Mervyn and me of a meeting with Erskine at three. Erskine wanted a delegation of students to meet with Bellamy to demand that some sort of action be taken against Maynes and Goering. We planned to meet the following morning in the library.

I was surprised to find Dreyfuss at the meeting. I'd had only one other personal encounter with him. One day at Zaney's, I was trying on jeans in anticipation of buying a pair. He came in and did the same thing. At one point he told me to keep the sales clerk busy. Later he came over to ask her for help. He winked at me. When he and I left the store, he asked me if I'd scored. I didn't answer.

On our way to the bus stop, his browless, lidless eyes a peacock blue—if he'd had tail feathers they'd have been spread—he opened his Adidas bag and showed me a pair of jeans. "You make me waste all my charm on her, and you didn't take nothing! Man, get a grip! I told her she looks like the girl that stole my heart and then moved away with her parents. The butter was fairly drippin' off her when I shut my trap. And you didn't take nothing! Man, you should be horse-whipped."

Our demands were mild. Too mild, Dreyfuss and Vince felt. Erskine said a symbolic victory was all we needed; our purpose wasn't to humiliate anybody. We would tell Bellamy that Maynes was the cause of Eddy's anger and was therefore partly responsible for Eddy's reactions. Goering should at least apologize to the students, at a school assembly, for his conduct. After all, he was the adult, Eddy the student. Vince was to make the appointment at recess and let us know the result at lunch.

At lunch Mrs Henry was present. Vince said Bellamy told him to get lost. He didn't negotiate with students. Before we could respond to Vince, Johnston walked into the library and broke into the meeting.

"I know what you people are up to," he said, passing his hand over his closely cropped brown hair. He squinted badly and looked even shorter; his blue suit, probably the same one I had seen him in my first time at General Wolfe, hugged his waist tightly.

"Don't think we don't know what you folks are up to!" Johnston said, his voice cracking.

"Mr Johnston," Erskine said, his teeth clenched, "we are in the middle of a meeting. You are interrupting us."

Flushed, Johnston removed his glasses, wiped them on his jacket, and left the library.

"They're not going to listen to us. We should start a petition to have Goering and Maynes and Saltzer fired," Dreyfuss said.

We bought the petition idea but mentioned Saltzer's name only in connection with the kick he'd given Priscilla, about which nothing had been done. We would demand the suspension of Goering and Maynes and the reinstatement of Eddy. That afternoon (Thursday) Mrs Henry and Vince prepared the petition.

By Friday morning it was ready and in circulation. Students signed it eagerly. We were aiming for five hundred signatures. At 2.20 a student came to world history class to say that I was wanted at the principal's office.

Vince, Dreyfuss, and Mervyn were already in there. Five copies of the petition were spread out on Bellamy's desk.

"Do you know anything about this?" Bellamy asked, holding up one of the sheets, his nose like a beak in his triangular face, his artificial arm in his lap, its doll-pink fingers looking more alive than his own fishbelly white.

I looked at Mervyn, Dreyfuss, and Vince.

Mervyn nodded.

"Yes."

Bellamy crumpled the sheet he held and three of the others. "All of you go get your books and report back here. I'm suspending the whole kit and caboose of you—for two weeks! Whippersnappers the whole bunch of you! The nerve! Not yet toilet-trained and think you can run the school system!" He picked up the telephone receiver and told his secretary to find two substitutes to cover Mrs Henry's and Mr Erskine's classes, and to ask them to report to his office at once.

While we waited for our suspension letters, we heard loud shouting in Bellamy's office.

25

IT WAS PAST 3.30 WHEN Erskine and Mrs Henry left Bellamy's office. Erskine's forehead was glowing and his eyes contracted with rage. We headed to the McDonald's at the shopping centre.

"Sir, why're we taking all this garbage?" Dreyfuss asked. "Why we don't have a student strike?"

"Yes," Vince agreed. "Why don't we?"

Mervyn and I were silent. All four of them looked at Mervyn and me. "It's not a good idea. They'll make you out to be the villains. Take it from me. I'm talking from experience," Erskine said.

"We won't involve you. You won't have to do nothing. Just cooperate with us," Dreyfuss countered.

We planned to meet again at McDonald's at lunch the following Monday. There were about twenty-five students in all attending the McDonald's meeting. Our suspensions banned us from the school premises, but Dreyfuss and Vince had gone there that morning, told the students that a walkout was planned for Wednesday, and had even managed to recruit class reps to disseminate information. Vince had also written a parody of the school song, which he'd photocopied and now gave to us.

Mrs Henry and Erskine continued to insist that the walkout wasn't a good idea. "I for it," Mervyn said in the dry, unemotional, hesitant way he spoke. He folded his arms and pressed them against his diaphragm. Most of the students applauded.

Once Mervyn got on board I too had to embark.

We told the class reps to come back at three for their final instructions. The four of us, "leaders," stayed on at McDonald's to work out the plans. Dreyfuss would inform the radio and television stations, Vince would make copies of the petition and suspension letters for the media, I was to compose the chanting slogans. All the class reps had been asked to get three members from their classes to supervise the students, to prevent them from harassing teachers and students who wanted to enter the school. We wanted no damage whatsoever done to school property.

Our plan was to walk around the school chanting, "Goering's a criminal; he sent Eddy to hospital" (actually Eddy was at home with his jaw wired, but the students wouldn't have known the truth). "Adolf-Hitler-Bellamy, we're not in Nazi Germany." Those were the only two of my slogans they kept. *"Slavery went out with the nineteenth century"* was one that wasn't kept. I laugh now at the naïveté of it. "Want a bit of advice?" Dreyfuss asked. "Next time you making slogans, smoke a little pot. You ain't writin' for Ms Mackenzie's class." Dreyfuss, his eyes at their bluest, offered to rent a bullhorn and lead the chanting. It suited his booming, gravelly, growling voice.

On Wednesday morning when we arrived, police cars were already blocking all access to the school premises. Twenty-five police officers were at the site (close to a hundred more arrived during the course of the morning). Every TV and radio station and newspaper had sent a reporter. We were not allowed to cross the police barricade.

Erskine, Mrs Henry, and, to my surprise, Ms Mackenzie were there. About a hundred students were already on site. The police threatened to arrest us. We looked at Erskine in dismay and he shook his head. Ms Mackenzie stayed closest to the police.

Within half an hour, there were at least five hundred students at the scene. Dreyfuss waited in the shopping centre, aware that the police would have otherwise confiscated the bullhorn. By a quarter to nine, Dreyfuss began the slogans, and reporters with cameramen in tow began climbing over one another to interview us.

Dreyfuss managed to get in twenty minutes of slogans before the police seized the horn. But the chanting continued, and when the crowd got tired of the group's chants it improvised its own, like "We want Bellamy. We want the mother fucker." We sang Hollis's "Salami Song" about Bellamy's complexion, which was fish-belly white. When he returned in September, it looked soiled, but within a couple of weeks it was again fish belly. Hollis in the lead, we'd sung the "Salami Song" hip-hop style on many occasions when the teacher on duty was out of earshot:

Fishbelly
Bell-a-my
Is a white
Sa-la-mi
Wrap 'im inna plastic
Fo' his mam-my

Now with Hollis leading us we chanted it at various tempos, even in call-response with spurts of applause in between—variations Hollis hadn't dreamt of.

We followed with Priscilla's:

Two-four-six-eight:
These damned teachers are full of hate.
Eight-six-four-two:
We hate the sons-o'-bitches too.

And Vince's send up of the school song:

Land of the north, we've stolen you
From folks who gave hospitality.
And from then till now it's all about
Disease and liquor and being knocked about.

Teach us to bear the yoke in youth
To withstand scorn and awful brutes,
That we may spread humanest creeds
And undo our parents' abhorrent deeds.

Land of the north, we wish to say,
We'll struggle for justice every day,
Respect all races, return natives their places
Be circumspect in every way.

We were proud of Vince.

By eleven there were well over a thousand people at the site, a third of whom were not students. Many were skippers from the other, nearby high school. At one point we came upon a reporter, wearing a white shaggy coat, looking every bit like a polar bear, urging students to hurl stones at the police. When a couple of women intervened, the reporter and his cameraman, dressed in army fatigues, pushed the students violently to escape from them. I later found out that Ms Mackenzie had placed several adults at strategic points to prevent us from becoming overenthusiastic and to discourage the police from clubbing us.

At 11.45 word reached us that Goering, who along with the rest of the staff was inside the school, wanted to talk to us. Vince told me to go tell Erskine. He was at the opposite end from us. The police stood like a blue wall in front of us, their batons dangling. The least difficult route to get to Erskine would have been to walk in front of them, but I'd heard too many stories of the police hitting or firing first and asking questions later. As long as I wasn't naked I could be armed; and about the first thing every black boy learns about Canadian society is that it considers him dangerous. Eventually we proceeded without telling Erskine.

Using the horn the police had taken from Dreyfuss, Vince told the crowd, "Mr Goering's in there. He's gonna talk to us."

"No!"

"Fuck him!"

"Get Goering!"

"He's coming to talk to us," Vince insisted.

"Sellout! Sellout! Sellout!"

A chant, a veritable boulder crashing into a lake, swept the crowd:

Two-four-six-eight:
We won't negotiate.
Eight-six-four-two:
What the fuck is wrong with you?

Goering came out the main door, moved slowly under the archway as if in pain, and came towards us. He was hit by about half a dozen snowballs and a couple of eggs. Most fell in front of him or shot past on either side of him. "Stop throwing things!" Vince told the crowd. The odd missile continued to be hurled.

Goering took the horn, yellow egg yolk dripping from the right sleeve of his black overcoat. "I'm sorry, very sorry, that my conduct is responsible for you being here today." He stopped as if he didn't know what to say. He seemed drained of blood and his voice quavered. "Believe me, I'm ashamed of myself. I always intended to apologize for my conduct." For a moment he seemed unable to continue, but he added, "While walking out here, I decided I'll not return to the classroom for the rest of this school year. That's all I want to say. Forgive me for the trouble I've caused you."

He gave the microphone back to Vince and headed back to the building. There was total silence.

"You've all heard Mr Goering," Vince broke the silence. "I think Mr Goering did the right thing. We thank all of you for coming and supporting student rights. Now we ask you to go home peacefully. Tomorrow when we come back to school, we must respect our teachers and put all this behind us."

"You behaved yourselves well. Now we want you to go on home like good boys and girls," a police officer said.

The odd student gave him the finger. The talking returned and the crowd began dispersing. I went over to where Vince was talking with the police officer. Within the minute Mrs Henry, Dreyfuss, Erskine, Ms Mackenzie and Mervyn joined us. The police officer, his eyes bulging as if he'd taken speed, complimented Vince for doing a fine job maintaining order.

"You're not afraid to teach them?" he asked the teachers.

"This one," Ms Mackenzie said, placing an arm around me and giggling girlishly, "is my best student. Come on all of you. I'm taking everybody to a Chinese restaurant for lunch. I want to celebrate! This is the greatest day of my life! I will get my old-age pension after all. I didn't think you young people had it in you. You chaps have got guts. Aren't we proud of you!" She turned and did a little dance.

Erskine nodded, suddenly looking boyish.

Mrs Henry beamed.

The Monday following the demo, Mervyn told me that Erskine wanted to see me the next day at lunch to discuss my CEGEP (college) application. I had already seen Mrs Black about it, and she had suggested I apply to Dawson. "For some reason Blacks and Italians seem to prefer Dawson." She grinned her gargoyle grin, showing her teeth at their worse.

Next day Erskine read my application, swallowed three of his soda pills, and took a deep breath. His first explosion was at me for choosing to go into the humanities. "What is it with you black children? Why don't you all have any ambition? You leave everything lucrative and prestigious to white people. Why are you all so afraid of competition?"

He stopped speaking and looked down at the application. "Why your first choice is Dawson?"

I told him what Mrs Black had said.

"She didn't tell you anything else?"

"No."

"You're sure?" His stare was intense. He shook his head as if he was trying to dislodge water from his inner ear or undo stiffness in his neck. "You and I will go to see her tomorrow."

Next day Mrs Black, smiling cautiously behind her desk, said, "Be reasonable, Mr Erskine. If you want to discuss my job, we will have to do so alone."

"Why didn't you tell this boy he has the grades to win a scholarship to Marianopolos?"

She shrugged her shoulders.

"And what is this 'Blacks and Italians prefer Dawson?' What's Vanier? A Yeshiva at public expense? The other day you declared in the staff room that Palestine belongs to the Jews by divine decree —there's no divine decree that says Blacks must be ghettoized at Dawson. You already programme enough of them into dead-end courses."

"That's unfair."

"Unfair! They are twenty percent of the school population. They make up eighty percent of the general and vocational classes. What are you doing? Preparing the next crop of maids and factory workers?"

"This is absurd."

"Only to you. You will hear about it. I need a blank application, please."

She turned around, took one from a folder and gave it to him.

"Thanks. Let's go, Pedro."

Back at the lab, he said to me, "So you're going into humanities! What sort of lunatic are you? If you work hard you won't have trouble getting into medicine or agriculture. Look, humanities is about words, words white people use to make Blacks hate themselves. Words don't feed hungry people. They don't cure sickness." He grew quiet for a while. "People with power hold on to it—to enrich themselves and control others. The advice they give is always in *their* interest. Intelligence," he continued, his voice now tinged with sadness, "must benefit the community, not the caprices of the few lucky to have it. You and I must use it to better the lot of *our people*." I couldn't argue with him, but I knew I wanted to study literature.

26

HOLY THURSDAY AFTERNOON, about six weeks after the demo, I was returning to my locker to get a textbook I'd forgotten and ran into Alfred. He accompanied me back and told me he expected to fail his courses.

"Why?"

"I don't do homework. And sometimes I doze off in class. Commitments, man!"

"What sort of commitments?"

He laughed. He placed a finger behind my ear, held it up, and looked at it. "See? It's still wet behind there. You ain't gonna understand. Let's leave it at that."

We walked to the shopping centre, where I'd intended to buy a shirt. Alfred bought me a coke. While I was trying on a shirt Hollis came by. I changed my mind about the shirt I'd selected. I was afraid they'd criticize my choice, since I couldn't afford the latest styles. I'd seen the scorn they heaped on others and protected myself from it. They left shortly before I did.

I picked up my school bag and headed for the exit. When I got to the door, a buzzer went off, and two security officers came towards me.

One of them, flushed, overweight, and wheezing, with pistol in his holster, pointed to my school bag and said, "Open her up." I did and saw a shirt in it.

"Let's see the bill."

"I didn't put it in there."

They both laughed. The one who'd accosted me said into his pager, "We've netted one." *Y'en a un dans la trappe.* Within a minute, a short, square-faced, white man with a craglike forehead and a lancelike goatee came. A scar in his left eyebrow separated it into roughly equal portions and continued for about an inch up his forehead. His eyes seemed never to blink. "Get the police," he ordered in French to the one with the pager. With thumb and forefinger he played with his turquoise tie, as he stared at me in silence. I concluded he was the manager.

People, including some General Wolfe students, began to gather around. The manager told me to follow him. In his office he gave me a seat and asked whether I was a student at General Wolfe. He took my student ID, copied some information from it onto a pad, and, without looking up at me, said, "Your mother's name?"

"Millicent Brady. No, No, Isis Moore."

He frowned, smacked his lips, and gave me a prolonged stare.

"I didn't put that shirt in my bag," I said.

He said something into the intercom on his desk. A security officer showed up a couple of minutes later. The manager went into an adjoining office and closed the door. I sat there under the surveillance of the security officer until the police, two young, smiling French Canadians—one tall and wellbuilt, the other short and already overweight—arrived.

The tall, well-built one, his auburn hair slicked down, his brown eyes amused, asked the manager in French if it was my first time.

The manager nodded. Next they checked out my ID and spoke my name into their cell phone. The voice coming back said in French ". . . One of the organizers of the school demonstration. . ." *Un des organisateurs de la récente manif.*

"Are your guys through with him?" the short officer, who had been silent, gleefully asked the manager and winked, his black short hair standing on his head like bristles, his skin a pasty white.

"Yes. Only when they're repeats," the manager replied.

Both officers smiled. They searched my pockets, told me to put my hands behind my back and handcuffed me.

"I didn't put that shirt in my bag."

"No, you didn't. The Holy Ghost did," the short, pasty skin one said. *Ouais, cétait le Saint Esprit.*

"And the name of your mudder is la *Sainte Vièrge*, hein?" the tall one mocked.

"'E don't got no mudder," the short one continued, switching to English.

They led me out to the police car.

My forehead felt cold. Sweat ran down my sides and dripped from my fingertips behind my back. Keep calm! Keep calm! I repeated to myself, my eyes closed. I didn't want to see anyone I recognized. When I got to the police station, I told myself, I would call Mr Erskine. At summer school the black studies teacher had told us it was my legal right and I should refuse to answer their questions if a lawyer wasn't present. A student had told him he was joking. "When those guys arrest us, man, the only thing they don't do is leave marks on our bodies."

They helped me out of the car, and I walked stiffly into the station, my arms shackled behind me. They sat me down hunched forward in a shallow chair, left me in handcuffs, and ignored me for more than an hour. A policeman came by then and asked how I was doing. I didn't answer. "Christ de nègre hautain! Taberwette! You know the rights!" he said, laughing as he turned and headed down a corridor.

Half an hour later, three officers—not the ones who'd arrested me—took me into a small room. In it were a cupboard, on which stood a circular, loud-ticking clock; a desk no wider than a foot with three chairs on the side where they were and a single chair on the side where they made me sit at times and at times stand. They left on the handcuffs.

"I would like to make a phone call," I said, my head lowered.

"Did we ask you a question?" the shortest of the three shouted at me. He lifted my chin brusquely and held it in his hand for about ten seconds and began to smile. "Hey guys, check this chin out. What's wrong with your chin, matey? Some white man caught you humping his wife and rearranged it?" He was stoop-shouldered and had a muscular frame that reminded me of Goering. He was obviously not French Canadian, was from Australia, South Africa or Rhodesia, some place where *a is pronounced i* and *e* has a soft *a* sound. His colleague in the middle had short blond hair, an oval face with a round chin, green eyes with tiny pupils, and bad breath. Their partner, on the left, had glossy black hair, a cherublike face with a thick handle-bar mustache, double chins, and a big gut. None of them wore badges or nametags. The anglophone cracked his knuckles occasionally, and Cherub balled his fists and boxed his knuckles gently against each other, all the while staring at me. This lasted for about ten minutes. They would do so for a few seconds, then become totally silent for a minute or two, intervals in which the clock's ticking behind me sounded increasingly ominous, and then resume, never taking their eyes off me for more than a split second.

Following this, the anglophone, seated directly in front of me, began opening up a set of files that he'd taken from the cupboard directly in back of him. He showed me pictures of several people and wanted to know if I knew them. Several times he made me stand and looked me over. "Hard to tell you guys one from another." Then he stood me against a measure on the wall and took my height and recorded it.

"Now, Matey," he said, about twenty minutes into the interrogation, "see this lass here." He pointed to a photograph at which I barely looked. "A real bewte, en't she? Women like her can send a man to jail. And some men will swear it's worth it. Now tell us what colour drawers she had on the night you fixed her, like the real he-man you are?"

"How you expect him to notice that?" Roundchin asked, his eyes like green marbles. "You wasn't interested in the colour of her drawers, right, Matey?"

"Come on," Cherub added, "set us straight, Matey. No black man about to screw a white woman got time to note the colour of her drawers. You guys head for touchdown from the go. See! Just looking at the picture gives him a hard-on."

"You have a hard-on, Matey?" the anglophone asked. "It's nothing to be ashamed of."

"He's too excited to answer."

"See, he's coming already."

"Seriously now," the anglophone resumed, "what was the colour of this lass's drawers? If we show you her drawers you think you'll recognize them? She described her attacker as someone like you. She said you were good."

"You're always this silent, Matey?"

"He's deaf. He needs a hearing aid," Cherub said as he brought his open palm forcefully towards my right ear.

I tried to duck.

They laughed.

"Here you're deaf, and I'm fitting you with a hearing aid, and you're pulling away your head. I swear, Matey, you're like your people: you got no gratitude."

"Give him a couple more seconds. See his face? He's still coming. Don't know why white women excite you guys so," Roundchin interrupted.

"Suppose we got it wrong," Cherub said. "That she wasn't wearing no drawers when you grabbed her; no drawers, no remember. Right?"

"You don't have to open your mouth. Just nod," Roundchin urged.

The anglophone moved from rapes, to break-ins, to muggings. I refused to answer until one of Cherub's hearing aids made me change my mind.

"Blacks don't remember much what they do, do they? You forgot your mother's name a while back. You probably forgot you committed these crimes, right? Too much of a jolly good time to remember. That girl you were coming over just now, she told us it was you who raped her. See, Matey, we want you to confess and then tell us your secret for sending white women wild. They say you're the greatest. They roll their eyes and smack their lips when they talk about you."

The anglophone got up then and Cherub took his place. Here and there in his speech you saw he was French Canadian, but his English was more or less perfect. "Now we seen some films," he began, "where Blacks is great actors. We want you to do a little acting for us. With your eyes mostly. See how well you been hiding the truth from us? We know you're a good actor."

"You can say no, if you don't want to act. We'll be disappointed but we'll suggest something else, like drumming the ribcage," Roundchin added.

"Ya," the anglophone said, rubbing his palms. "And get you to dance the sambo-mambo after. On your hands. Vup! Vup!" He made a couple of obscene hip thrusts.

"Naw," said Roundchin, "I want to see you roll those eyes." He turned and took out a torch and a high stool from the cupboard." With his forefinger he motioned for me to get up from behind the desk and mount the stool. He helped me onto the stool; it was high and the handcuffs made getting on it awkward.

"Yeah, let's see you roll them eyes. No blinking now, Matey, or we might push our fingers behind them to keep them still," the anglophone said as Cherub beamed a hot torch into my eyes.

"Now roll!" Roundchin commanded.

"Good. Keep 'em rolling, Matey."

"Ain't he a bewte? Matey, you keep that up and you can have my sister. Got stallion hips. Roll them eyes. Yeah. Don't stop. I'm a man to my word."

I blinked once and found myself off the stool onto the floor, blind momentarily, and afterwards seeing stars. Because of the handcuffs I could not break the fall.

"Next time, Matey, we'll look behind your eyeballs to see why they're blinking," the anglophone informed me while he and Roundchin repositioned me onto the stool.

"Hey," Cherub added, "is it too much to ask for a little cooperation? This is a important service. Improve your vision."

"Your memory and intelligence too, Matey," the anglophone taunted, "so you can tell the difference between what's yours and what's not. Between what's rape and what's not. You'll leave here a wise lad. See? It's for you own good. What you say? Shall we continue to improve your vision and your discernment?" He took the torch briefly from Cherub and raised the beam a notch higher.

"Look at the whites o' those eyes! Matey, you're turning white. Guys, we'd better stop. Matey's turning white. That wasn't our intention."

"Another couple o' hours, Matey, and you'll be a blue-eyed, blond, bona fide, law-abiding man. Your Ma'll disown you."

They laughed.

"What say you, pals, do we turn Matey here into a white man?" The light beam was searing now and my vision was completely blurred. "Sing a little, Matey, while we work your change over. We like music. Makes the time pass quicker. 'Wash me in the blood of the lamb and I shall be whiter than snow—'" Laughter foiled his attempt at song.

"Naw," Roundchin said. "Matey'll miss all that sex. Won't be satisfied with a ordinary hard-on."

They switched off the torch, and I had trouble getting my eyelids to cover my eyes. My eyeballs pulsed with pain and for a couple of minutes the air around me seemed to have turned into glowing pearl-white confetti.

They returned me to the desk. "Now let's see if your memory's any better," Roundchin said spraying me with spit and swathing me with his shit breath.

They chuckled. "All that light in your eyes bound to improve your sight, Matey. It's so good, Matey, your brothers keep coming back soon as they begin having trouble figuring out what's theirs."

Again the files, the same questions, the same taunts.

"Well, Matey's memory's just as bad, maybe worse. No good came from our little operation. I have another idea. A little exercise," Roundchin suggested, his spit doing its job.

"A little sambo-mambo," the anglophone added.

They took me into a narrow room, where they removed my clothes. "You're full of surprises! What this?" Cherub asked, lifting my penis with one of his fingers. No wonder that woman came to the station! If these surprises keep up, we'll soon find a' honest nigger."

"Tch! Tch. Don't call Matey that. Matey's my friend. I won't have it. What happened to your prick, Matey? Matey, if I was a woman and you raped me with a prick like that I'd be bound to get mad."

"Now we are going to put you back in your element. You'll never feel so normal again."

Cherub took something from a canvas bag that was lying in a corner of the room. Roundchin mounted a stepladder and affixed an extensible bar—the kind used for chin-ups—with two mobile rings to what must have been brackets in the wall. They unlocked my handcuffs, stretched me out on a table, and attached something to my ankles. They fitted a foam helmet onto my head, leaving only my eyes, mouth, and nostrils uncovered. They hoisted me from the legs and flipped me so I was hanging upside down. Then they relocked the handcuffs.

"That's your natural position, Matey."

"Don't remind him. He won't want to come down."

"And while we're at it, would you like a chunk of salami and ice cream from this end? Bet you nobody ever treated you so well in your life? There are kind white people on this earth. Let me tell you." He pushed what felt like three fingers into my rectum. "You've been having a lot of sausage lately, Matey. Not good for you. Full of cholesterol."

From the canvas bag they took three truncheons. They pushed my body towards each other, raising their sticks menacingly each time my head got close. That way I was in a perpetual sway. It was as if my nostrils no longer dilated; I breathed through a paper-thin sliver in my mouth, and my head felt like a painful, pulsing bladder. With each pulsation of my heart, my eyes threatened to explode. I tasted blood and tried to spit, but the helmet clamped my jaws almost totally. My entrails pressed against my diaphragm, compressing my lungs, choking me.

I tried to gurgle out, "I didn't steal that shirt," but only succeeded in stirring up the blood and saliva in the mouth. It was futile.

Even so they heard the gurgling, for Cherub screamed, *"Ferme ta boîte!"*

"Sing for us, Matey. 'Swing low, sweet chariot, coming for to carry me home.' Are you over Jordan yet, Matey? Tell us what you see. You're having a jolly good time, Matey. We can see that."

"We should videotape this, and give you half the profits, Matey."

"Naw, with a prick like that, nobody'd be interested," Cherub said.

"I'll not have you putting down Matey's family jewels. Don't mind him, Matey. You don't have the kind o' jewels to make him jealous."

They laughed.

There were several sharp spasms in my stomach then, followed by burning vomit in my throat, mouth, and nostrils. I strained to let drip out what I could between the spaces of my teeth and the sliver in my lips.

"Regarde! Il a vomi sur nous!" Cherub screamed. "Christ de cochon! Corliss!"

"Naw, it's kaka. Matey's mouth's up here, waiting for sausage," Roundchin said.

Cherub gave me a real blow then, cleared his throat and spat on me. My body went limp.

"That wasn't vomit," the anglophone said. "That's come. Matey's highly versatile. You can come from anywhere. Right, Matey?"

"That calls for a hunk of sausage, Matey; to keep you coming," Cherub added.

After this they lowered me, seated me hunched forward on the edge of the table, my handcuffed hands pressed behind me against the table because I was trembling, and removed their paraphernalia.

"Matey," the anglophone said, "you must be hot and sweaty, what with all this fun." (I was ice-cold.) "My pal here"—he pointed to Cherub—"will take you for a shower and send you back to your Ma a sweet-smelling, innocent, clean black boy. Hope she doesn't reject you.

"We treat everyone here like royalty. Of course, this time you only got the hors d'oeuvres. Next time you'll have main course and maybe dessert."

Cherub draped my clothes over my handcuffed arms behind me. Naked I followed him to the shower. A hose hung coiled in front of it. He removed my clothes, hung them on a peg outside the shower stall, unlocked the handcuffs and pointed to the inside of the shower stall, where I finally spat out the remaining vomit in my mouth. A jet of cold April water knocked me against the side of the shower. When the water stopped I could not move. Cherub helped me out of the shower, but I could not dry myself. He dried me. Gradually the numbness became a burning sensation. He handed me my clothes. I fumbled with them but could not put them on. He dressed me.

"Try to stay clean." He took my chin in his hand. "I have a mind to adopt you. I could protect you. *Icitte, on est tous des pères de famille. J'ai rien contre les Nègres, moé. Je fais ma jobbe. Le monde est comme il est et je dois vivre en dedans.*" Then he was silent, in reflection. *"Allons en avant."*

I began walking.

"Tu parles français, toé?

I didn't answer.

He seated me where I'd sat when they first brought me to the station.

Now my teeth were chattering wildly. The nylon windbreaker I had on was useless. It was 11.45 by the station clock.

My mother arrived around 12.30 and found me shivering. My tears began as soon as she entered, moving like a mannequin. Her face a mahogany mask carved with deep wrinkles, she signed the papers they pushed in front of her. They spoke to her, too low for me to hear. She never once opened her mouth.

"Why you didn' call me earlier?" she asked when we got outside.

"They didn't let me."

"The officer says you made fun of them and refused to give them my name and phone number."

As soon as I stepped outside the police station, I leaned against my mother and began to howl. Thick snowflakes were falling and melting as they hit the ground.

"Quiet! People will see us!"

I ignored her. We got to a building a block away and I sank down on its steps and continued to bawl. I retched a few times, and my body went limp.

The next day Erskine came by, took me to his home, and found out that Hollis, urged on by Alfred, had put the shirt in my bag. When Erskine brought me back, Ma told him she appreciated his interest in me but didn't want him to involve me with anything that concerned the police. "I, a grown woman, wet myself when I go to get Pedro at the station. Mr Erskine, *you* must know 'Cockroach don' get justice in fowlcock court.'"

Erskine nodded gravely then looked at me and bit his lower lip.

That weekend I spent a long time thinking about what Alfred and Hollis had done to me and of my experience at the police station; and without knowing how I did it, I compressed my dignity to a kernel, encased it, and shoved it deep within myself, far from bigots' spit and spite.

If this morning's nightmare is any indication, the casing has broken, but I must not panic. Perhaps it's not a bad thing.

27

ON THE TUESDAY MORNING after Easter, there was a school assembly. Bellamy and Johnston were on the stage. Johnston, still wearing his blue suit, told us that the warm weather was already upon us and he would step up his measures to cut down on skipping. That was all he said.

Bellamy rose to speak. "Some things have been bothering me about this school." He pounded the lectern with his live hand. He put on his reading glasses, looked at his notes, and then removed his glasses. "Lately there's been a rash of shoplifting incidents. Now the student leaders are in on the act. If the leaders shoplift, what will the followers do?"

"*Help sell the stuff,*" someone in the back whispered. A few students chuckled.

A choral whisper swept through the assembly, and several students turned to stare at me.

"This is one of the oldest surviving schools in Canada, and used to be one of the most prestigious. Built in 1801. 175 years ago. We ought to be celebrating. Instead we're drowning in filth. You raving maniacs bent on destroying civilization, you won't destroy this school. I will make sure you don't.

"When I studied here, we walked on tiptoe through the foyer. We felt unworthy in the presence of the eminent personages there. YOU TRAMP THROUGH THE FOYER LIKE PIGS TO THE TROUGH!"

"*He's lost it,*" the student behind me whispered.

"Each year we spend thousands of dollars removing the graffiti you soil it with."

That was certainly true. Paint and graffiti bleach weren't always able to cover or erase the penises and "Fuck you! Bellamy!" that students left there.

"When I came here as principal fifteen years ago this school out-performed every other public school in this province."

"Time for you to go then!" the whispering student said.

"Then, students were proud to say they were from General Wolfe. From all over Montreal people sent their children. Today the residents of NDG are sending their children elsewhere. Why? Because when they ask about General Wolfe, they are told, 'The students at General Wolfe are shoplifters'; 'the students at General Wolfe have no discipline'; 'the students at General Wolfe behave like animals in school and in public'; 'General Wolfe is infested with thugs.'

"And that is only half of our problem. Now we are overrun with drugs. Those of you who buy it and those of you who sell it know who you are. I'm putting you on alert. There will be no mercy for you when you get caught—and caught you will be. And although I think the best place for many of you is reform school or even prison, I'll still advise you to quit while you're on this side of the bars."

The whispering began again. But no particular person that I knew of was singled out this time.

"Again, I wish to remind you that anyone caught loitering in the foyer will be suspended."

On Wednesday morning, there was a freak April snowstorm. I was standing in the third floor stairwell on the southern side of the building, staring at the tossing twigs of the leafless trees on the rear school ground and the wind-driven snow piling up around them. The land was like a prisoner which its captor was exulting over. A day earlier the earth had been green with the first grass of spring and now it was back to winter. Winter! I merely had to see that the sky was sapphire, the sunshine a clear glitter—know, in other words, that it was flesh-freezing weather—and my skin got bumpy and my hands sweaty; six or seven months of freezing winds that were worse than the hurricanes I'd left behind. Now spring seemed hesitant, and I longed for the reassurance of tulips and lilacs.

I felt a hand on my shoulder and jumped. It was Vince, his usually bright amber eyes contracted; his cherubic, innocent, often smiling dark face tense; his thick, usually wavy walnut hair that ordinarily reached down to his shoulders bristled outwards. His sweater protruded in a black border below his open azure jean jacket.

He beckoned with his forefinger that I should follow him and placed a finger on his lips. I followed him down to the foyer and suddenly saw General Wolfe with a black face and gobs of paint, like black blisters on his chest. Above the auditorium door, Queens Elizabeth and Victoria had grown black beards. Vince nudged me and whispered nervously, "Whoever did this is way past his nostrils in shit." I felt like laughing but was checked by fear. We headed out of the foyer quickly and up the stairs to the third floor.

On Memorial Day, Bellamy, dressed in military togs—he was a World War II veteran— assembled us in the auditorium, made us sing the national anthem and the school song ("Land of Our Birth We Pledge to Thee"), lectured us on patriotism, made us vow to remember the war dead always, and marched us single file out of the auditorium into the foyer to salute General Wolfe and the names of the dead on the war memorial plaques.

During homeroom Bellamy sent for me. I met Mervyn sitting outside his office, his eyes squinted, his forehead creased and shining, his hands cupped and lying listlessly in his lap. With his eyes he interrogated me. I shook my head slowly. He swallowed, making a sound.

"Did you do it?" Bellamy asked me when we were in his office. He sat at his horseshoe-shaped desk. He held his dead arm in his right hand. At his back, through the glass I could see the snow swirling violently across the front playground and the shopping centre parking lot.

"Do what, sir?

"What happened in the foyer?" He eyed me skeptically. His eyes were grey slits in his triangular fishbelly-white face. He wore a black blazer with brass buttons and a grey turtleneck sweater.

"Sir, I don't know anymore than you what happened in the foyer."

He waited a long while in silence.

"Wait outside my office. The police are on their way to question you." He smiled disdainfully.

My knees knocked, my fingers trembled, my hands sweated. Fifteen minutes later, two detectives dressed in civilian clothes arrived. They took Mervyn into Bellamy's office and questioned him first.

When Mervyn left they turned on me. They hadn't taken off their trench coats, and I knew instantly it was because they concealed recording equipment. They asked me to account for everything I'd done the afternoon and evening before. They made me repeat myself several times. Later they interrogated Dreyfuss and Vince. By late afternoon a bulletin sent to every class asked students to name anyone they might have seen hanging around or entering or leaving the foyer on Tuesday afternoon or evening.

All four of us were again summoned to Bellamy's office at 2.30 pm. We were asked if the clothes we had on were the ones we'd been wearing on Tuesday. We were photographed and told we had until 4.30 to go home and change our clothes and bring them back to the office.

Next morning General Wolfe was encased in orange plastic bags, as if ready to be hauled to a garbage dump. (Two weeks later they had him all cleaned up, but he acquired a beige tan, as though he'd been marauding in the tropics instead of languishing in a frigid-zone foyer. Queens Elizabeth and Victoria left for good. Photograph portraits of Prime Minister Pierre Trudeau and Governor General Jules Léger took their place.)

On Thursday we were again interrogated. The detectives warned us that if by the next day they did not have any leads, they'd take us to the station and continue their questioning there. "You guys won't like that." One stared at me a long while, a hint perhaps that I should explain what it was like.

On Friday no one sent for me. In the afternoon, on my way to my last class I ran into Mrs Henry, who told me that the person who'd done it had confessed.

"Was it a black student?"

"Why a black student?" she snapped. "I don't know." She went down the stairs in a sudden hurry.

Accompanied by his father, a physics professor at Concordia

University, Tim Chang had confessed.

In history class he'd sometimes laugh at some of the things Saltzer said but offer no commentary. Saltzer's eyes would blink rapidly in response. Madam Shank, our biology teacher—she said she was cousin to Chiang Kai Shek—regularly sent students with incomplete homework to the foyer to apologize to the portraits there. One Monday morning she'd sent Tim. At first he looked stunned. He stood up and his jaw fell. His face turned white. He was gripping his desk so hard that his knuckles went bone white. A tremor started in his lips and he made a loud hiccupping sound. Then abruptly he left the class.

All those faces of dead white men in military uniforms, clerical collars, judges' robes—staring at him, judging him, diminishing him, accusing him of betrayal! He had to fight back. He could give them the finger, but who'd know he'd done so?

He and I were the only non-white students in Ms Mackenzie's advanced English class, but we rarely spoke to each other. On Remembrance Day in 1975 our class with her had been right after we'd saluted General Wolfe. We'd discussed three of Wilfrid Owens's antiwar poems and, for homework, we'd had to write a poem expressing our feelings about war. Tim's was one of the most memorable:

Lions kill antelopes
Because they need the meat;
They protect their territory with roars.
We, with trumpets, bugles, pageantry
And forty percent of our GDP,
Slaughter humanity
And dump the meat.

(In my second year at McGill he and I nodded or waved to each other when we crossed paths on campus. I would have liked to know how his father dealt with his act, whether he'd punished him, and where he went to after he was expelled from General Wolfe.)

Seventeen days after my experience with the police, I caught up with

Alfred. He'd been deliberately avoiding me. "Why'd you and Hollis do that to me?"

"'Cause you need to come down a couple o' pegs. That's why. Now you know what it's fucking well like to be black and struggling."

Struggling! Your mother's a university professor. Your father's an MD. You wear designer everything. You have over twenty thousand dollars worth of gold around your neck, wrists, and fingers. "You're not serious. Remember, it was you who insisted that I change my out-of-date clothes! Remember how you figured out that my mother's a live-in maid!"

"That ain't got sweet fuck-all to do with nothing. I'm talking about success. Achieving! You know what I mean? You write fucking better than white people. You might even be valedictorian. That's what count!"

"And you're angry with me!"

"Yes!" He said it with venom.

"Why, Alfred?" A feeling close to despair filling me.

"Because I was born here. See? I have rights you don't have. But, see, you're the one with brains, the discipline. Life ain't fair. You're going places. You know where I'm headed? Jail! That's where, man—*if they don't kill me or I don't kill myself first.*"

I shook my head slowly, stunned by what I was hearing.

"You're shocked, eh? Well that's why we put the fucking shirt in your bag. And if we get a second chance we'll do it again. And if I catch you sitting on a bridge I'll push you off!"

Then, after a silent moment, he said softly, in a calmer tone, "You ain't nothing special, you know. Goody Two-Shoes! *Archie Bootlicker!*" It was the first time I'd heard this expression. "We've all made the trip to the station, one time or the other." He sounded weary. "Got whacked by the cops. Heard them call our sisters and mamas whores. Get what I mean, man? We did you a favour. It's a important part o' your education. A initiation. Into blackness. Valuable schooling, man." A sick grin had spread across his face.

(I could have been spared the lesson but four years later in a social psychology class I was taking at McGill as one of my electives, my mind returned to this conversation. There was more truth in it than

I wanted to believe. By then I'd been shocked too many times out of the dreamland I wanted to inhabit. I was alright as a comedian—a joker—or an ever-ready sex partner; I should have desired nothing better than to cool down white women in heat; had to be a good dancer, musician, and a drug user. Was the Yellow Pages for boogie-woogie underground haunts filled with black studs; a seller of "stuff" or a directory for sellers of "stuff."

Yes. Alfred was right about the lesson. A lesson in how power works: power that could arbitrarily decide what my orifices could be used for, power to torture me to conform to whatever fantasy Whites think Blackness is or must be. "O but you are so refined [for a black man, black woman, that is]!" I used to be flattered when my professors asked me where in England I had studied, until I realized they were implying that Caribbean schools were inept. A few even assumed I was the product of privilege.)

The evening of June 19, I was home preparing for my very last high school exam, when the phone rang and Erskine told me not to be surprised if the police came by for a visit. If they came I should call him before I let them into the apartment. Bellamy had found drugs in Alfred's locker, and since I was supposed to be one of his friends, Bellamy had given my name as well as Hollis's to the police. They'd searched my locker as well.

The police tried to arrest Alfred that same night. He was past his eighteenth birthday. Two days later, near Boucherville, in a marsh bordering the St Lawrence River, they found his body with a bullet hole in his skull, and the gun beside him. The coroner said it was suicide.

The Montreal Star devoted a full page to him, including excerpts from an interview with his mother. She was Jamaican, and *Alfred had come to Canada when he was nine.*

Finally the end of June brought some good news: a full scholarship to college. When I phoned Erskine to tell him the news, he came to the apartment and took me to a Caribbean restaurant in NDG. There he told me that his father was a Barbadian planter and his mother a field hand who, to keep her job on the plantation, had slept with his father. "I was lucky to be bright and to have teachers who encouraged me. My father never acknowledged me until I came here to study; he asked my mother for my address and wrote me. I never answered his letter." He fell silent.

"I'm leaving General Wolfe. I'll be at Howard in the fall, studying medicine."

"But you've been so good to us." I felt saddened at the thought that he'd be leaving.

"Mrs Henry will be there. Teaching was temporary. I always knew that."

He asked if I was still bent on studying literature. Looking away, I told him yes.

"Look me in the face," he said, without his usual authoritarian tone.

I stared into his eyes. I recalled that a year earlier I had been standing on the sidewalk of Ste Catherine Street near Drummond watching the Carifesta floats come along, when I felt a hand on my shoulder and turned to see Erskine. "What a waste o' energy!" he said, waving his hand dismissively at one of the floats—a group of speckled yellow butterflies dancing in a circle. He was tired, he said, of seeing black people "forming the fool" for white people. We should pool our money and buy apartment blocks so white land-lords don't have to overcharge us and insult us, open stores to keep our money in our community. "All this spreeing! Making asses o' weselves for white applause—makes a body nauseous."

"All right, study literature then," he broke into my reverie. "But get a doctorate in it. Become a scholar."

I nodded, more to please him than anything else.

He's curing physical sickness—he wouldn't have patience for the psychical—in Harlem. He and Mervyn are still in touch.

28

WHEN I RETURNED TO GENERAL Wolfe it was to receive my diploma in October. From Washington, Erskine sent me a telegram of congratulation. He'd persuaded the Little England Society, of which he'd once been president, to give me its annual scholarship for an outstanding student of Barbadian origin. He'd concocted some sort of story to make me Barbadian. My mother, looking refreshed like a garden after rain, wore a burnished gold dress. For the occasion, she'd straightened and dyed her hair, a radical gesture for her. Brother Solomon was my other guest. I won three academic prizes but Vince was valedictorian.

When we got home Ma announced that she had rented a two-bedroom apartment on the third floor of the building with the large lawn and beautiful garden down the street—the same apartment I'm in today—and we were going to move into it on November first. That was her graduation gift to me: my own bedroom; the rent would be paid as long as I stayed in school and she had a job. I wondered how she would afford the rent. For some time she had been working Saturdays as well. Now she told me it was to make the extra money she needed to furnish the place. I was glad we would finally quit that basement, live where real daylight could enter, and stop inhaling carbon monoxide.

Three days later I was on my way to Isabella Island to attend Grama's funeral. The day after my graduation she'd had a massive stroke that killed her almost instantly. The flight was delayed for several hours in Barbados, and I arrived on Isabella Island two hours after my grandmother's interment. I'm not sure if there were facilities on Isabella Island then for refrigerating corpses. But that would have been too costly an option for my mother. Vanity was not her weak point, and holding back a corpse from rotting in order to see it, or because people would applaud her for doing so, would have been out of the question for her. She'd have had to choose between keeping Grama's body on ice and furniture for the new apartment. It must have stressed her financially to have to buy my ticket, but when I got home from college and she announced the news of Grama's death, she'd already booked my flight for the next morning.

It was dark when I visited the graveyard, accompanied by Mrs Duncan's nephew, who showed me the grave with a flashlight. On my own next day I returned to the cemetery and watched the grave covered with flowers, and I thought of my grandmother in the ground underneath, no longer in need of medicine. The lilies in the wreaths had already wilted. The sun poured down from a cloudless sky and Hanovertown, shaped like a C, stretched peacefully up from the sea, up the slopes on all sides. In spite of the heat pouring out from the sun, I felt cold as I reflected that here was the end of all human life and ambition.

Mr Sam's grave was a few feet away, enclosed by a beautiful tomb, a tree etched in the black granite headstone donated by his Shango society. I sat on it. But it was not Mr Sam that I remembered. It was Ansel. Perhaps because the day of Ansel's funeral had looked exactly like this one. Two men whose stories were a vital part of my education. Looking around at the tombstones, in this vast abode of the dead, I understood for the first time my own entrapment in the unalterable process of growth and decay. "Oh Death where is thy sting? Oh, grave where is thy victory?" They were words of hidden desperation, I now realized—the need to deny the obvious. Till then, I had merely believed that God was a benevolent father, and all the various religions that fought one another were victims of their own foolishness. A depressing paralysis descended on me then. I had walked to the cemetery earlier, but I was obliged to take a bus back to Mount Olivet, to Mrs Duncan's place where I was staying.

When I got back from Isabella Island and recounted everything to my mother, she was silent for a long while, then she invited me to sit on the sofa bed beside her. She placed her hand on mine and said, "I want you to forgive me for not telling you your father name. Yo' father is Patrick Percy. I didn' want you to know that before you graduate from high school. I didn' want it for affect you. I was worried that you was too fragile when you first came, and I myself was confused. Oh, I had a pretty good idea what you been going through. It not easy to move to a new country with racism and all that." Her tears flowed then, quietly. I saw them as a plea for forgiveness and I forgave her. I wondered why I had first felt and then doubted that Patrick Percy was my father. *Everyone would go to great lengths to prove his father is not a murderer.* I cannot but think of him each time I hear of bank robberies, murders, and other heinous crimes. My mind turns too to the burdensome knowledge children of criminals must carry.

Only once afterward did I bring him up in an awkward attempt to tease my mother over her prudishness. I told her that with a name like Isis, she should have asked the executioner to save my father's penis. I'd wanted to see her freeze with embarrassment, but she replied, "And do what with it?"

"Resurrect him."

"So he could come and father you? Where you get these ideas from?"

I told her the Isis-Osiris story. When I finished she said, "So you would like to be Horus? Well you is just Pedro, and now that I know what your name mean, I hope you know that the only foundation rock and key you got is your ambition and the use you make of it."

"And your name? It means throne."

She smiled. "All young girls dream o' becoming queens, but they soon realize the only throne they will sit on is a toilet seat, and if they don' watch it *they* become toilet seats."

My mother. By then I truly admired and respected her.

29

ALL THIS CULMINATED IN 1976, almost ten years ago, ten years in which I have been wondering whether there's any meaning to life. I got my DEC, three years later a BA from McGill, because education should have been my visa out of indigence (at any rate I hope it will be), and returned to Isabella Island in search of salvation. My years in Montreal, I'd felt, had been an immersion in shit, an image I retained from a dream in which Dreyfuss and his Nations had thrown me down a manhole and I'd landed in a reservoir of shit. But the cleansing and nurturing I went back for didn't exist. This time Isabella Island was green, but with my new eyes I saw that it was in many ways a desert, had always been. The oases that had sustained me in childhood were now shrunk. I felt like a nomad who'd found larger pastures, whose vision had travelled beyond the insular horizon and could no longer fit inside the smaller world. I saw pettiness and cruelty everywhere—worsened by poverty—and I saw the squalor and despair which had been hidden from my child's eyes and mind. One night during my second week I dreamed I was on a hilltop preaching a sermon of self-improvement to people assembled below, when someone suddenly screamed, "Let's stone the fool," and the crowd started up the hill with rocks in their hands. I screamed so loud that Mrs Duncan awakened and came to see what was wrong. And so I came back to Canada with a thickened coat of shit. I obtained an MA and a degree in education, largely because I knew how to study and nothing else. Now I wait for a teaching position and wonder, if I ever get one, whether I'd be for my students what Erskine and Mrs Henry had been for me.

Except for my mother's death, the details of the last ten years are not worth recalling. I suspect too that life is comprised of a few events that repeat themselves rearranged differently. Mine of the last ten years followed the pattern established in the first sixteen years of my life: a triangle, traced clockwise, of expectation, deception, awareness. The matrix is time, in which we all ripen towards maturity, also called death.

On November 9, 1985, Ma collapsed in a Hampstead home she was cleaning. A couple of days later, the doctors diagnosed stomach cancer that had already metastasized into her pancreas and liver.

She reacted as if the doctor had merely forecast fine weather. Half an hour later she grew pensive and said she'd better begin to tell me what she had to say. She told me to bring my chair where she could see me, and I could hold her hand.

"First thing, I want you to trust yo'self. I been watching you these last eleven years, and you been steady as a rock, even when you went back home thinking peace and contentment was there."

I knew otherwise, but said nothing. She stared at the ceiling for about a minute then continued.

"You used to tell me all sorts o' things 'bout the church—to shock me, but they open my eyes and make me think. One time you say to me, 'Ma, you know there are more non-Christians in Asia alone than all the Christians in the world put together? And you really believe God will send all those people to hell?' For weeks I think 'bout that, but I am a weak woman without learning, and I need the church to lean on." She stopped talking for a while, stared at the ceiling, wrapped her left fingers in the bed sheet, undid them, and then smoothed out the folds.

"You remember the time when Elfreda was praying her stupidness 'bout South Africa? I did 'gree with you when you say it wasn't God they need, was machine guns."

The Soweto massacre. Then Montreal was euphoric about the upcoming Olympics. The same time the police were looking for Alfred. I'd expected them to show up at the apartment any time. Elfreda had prayed aloud that Sunday asking God to "show Black South Africans the evil of their ways; turn them from idol worship, so you, the God of Abraham! and Isaac! and Job! will intercede and deliver them from the hands of their oppressors." I'd wanted to interrupt the service and walk out of the church. At home, I vented my anger on my mother.

"In Isabella," Ma resumed, "it was blasphemy to question the teachings o' the Bible. When you travel out you see things differently.

"I was proud to have a son who could question things that was all fuzzy to me."

"Why you never told me this before?" I found this astonishing.

"I did, you know. I stopped pestering you about going to church after you finish high school, and I make every sacrifice for yo' schooling? *You* wasn' listening."

My eyes filled. I didn't want my tears to distress her, so I went to the bathroom.

"I would o' like to see you with a paying job before I go," she said when I got back; "but that is not to be."

We lapsed into a silence which she broke. "Life, what a burden! I eager to put this one down. It always been too heavy for me to carry."

I was uncertain whether I wanted her to go on or to stop.

"I always wanted to be a independent woman. But the body and the mind is two different things, and they always fight, pull in opposite direction. And the body always win. I used to watch women get beat, and I used to say, 'Not me.' And Mama used to say, you have for have a man to protect you. A man! Daddy deserted, and everybody was too kind to tell her what it mean. I love my father. He was so dignified! Papa couldn't o' find it easy in the army. They used to use black soldiers for carry load. He couldn't be white people donkey. I wanted to be like him. I know one thing: if he did come back home, I wouldo' been educated. 'No child o' mine,' he uses for say, 'will end up in white people kitchen.' In the end war get too heavy for him. Not even his love for me could o' make him bear it. He run off, straight into the desert. I understand now why he do it. Life in Canada explain all that to me. I forgive him.

"If he been seeing me all these years, he must be a unhappy soul. Rich people give orders and poor people dream."

She'd never spoken to me about my grandfather. Now I understood why. She was ashamed of how far short her life had fallen from the ideals he'd had for her, and probably hadn't fully forgiven him for placing his pride ahead of her future.

"When we find out that Daddy went AWOL and the allowances stop coming, Mama had to spend what they put aside for enlarge the house and pay for my schooling, and go right back to changing the nappies o' white children. The first few weeks she used to come home, throw herself on the bed and bawl."

She wasn't looking at me. She was unrolling the scrolls of her memory. "In the meantime I was getting big, and it cost more to go to high school than Mama was earning. She used to say, 'You better pray some man with money married you.' Things was arranged so black people couldn't have money. She did mean men like teachers, policemen, and the few who was civil servants. Mulattos had the first pick o' the good jobs. Educated black men use to get what leave over. And all o' them use to marry light-skinned women. The arrowroot, cane and cotton field—weeding, chopping, ploughing in sun and rain—was where everybody else work, and where the mulattos and white people spit on them, and when they come home they had their wives and women to beat. No thanks. Pedro, I didn't want any o' that, unless he was a man like my father. He and Mr Duncan been the only two decent black men I know. Brother Shiloh, too, but he in another class. And when you married in those days, you couldn' leave yo' husband. The community shun you if you do. Even when he beat you. You was expected to take the blows, cry until they cool, until he give you more. And believe me, Pedro, the white men didn' treat their wives any better. Mama did know all 'bout it.

"Well, I fall like every other *jackabat*; for somebody on a dung heap." She took a deep breath, one full of emotion. "And I been trying to wash myself clean ever since. Ever since. Life!" She compressed her lips and her facial muscles bundled with emotion. "The colour you born with, where you born, the class you born in—make all the difference in what you turn out to be." She paused.

"How come I so talkative today?"

"Everything you say is meaningful."

She smiled. "Pedro, I'm proud o' you. I better tell you now while

I can say so. I hope that whoever you share yo' life with you all will make each other happy. A single life is a lonely life, but a unhappy relationship is terrible. Keep this in mind when you take up with a woman"—she paused, took a deep breath— "or a man." A long silence. "I suspect that 'bout you a long time. I not the foolish woman I was when you first come here."

She touched an issue I'd put off resolving. I'd never discussed my confused sexuality with her or anyone—hadn't even fully explored it in my own head. I found it easier to avoid sex altogether.

It was a long while before she resumed.

"How long you think I will live?"

"I don't know. The doctor said about six weeks."

"Two weeks at the most. I had two things to do: take care o' Mama till she died, and look after you till you grow up. I don't have a single other reason to hold on to life. I ready to lay this burden down.

"When I feel the end near I have something important to share with you. If life play a joke on me and I don' tell you before I go, it all written down on a sheet of paper in the envelope with my insurance policy and my will. But I won't go before I tell you with my own voice. And, you know something, I won't live long after I tell you. It will be my last burden before I go, light as air.

"Tomorrow I want you to go to the bank at the Plaza and bring me a withdrawal slip. I have a little bit of money there I want to give you now, because they have a way o' tying up these things when people die."

I usually got to the ward to see her every day around one and would leave the ward around six, as soon as the members of her congregation began arriving. A week later, at ten am, the head nurse of her ward phoned asking me to come to the hospital right away. When I got there, Ma was hooked up to oxygen and being fed intravenously, but she was lucid. I remarked something I hadn't allowed myself to see—that she was no bigger than her skeleton. Her facial flesh had melted; her skin, yellowish and puckered with shallow connecting lines, looked in spots like cracked antique china. From deep within their cavernous sockets, her eyes shone with a luminosity I'd never known them to have.

Her windowsill was lined with the flowers her church brothers and sisters had brought. The lavender in them scented the air. Her bed was raised to a sitting position. Breathing through her oxygen mask, she beckoned to me to come closer. I approached her and took her free hand in mine.

She motioned to me to pull the mask below her chin.

I did.

"I have for have your forgiveness so I can start my other journey," she said, her voice rasping.

"You don't need to." I meant it too.

She raised her hand in a gesture of silence. "When I found out I was making you, I drink chlorine bleach two times to . . . to get rid of you. It wasn' that I wanted to." She paused for breath. "When I took up with yo' father, he promised me the moon and I did believe him. Don' ask me why." She stopped and fumbled with the mask. I put it back on and she breathed through it for about a minute before motioning with a nod that I could remove it. "I did already see the women-them yo' father fooled. But I did feel I wouldn' be one o' them." Her thoughts were clear but she was tasked by the effort to voice them; her chest heaved and her voice rattled slightly.

"When I find out I was pregnant with you, I tell him.

"Don' expec' child maintenance from me,' is what he said to me.

"'But you say you love me, and when things improve we going get married.'

"'Well, they not improve!'

"'What about the future?'

"'I live in the present. We better break this off right now.'

"We were sitting on the Hanovertown wharf. It was already past ten pm, and not a soul was around. Your father got up and left me sitting there." She stopped, a heavy rasp in her voice. I replaced the mask for about two minutes.

"And he never draw his breath to me again. The hate I feel for him I turn on you inside me. I drink the chlorine but all it did was burn my throat. And I was wondering who might o' been able to help me before it get too late.

"I didn' have much time to think, 'cause two days later, Mother Branch, Ishtar Saul mother—she was always deep in her African religion; even go to jail for it—come into our yard. Mama wasn' home. 'Daughter,' she say to me, 'I have a message fo' you from the other side. In my travels there, I come upon a middle-height man, wearing war clothes. He say to me, "Tell Isis for keep the pickney."'

"Mother Branch come to live in Mount Olivet long after Daddy went off to war, so she didn' know him."

She stared at the ceiling silently. I put back on the mask. She kept it on for about two minutes, then resumed. "After you born, I use to hope the chlorine didn' damage yo' brain, but I couldn' bring myself to nurse you. The old heads say goat milk is the best, so what little money I could spare I spend it on goat milk to nourish you." She paused and I replaced the mask. This time she kept it on for about fifteen minutes. "When you first come to Canada, I realize how strong my feelings against yo' father still was, and not just against yo' father; no—against my own self. I never used to come home on evenings because." She left the statement incomplete. "I didn' have to prepare no breakfast for Mr Wilton. You remember that?"

I said nothing.

"Afterwards I used to feel that God didn' let me succeed with the abortion, so I wouldn' damn my soul. When Louisa take me to Saints Militant Church, I use the chance for purge my soul." She stopped talking. "It didn' work. My conscience used to sink into me like claws when I least expect. And the nightmares used to come often."

For a while she breathed quietly through the mask.

"I never tell Ms Wilton 'bout you. The first question she asked me: 'You have any children?' I tell her no. And she said, 'Good, because I don't want anybody of questionable morals around my children.' She was always running off at the mouth that West Indians have lots o' bastard children. I was always afraid she would o' think I was a cheap woman and would o' fire me, especially seeing that I did done already lie to her."

Silence.

"You not ashamed of me? You don't hate me?"

"For what? You did what you had to do to survive. Have you forgiven my father?"

"Yes. But I never forgive myself for what I let him do to me. A bag o' dung, that is how I feel from that time on. Not even Christ born-again blood could o' change that. Now I feel all right. Confession good for the soul."

She'd emptied her secret bag.

I squeezed her hand. Her face assumed a peaceful smile and her eyes closed. I replaced the oxygen mask for the last time.

She'd had a nightmare the week after Mrs Wilton had fired her. Her screams had awakened me. "I am not going! Take yo' filthy hands off me!" She'd sat up in bed for about fifteen minutes before saying anything.

"Oh what a frightening dream! I was in church, and in the middle of a hymn. And a mysterious hand pulled every thread out of everything I was wearing, and all my clothes drop in a heap around my feet. The congregation stop singing and look at me like if I was the Antichrist or worse, and run out of the church. The next thing I know is I see these policemen with handcuffs. And they start to put them on me. And I was just as determined they wasn't going to put no handcuffs on me."

I remembered too her nightmare my first week of school in Canada, in which she'd dreamt she'd killed me.

I continued to hold her hand while she dozed, fearing that I would wake her. My mind wandered back to the story of why Mavis had gone mad, to our earlier conversation about her dreams and disappointments, to Grama and Grampa, to conditions when she was growing up—these were important for me. But what she told me on her deathbed was important for *her*. She was right. It was her burden. Repressed sorrow: deep, silent, innocuous in its chasm until it overwhelms our barricades and our being; tectonic plates moving silently in the subliminal turbulence of our psyches—until we quake. Never mind.

She slipped into a coma while I held her hand. By eight pm she was dead.

30

"IN MY BEGINNING IS MY END." The other way too. That's harder to envisage. My mind turns to the nightmare that awakened me at 4.00 am. Reality's twin pivot: destruction and salvation.

Ma's funeral turned out to be a reunion: Agatha, now an RN; Mervyn, a mechanic with Canadian Tire; Hollis, sober, thoughtful, shorn of his adolescent fantasies (I guess that's what adolescence is for—unbounded fantasizing before existence sets our limits: *"I know one thing. It ain't no schoolwork that going make a woman keep coming back. I know another thing too: if I satisfy she, she go work for me and she."*) caring for his mother, an MS sufferer, during the day and singing for a living at night; he brought along his seven-year-old daughter, who did not have school that day; Priscilla, a good twenty pounds heavier and now married to Dreyfuss, whose shoulders have doubled in expanse; he heads the Longshoremen's local at the Port of Montreal, she's a social worker; Vince, now an engineer in Toronto; even John-Giovanni, looking every bit the same, except for a beard, still rocking from the hips up, still stomping the earth with his turned-out feet, still working at his father's garage, but no longer swearing and grabbing his dick—or perhaps the occasion was too solemn; Ellen, who did a degree in nursing at Université de Montréal and now works in cardiology at the Jewish General. No one knew what became of Eddy. Hollis wanted to know how often Dreyfuss calls 911 to report husband abuse. We laughed. And Ellen reminded us that we'd thought she was destined for another occupation.

Alfred seemed most present in his absence, because we avoided mentioning him. I still wonder, during my bouts of insomnia, why, with his intelligence, physical beauty, brilliant and successful parents, he destroyed himself. To think that in the end he hated me!

Would have pushed me off a bridge, he said, if he'd met me sitting on one. *His* funeral had been by invitation only, and we had not been invited. My father's a murderer, his a homosexual. Strange he should have thought it a crime, disgrace, what have you. Did he hide things from me, things too reprehensible to mention, things that drove him to self-destruction? Would I be thinking this, if my mother hadn't told me *her* secrets? Time might have dulled his hate, might have mended him.

I hadn't expected my ex-classmates to show up, and certainly not Vince, coming all the way from Toronto—now with close-cropped hair, fat cheeks, a double chin, rounding belly, and meaty hips—a solid citizen who'd put away childish looks and things. He wanted to be assured that I wasn't staying at the flat alone. I lied.

Back home, alone in the apartment, after the wake in the basement of the church (a former Westmount Presbyterian Church building, adorned with pale oak pews, marble tiles, and stained glass windows, which the Saints Militant were renting), I stared absently outside at the blackness of falling rain splotched yellow by the glow of street lamps and antiburglar lights, thought about my classmates being there for me, and began to understand what fellowship means. It was why my mother, Sister Andrews, Sister Agnes, and Elder Elfreda dissed one another (aggression was another of those things the blood-of-the-lamb could not curb), tossed their psychic excrement—like chamber-pot stuff in medieval streets—onto the ones who wouldn't retaliate. They too had their pecking order, overruled only by their need to aid and be aided by one another.

That night I dreamt that Bruisee and I were together as in the old days. At some point Bruisee became Hollis, and we were asleep in the same bed and holding each other, and I got an erection and ejaculated, and became worried that Hollis probably knew and was thinking I'd abused him. Later Ellen came, placed her hands on her hips, and laughed at me until I awoke. What on earth was happening in the nether regions of my psyche? Had I been attracted to him all these years without ever knowing it? The next night I dreamt that we were at the Calgary Stampede. Bruisee, Alfred, Hollis, Dreyfuss, and Mervyn were there and rode bulls. Twice Hollis stood astride the horns of his bull. After dismounting, each held his bull by a single horn and confidently led it out of the compound while the stands encircling them exploded with the spectators' pleased applause. The microphone announced me as the next rodeo. There was a moment of tomblike silence, when time itself stopped. I tried to run out of the compound. The spectators booed. Powerful arms gripped me and sat me on a bull, which instantly tossed me into the air. I woke midway through the fall.

And so, as my fears become stage, spotlight and characters when sleep unlocks the cages barred by wakefulness, I am beginning to see some of the issues I'll have to resolve.

When burdens get too heavy you have to put them down—my mother's signature phrase. There were burdens she couldn't put down. Our needs devise the frames we live our lives in, and it's the lucky few for whom they're not prisons. I'd once heard her pleading with Sister Andrews to have pity on a church sister who'd fled the church to become the mistress of a married man. Yet she pronounced herself a whore, a *jackabat*, because she'd yielded to her need for sex and companionship, and thereafter spent her life atoning for and stifling such needs. *Her fall.* I the fruit of frailty: Cain's mark; a drop of live acid in her psyche. And fundamentalist religion, where she sought peace, exculpation, balm, became the ultimate prison. Did she find hope in its maze, or merely *"the end of her rope?"* Not that, I sincerely hope. *Brother Solomon raising his children by himself. Children gotten twixt lawful sheets*—no drops of acid in his psyche. At the funeral he sounded self-satisfied, proud of his two grandchildren, boastful of his sons: one co-owns an engineering firm, one's intern-ing at Toronto General, the third is finishing a PhD in history at the University of Chicago, "on a scholarship, everything paid." Besting those whose children would not or could not shine—even if at funerals and weddings we update ourselves about our acquaintances. What if one or all three had become pushers, thieves or pimps? He was "high up" and, from the sound of things, did not fear falling. But I'll always be grateful to him for straightening out my mother, for sup-porting me, the summer I arrived here.

Needs. Pleasure brings its complement of pain, privation its mix of freedom and enslavement.

What advice would Mr Sam give me now?

What are my other needs: those I can tackle? My Isabella Island math teacher used to say, "Solve the easiest problems first. They'll warm up the brain for the harder ones."

A place to sleep. Food to eat. Books to read.

What would I do if these needs were met?

Study for a PhD. I've promised Erskine I would. Circumstances force us to alter our expectations and our promises.

Why not begin work on your PhD while you wait for this elusive teaching job?

Why not? Lessen my expenses, find a cheaper place, rid myself of my mother's things.

Yes, your mother is dead. She needs nothing. It's you who who're carrying what the dead put down.

Put them down. "Simplify! Simplify! Simplify!"

My stomach growls. I'm hungry.

My mind returns to the eve of my departure for Canada. Grama is saying, " . . . I waiting patiently till Pedro come back home to prescribe medicine for me in me old age." I feel utterly alone. Adulthood. Occidental Adulthood. You leap into aloneness or replace the guardians of your childhood.

January 6. My birthday. I get up from the kitchen table to find something to eat, but instead walk to the living room window. It's surprisingly bright outside. The snow has stopped. The rumble of a snowplough and its revolving yellow light momentarily distract me. The sky is again blue. Up the hill to the southwest, to my right, a short distance beyond the Westmount summit, the sun is an orange ball less than a hand's breadth above the horizon. Its glow puts the naked trees in relief. Their bare stalks are tossing. In winter, you're aware that trees are paralysed from their trunks down, and they scream in pain as glacial winds strike them. *Their prison is their sustenance.* And they endure December with the certainty of June. Their naked-ness chills me. But nature compensates them: they grow perpetually, must be the objects of the amputee's and impotent lecher's envy. But trees of the same species fare differently in different soils and different climates. *"If winter comes can spring be far behind?"*

I stare until the sun dips behind the summit. They are unfair, I see now, and useless—bitter feelings about unpleasant, unalterable phenomena. *The hill's now without the sun's glow.* I remember my earliest fantasies about sunrise and sunset—the sun tired at day's end, drowsy at sunrise; asking Grama where the wind comes from and her telling me it's God's secret—and I think of the many animals hibernating in the earth. All summer long they wisely turned the earth's fruits into stored energy, and now they find refuge beneath its ice-bound hide. Like the trees (those at the very top of the summit are even more spectacular, now that the sun illuminates them from behind the summit) with all that's vital for their spring revival safely locked away inside. Shedding their leaves—first to blanket, later to feed, their roots; thickening their bark to cushion the wind's blows and seal their life-sap away from winter's freeze. Even so, many of their tenderest shoots will die.

Hibernal musings.

All worthwhile instruction comes from nature, the Romantics say.

One season brings dearth. Another plenitude. Nature's creatures have figured it out. Besides, we must all share the sun's heat: northern cold and southern heat, southern cold and northern heat, each an end of the heat-cold seesaw. Nothing could be fairer. Anything else is greed.

Ansel, back on Isabella Island, understood it.

"Who is yo' father?"

"The sun."

"So if we ask you, 'Who yo' mother is?' you will tell us 'the earth'?"

"Absolutely correct."

"And the sea, and the rain, and wind?"

"They're my uncles and aunts."

When I studied *Walden* I began to valorize him. Unlike Thoreau, he left no record of his thoughts.

My mother lamented her inability to dissect the doctrines she'd been fed, but knew poor people weren't sparrows or lilies of the field, had to "tell lies just to eat sometimes." Isis Moore had to become Millicent Brady, leaving no paper trail for Canadian immigration to track her down; and deny she was an out-of-wedlock mother to suit the bigotry of her employer; and "lean" on Christ, whom she both believed and contradicted.

But for reasons that defy all reason we need to believe that lilies of the field neither toil nor spin (botanists tell us otherwise), that we are the authors of our suffering—a handle, a container, for existential pain, evident in our ongoing authoring of Buddha and Christ.

Most humans lead lives of quiet desperation, Thoreau felt. And he blamed them for it—undeservedly, I think. But understanding these matters lessens no one's pain. *Sufficient unto the day is the evil thereof.* Ansel understood this. Otherwise he couldn't have lived as he did. So did Mr Sam. He fed Misfortune and was nevertheless its food.

Existential dues, the cost for living, as dire and inevitable as birth pains.

Droplets of perspiration collect on my forehead and sweat trickles down my armpits. I watch the sweat drops coalescing on my fingertips.

Acknowledgements

I would like to thank Nurjehan Aziz and M G Vassanji for their valuable editorial suggestions.

H NIGEL THOMAS was born in St Vincent. He attended university in Montreal and for ten years was a teacher with the Protestant School Board of Greater Montreal. He is now professor of literature at Laval University. His published works include the novel *Spirits in the Dark*, which was short-listed for the 1994 Quebec Writers' Federation Hugh MacLennan Fiction Award; *How Loud Can the Village Cock Crow*, short fiction; and *Moving through Darkness*, poetry.